The Grand

GRAND SPRINGS, COLORADO   Vol. 103. No. 265   **35 cents**

KIDNAPPED!

Mayor's Daughter and Granddaughter Missing

Interdum volgus rectum videt, est ubi peccat. Si veteres ita miratur laudatque poetas, ut nihil anteferat, nihil illis comparet, errat. Si quaedam nimis antique, si peraque dure dicere credit eos, ignave multa fatetur, et mecum facit et lova iudicat aequo.

Non equidem insector delendave carmina Livi esse reor, memini quae plagosum mihi parvo Orbilium dictare; sed emendata videri pulchraque et exactis minimum distantia miror. Inter quae verbum emicuit si forte decorum, et si versus paulo concinnior unus et alter, iniuste totum ducit venditque poema.Interdum volgus rectum videt, est ubi peccat. Si veteres ita miratur laudatque poetas, ut nihil anteferat, nihil illis comparet, errat. Si quaedam nimis antique, si peraque dure dicere credit eos, ignave multa fatetur, et sapit et mecum facit et lova iudicat aequo.

totum ducit venditque poema. Interdum volgus rectum videt, est ubi peccat. Si veteres ita miratur laudatque poetas, ut nihil anteferat, nihil illis comparet, errat. Si quaedam nimis antique, si peraque dure dicere credit eos, ignave multa fatetur, et sapit et mecum facit et lova iudicat aequo.

Non equidem insector delendave carmina Livi esse reor, memini quae plagosum mihi parvo Orbilium dictare; sed emendata videri pulchraque et exactis Interdum volgus rectum videt, est ubi peccat. Si veteres ita miratur laudatque poetas, ut nihil anteferat, nihil illis comparet, errat. Si quaedam nimis antique, si peraque dure dicere credit eos, ignave multa fatetur, et sapit et mecum facit et lova iudicat aequo.

Non equidem insector delendave carmina Livi esse reor, memini quae plagosum mihi parvo Orbilium dictare; sed emendata videri pulchraque et exactis minimum distantia miror. Inter quae verbum emicuit si forte decorum, et si versus paulo

Investigation into Mayor's Murder Continues

Non equidem insector delendave carmina Livi esse reor, memini quae plagosum mihi parvo Orbilium dictare; sed emendata videri pulchraque et exactis minimum distantia miror. Inter quae verbum emicuit si forte decorum, et si versus paulo concinnior unus et alter, iniuste

INDEX:

Business	B
Sports	C
Real Estate	D
Entertainment	E
Classifieds	F

HERALD EXCLUSIVE: Father Discovers Child—Only to Lose Her Again

concinnior unus et alter, iniuste totum ducit venditque poema.Interdum volgus rectum videt, est ubi peccat. Si veteres ita miratur laudatque poetas, ut nihil anteferat, nihil illis comparet, errat. Si quaedam nimis antique, si peraque dure dicere credit eos, ignave multa fatetur, et sapit et mecum facit et lova iudicat aequo.

Non equidem insector delendave carmina Livi esse reor, memini quae plagosum mihi parvo Orbilium dictare; sed emendata videri pulchraque et exactis minimum distantia miror. Inter quae verbum emicuit si forte decorum, et si versus imis antique, si peraque dure dicere credit eos, ignave multa fatetur, et sapit et mecum facit et lova iudicat aequo.

Non equidem insector delendave carmina Livi esse reor, memini quae plagosum mihi parvo Orbilium dictare; sed emendata videri pulchraque et exactis minimum distantia miror. Inter quae verbum emicuit si forte decorum, et si versus imis antique, si peraque dure dicere credit eos, ignave multa fatetur, et sapit et mecum facit et lova iudicat aequo.

Dear Reader,

Sometimes your life can change in a heartbeat. For the residents of Grand Springs, Colorado, a blackout has set off a string of events that will alter people's lives forever....

Welcome to Silhouette's exciting new series, 36 HOURS, where each month heroic characters face personal challenges—and find love against all odds. This month an industrious reporter has only one chance to save his high school sweetheart...and his newly discovered child. Rio Redtree would do anything to rescue Eve and his beloved daughter, Molly. But the sacrifices might be great....

In coming months you'll meet a bride on the run who must depend on a sexy stranger for protection; a loving nurse who marries a co-worker to gain custody of the baby she helped deliver; and a rough-edged cop who could mean the difference between life and death for a woman unjustly accused. Join us each month as we bring you 36 hours that will change *your* life!

Sincerely,

The editors at Silhouette

36 HOURS

FATHER AND CHILD REUNION

CHRISTINE FLYNN

Silhouette Books

Published by Silhouette Books

America's Publisher of Contemporary Romance

Special thanks and acknowledgment are given to Christine Flynn for her contribution to the 36 HOURS series.

For my brothers, Richard and Anthony.
You're both so very special.

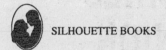

SILHOUETTE BOOKS

FATHER AND CHILD REUNION

Copyright © 1997 by Harlequin Books S.A.

ISBN 0-373-65011-6

This edition published by arrangement with Harlequin Books S.A.

® and TM are trademarks of Harlequin Books S.A., used under license. Trademarks indicated with ® are registered in the United States Patent and Trademark Office, the Canadian Trade Marks Office and in other countries.

Printed in U.S.A.

Christine Flynn

Award-winning author Christine Flynn is a former paralegal whose novels have appeared on bestseller lists, including *USA Today* and Waldenbooks, since her first book was published in 1985. The author of the number-one bestselling *A Father's Wish,* she resides in Arizona with her husband and two shamelessly spoiled dogs. *Father and Child Reunion* is her twenty-fourth book.

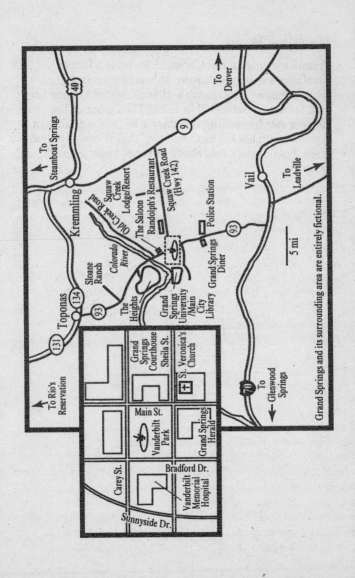

To Denver

To Steamboat Springs

40

9

To Leadville

Vail

Squaw Creek Road (Hwy 142)

Police Station

Kremmling

Squaw Creek Lodge/Resort

The Saloon

Randolph's Restaurant

Old Creek Road

Colorado River

Sloane Ranch

Grand Springs Diner

93

5 mi

Toponas

134

93

The Heights

Grand Springs University/Main City Library

Grand Springs and its surrounding area are entirely fictional.

131

To Rio's Reservation

Grand Springs Courthouse

Sheila St.

St. Veronica's Church

To Glenwood Springs

Main St.

Vanderbilt Park

Grand Springs Herald

Carey St.

Bradford Dr.

Vanderbilt Memorial Hospital

Sunnyside Dr.

Prologue

It was only a nightmare. An awful, impossible dream. Any minute, Eve Stuart was sure she would wake up in her own bed and the horror would be over. Since it was Sunday, she'd settle Molly, her five-year-old, in front of the television with a bowl of cereal to watch cartoons. Then she'd call her mom, as she did every Sunday morning, and they would chat for an hour about what was going on in their respective worlds.

. She knew exactly how the conversation would go. Her mom would ask if she had any new clients at the interior design studio, while sounds of coffee being poured filtered from each end of the line. After that, she'd want to know what Molly had done in preschool that week. Since Olivia Stuart was mayor of Grand Springs, Colorado, and on the board of nearly every charity in town, Eve would then get an update on the latest fund-raiser, along with an earful about how the city council was trying to railroad this issue or that cause. Grand Springs was more than a thousand miles from Santa Barbara, but she and her mom had never let the distance interfere. They had always been close.

Eve leaned her forehead against the window, too numb to notice the sunlight dancing off the puddles left by the storm. She'd been nervous about coming back, and her reasons had nothing to do with her family. But assuming she wouldn't be here long, she'd come to attend her brother's wedding and to spend the weekend with her mom. Instead, the wedding had been called off because the bride disappeared, massive mud slides had thrown the town into utter chaos, and she had spent yesterday in the chapel and this morning on a park bench across from Vanderbilt Memorial hospital trying to make sense of something that made no sense at all.

Her mother had collapsed on Friday night. A heart attack, Dr. Jennings had told her. But that was impossible. Her mother had never had anything more serious than a cold. Now she was dead.

"The lady says I'm suppose' to watch TV and let you take a nap. Can't I be in here with you, Mommy?"

At the sound of the soft little voice, Eve wiped her cheek with the back of her hand. Her pixie-faced little girl stood in the doorway of the bedroom. The pink bow of one long black pigtail drooped listlessly, and Ted, her battered blue teddy bear, dangled from her small fist as if he were hanging on for dear life. The lady Molly referred to was Millicent, the next-door neighbor who'd sat with her all night and most of yesterday.

Molly cocked her head, her little brow furrowing.

"Are you sad?"

Eve sank into the maple rocking chair behind her and opened her arms. Leave it to a child to reduce a myriad of emotions to their simplest term.

"Yes," she whispered when Molly climbed into her lap. "Yes, I am." The little girl smelled of bubble bath and orange juice, scents that seemed so impossibly normal. "I need to tell you something, honey. About Grandma."

Searching for the words she didn't want to voice, Eve smoothed back Molly's dark bangs. Her little girl was so small, so innocent, and every instinct Eve possessed screamed to protect her baby from such a harsh reality. But Molly would start asking questions soon. Lately, it seemed all she did was ask questions.

"Do you remember when they took Grandma to the hospital in the ambulance, and I told you she was very sick?"

With her chin on Ted's head, Molly gave a sober nod.

"Well, the doctors did everything they could to make her better...but they couldn't." Eve swallowed past the knot in her throat. "She died."

A frown swept Molly's delicate features.

"Do you know what that means?"

"I think so."

"You do?"

"Angela Abramson had a fish that died."

Angela was her little friend from preschool. Eve had forgotten about the fish. "Then, you understand that when someone...or something...dies, it can't come back again."

Innocent blue eyes turned troubled. "Did they flush Grandma down the toilet?"

"Oh, no, honey," Eve assured, hugging her close. "It's different with people than it is with fish."

"Then, where is she?"

"Well," Eve began, wondering how to explained something so complicated. "The part of her that we can see is still at the hospital. But the part of her that made her the person we knew...her spirit...is in heaven."

"Can we go see her spirit?"

"Heaven is where the angels are, Molly. People...living people...can't go there. You remember me reading to you about angels, don't you?"

Eve felt Molly nod and curl closer. Her daughter was familiar with angels from bedtime stories, and with the angel that crowned their tree at Christmas. What she knew about "real" angels, though, was that she couldn't see them. So Eve explained that her grandma was just like those angels now. Even though they couldn't see her, she would always be with them.

It was hard for Eve to know if her little girl could grasp such a concept. Though she tried desperately to find some comfort in it herself, intangibles provided little solace at the moment. The only thing that helped the ache in her chest was holding Molly. With her child's warm little body snuggled securely in her arms, she slowly began to rock.

"Mommy?"

"What, honey?"

"Is your daddy an angel, too?"

Eve had never known her father, and her mom had rarely mentioned him. He'd died so long ago that she had no mental image of him at all. "I suppose he is."

"So Grandma won't be lonesome up there?"

"No, honey. She won't be lonesome."

"Mommy?"

"Hmm?"

"How come I don't have a daddy?"

"You do have a daddy," Eve replied, numbness buffering the jolt she might have otherwise felt at the question. "Everyone does. Some of us just don't live with them."

"Oh." Molly wiggled in tighter. "We live with just us, huh?"

"Just us," she repeated, and let herself be grateful that her little girl hadn't pressed for more.

Eve had always known Molly would ask about her father someday, but the child didn't need anything else to shake her little world just now. And, just now, Rio Redtree was the last person on earth Eve wanted to think about. Not that she'd been able to avoid thoughts of him. Ever since she'd decided to come home, the enigmatic man who'd once stolen her heart had been very much on her mind.

It had been six years since Eve had seen him. Six years that seemed like a lifetime. Rio was an investigative reporter for the the *Grand Springs Herald* now. According to her mother, the most relentless reporter the paper had ever hired. Only her mother had known how close she and Rio had once been. And only her mother had known that he was the father of Eve's child.

But Rio didn't even know Molly existed.

One

Eve stopped in the doorway of her mom's bedroom, packing boxes in hand and a knot in her throat. She wouldn't think about what she had to do. She'd just do it.

The resolution made, she dropped the boxes by the lace-covered four-poster bed, whipped back the curtains overlooking the flower garden and opened the doors of a tall cherry armoire. The cubicles at eye level were filled with neatly folded sweaters. Cardigans and lightweights on one side, jacket-types and bulky knits on the other. Without letting herself recall the last time she'd seen her mother wearing any one of them, Eve put the lot in a box designated for the women's shelter. She set the small floral sachet she found tucked behind them in a smaller box for mementos she would save for Molly.

Keeping her mind carefully blank, she turned next to the narrow drawer beneath the now empty shelves. It held scarves. Soft squares of soft periwinkle, rose and yellow lay next to lengths of poppy red, royal blue and emerald green. Patterns were separated from solids. Pastels from primaries. Each color group was separated further by size.

She'd known her mother was efficient, even admired her innate sense of order. But had she ever realized she was this organized?

At the thought, Eve's resolve faltered. She wasn't a strong person. A little stubborn, maybe. Independent, definitely. And that, out of necessity as much as training. But she really wasn't strong enough to divorce herself from the ache in her chest. It was just that, after packing up most of the closet yesterday, blocking her mind to what she was doing had seemed the only way to get through the rest of the room without dehydrating herself.

She hesitantly touched a square of indigo blue. She didn't want to be here. She wanted to be home in Santa Barbara. Back in her sunny apartment with the tulips she and Molly had planted struggling to grow on their tiny patio. Back at work, arguing with jerky Geoff Enright about whether or not she could handle major accounts on her own. Back in the familiar world of shuttling Molly to pre-school and day care and to T-ball or tumbling class on Saturday, and spending evenings with the sketches she hoped would someday be good enough to sell.

What did she know about filing for probate and liquidating assets and whatever else the attorney had said she needed to do? She knew color and texture and space. She knew how to design interiors that were functional, appealing, stunning. Whatever the client wanted. She knew "Barney" and how to make cupcakes with smiley faces. But she still didn't know what she was supposed to do with all the things her mother had loved.

Squares of fabric turned into a kaleidoscope of color as the scarves blurred.

Blinking furiously, Eve pulled a breath and picked up a stack of silk. Her mother's possessions wouldn't pack themselves, so she'd best get on with it. After all, taking care of her mother's belongings was part of the reason she'd come back.

Shortly after the funeral, she had returned to Santa Barbara to finish what design projects she could, then turned over the rest to her boss and begged for a leave of absence from her job. She'd been so busy, she could scarcely think. But the numbness that had protected her during that time had vanished the moment she'd walked back through the door of the spacious, two-story house, Molly and suitcases in tow. Though she'd been gone for almost a month, and she'd had a two-day, thousand-mile drive in which to prepare herself for her return, she'd felt just as rocky when she arrived as she had the day they'd left. Nothing had changed. In the days following her mother's death, the unimaginable—the *unthinkable*—had become the reality.

Eve still couldn't believe what the police had told her. Her mother hadn't just had a heart attack. She'd been murdered.

"A lethal injection of potassium" was how the detective had so calmly described what the killer had used for a weapon. "Someone definitely knew what he was doing."

The last of the scarves went into the box. The senselessness of her mother's death only compounded the ache in Eve's chest. Or maybe, she thought, it was some sort of unacknowledged rage at whoever could have done such a thing that made it so hard to breathe whenever she thought of why her mother was no longer there. It didn't help that the police had yet to come up with a solid suspect; that whoever had robbed her and her brother of their mom, Molly of her grandmother and the entire town of a decent, caring human being was still running free. At least, she hadn't heard that the authorities had any leads. Her brother, Hal, who was the acting mayor and in a much better position than she to get that sort of information, wasn't speaking to her much these days.

The refined, two-tone chime of the doorbell cut off any consideration Eve might have given that disturbing development. As shaky as she was feeling, she could only handle one problem at a time, anyway.

The doorbell sounded again, the notes drifting through the house like a musical ghost.

One of the first things Eve had done when she'd returned a few days ago was enroll Molly in St. Veronica's summer day camp. That meant her little girl wasn't there to peek around the Priscillas in the living room and holler out a description of whoever was leaning on the bell.

For one totally indulgent moment, Eve considered not answering. Only the thought that Molly might be returning early had her shoving her fingers through her hair and heading for the stairs.

It wasn't Molly. By the time Eve reached the bottom step of the wide, carved oak staircase, she could see a shape visible through the pattern of beveled glass on the front door. It was definitely adult. Big adult. The top of Molly's head wouldn't have even reached the casing of the oval window.

She headed across the wide foyer, thinking it was probably Millicent from next door or, perhaps, someone from one of the many organizations to which her mom had belonged. That thought, belated though it was, had her wishing she'd checked herself out in the dresser mirror. Her mom certainly would have. Appearances were important, after all. And Eve, the prodigal daughter, wanted very much to avoid reflecting badly on her mother.

Her hand brushed the collar of her pink oxford shirt, then flattened over the single pearl on her necklace. Her white slacks were cotton and casual, but her attire should stand up to scrutiny. It was the rest of her that needed work. Her blue eyes were probably rimmed in red, and her short blond hair would have been more presentable had she not shoved her fingers through it, but it was too late to undo the damage now. Her caller could see her approaching through the door's window.

And she could see him.

Tall, broad-shouldered, dark. The impressions registered a millisecond before her heart bumped her ribs and her steps faltered to a stop.

Rio.

Her heart jerked again, her thoughts scrambling. She'd known she'd have to see him. Considering his work and her obligations, avoiding him for the next couple of months would be nearly impossible. She knew, too, that she had to tell him about Molly before he found out on his own. But she had no idea how to do that. Or what he would say when she did.

A thread of panic tangled with the other emotions knotting her stomach. She'd known she would see him. But she'd never thought he'd appear on her mother's doorstep.

Brass clicked when she pressed the latch. Pulling open the door, she glanced past the narrow band of a collarless white shirt to a jaw that looked chiseled from stone. A heartbeat later, she met eyes the color of midnight.

The scent of impending rain blew in with the breeze. Or maybe it was the man dwarfing her in the doorway that suddenly made the air feel charged. Rio seemed bigger to her, his lean body more powerful. His neatly trimmed black hair was combed straight back from his face, accentuating the bronze and beautifully honed features that spoke clearly of his Native American ancestry. But those features betrayed nothing.

His mouth, sculpted and blatantly sensual, formed a hard line when his glance moved from her pale features to the scarf in her hand, then locked on her face once more. Knowing she would see him didn't mean she'd been prepared. She realized that the moment she encountered the piercing ebony eyes that had always seen so much, and revealed so little.

"Hello, Eve."

"Rio." His name was little more than a whisper. "I didn't expect you."

"I don't imagine you did. May I come in?"

Another jolt of panic sliced through her at the question, her glance darting to her watch. Realizing that Molly wasn't due to return for half an hour, her next breath came a little easier. "Yes. Yes, of course."

She pushed open the screen, than backed to the center of the large maroon-and-blue Aubusson rug when he stepped in and closed the door. In the space of seconds, he'd scanned the high-ceilinged foyer, the perimeter of polished wood floor and the mirror reflecting the matching Ming-style vases on the long entry table.

"I'm working on a story for the *Herald* about your mother's murder." His voice, smoky and deep, held a cool edge of professionalism as he studied his surroundings. He clearly had a purpose. Yet, he didn't seem interested in knowing why she'd disappeared from his life without a word. Or why she'd refused to return his calls. When he turned to face her again, six years of silence screaming between them, he was all business. The look in his eyes as he noted the redness in hers seemed no less impersonal.

"I'm interviewing everyone who may have had any contact with her that last day," he added, making it clear he hadn't singled her out. "If you have a few minutes, I'd like to talk to you. Just so you know, I'm not willing to jeopardize finding whoever's guilty for the sake of a story. Anything you tell me stays confidential until the police investigation breaks."

He was here because of his job. Not because of their past. Eve slowly expelled the breath that had locked itself in her lungs. She knew she should feel relieved. Yet, even though she'd always known that he had mattered far more to her than she had to him, she didn't know what to make of his indifference.

Preferring it to the questions he *could* have asked, her glance fell to the length of crimson silk wadded in her fist. "I don't know what I could possibly tell you. I have no idea who would have wanted to kill my mother. Or why." She paused, her voice losing its steadiness as she drew the scarf through her fingers and held it up. Red had always been her mother's favorite color. "I was packing Mom's things. You wouldn't think cleaning out drawers would be that hard, would you?"

She tried to smile. Pretty sure the effort didn't match the result, she turned away, heading into the living room with its dark, polished woods and rich blue-and-burgundy fabrics. She could feel him watching her, assessing the way she moved, the tilt of her head. Yet, were she to face him, she doubted his expression would reveal anything that he didn't want her to see.

Given the way she was feeling just then, a little lost, a lot uncertain, she'd barter everything short of her soul for that ability.

She could hear him moving behind her, his footfall slow and measured. There was caution in the sound. Or maybe it was reluctance. When he stopped beside a navy barrel chair, that hesitation had entered his voice.

"I'm really sorry about your mother, Eve. Considering how close you were, I'm sure you must miss her."

She was right. Though some of the coolness had left his voice, his expression was still guarded.

"Thank you," she returned. "I do miss her. Sometimes so much that I don't think I'll be able to stand it. But I'm getting by." She managed the smile this time, even though it was a little shaky at the edges. "A lot of other people miss her, too. I think half the town attended her funeral."

"I'm sure more would have been there if some of the roads hadn't still been blocked." His glance skimmed her face, but the unwilling concern in his eyes vanished as he looked away. "I was on an assignment on the other side of town, or I'd have been there myself."

He couldn't possibly know how relieved she was that he hadn't been. The entire city had been affected by the mud slides that had taken out electrical power, roads and water lines. Though utilities had been restored for the most part and the roads cleared, like aftershocks of an earthquake, the effects of that fateful storm were still being felt. Which, she reminded herself, was the only reason Rio was here now.

"This investigation you're doing," she said, hurrying past the silence suddenly straining their conversation. "Have you found out anything yet?"

For a moment, he didn't respond. Looking very much as

if there was something else he wanted to say, he took a step closer. He must have changed his mind about whatever it was. That same step brought him right back to business.

"Nothing that leads anywhere specific. Since your brother is the council's liaison with the police, he has an inside line to what's going on. I'm sure you have as much information as I do. Maybe more."

"Actually," she replied, the hope he might know something fading to disappointment, "I know very little."

That didn't seem to be the response he'd hoped for. A frown slashed his forehead.

"So what has Hal told you?"

"Only that they're working on it. He said he'd let me know if anything comes up."

"That's all?"

"We really don't talk that much. Hal's been awfully busy since he took over Mom's mayoral duties." The explanation sounded like an excuse. She knew that, but it was the truth, as far as it went. "I've talked to one of the detectives a couple of times, and he's mentioned one theory they're following. Something about strip miners and some lease renewal Mom was opposed to. But I hate to keep bugging him." The hope sprang back, refusing to die. "If there's anything you know…"

"Why isn't Hal talking to you?"

His eyes searching hers, he moved closer still. He was a reporter, Eve reminded herself. He wanted a story. Yet, even though she knew that, even though Rio couldn't have made it any more obvious that he was there only because he had to be, the edge in his voice had softened. Something that sounded suspiciously like the concern she'd so briefly glimpsed moments ago had stripped it away.

It made no sense at all to Eve, but if he suddenly turned nice on her, she didn't know if she'd be able to handle it.

She drew a quick, steadying breath. At least, to Rio, it seemed she was seeking some sort of control just then. All he really knew was that he hadn't expected to see her this way. More than that, he hadn't expected her to matter.

Not anymore.

He had stopped an arm's length from her, forcing her to tip her head back to look up at him. He could tell she'd been crying. Or trying to avoid it. Yet, even with the telltale pink tinting her sky blue eyes, there was no denying how lovely she had become. She was no longer the girl he remembered, but she was still as small and slight as a fawn. Her pale blond hair looked shot with sunlight, and though the stylish, sophisticated cut was far too short for his taste, it framed a face of fragile beauty; a face that revealed far more than he wanted to see.

Between the grief she so bravely held in check and her obvious hunger for anything she could learn about her mother's murderer, she looked desperately in need of a pair of arms. Realizing that he was actually thinking about easing her into his, he shoved his hands into his pockets. Even if he could get past what she'd done to him, his touch could well be unwelcome.

"Are we on the record, or off?"

"None of what you say to me is going anywhere right now. I already told you that."

"But this doesn't have anything to do with your story."

"This isn't about the story. It's about why your brother has cut you out of the loop."

His words seemed to magnify the distress in her eyes. She already looked far too vulnerable. Far too alone.

Balling his hands into fists, Rio took a mental step back, regrouping, reassessing. Any investigative reporter worth his byline knew how important it was to remain objective. And he had been so sure his objectivity was in place where Eve was concerned. Obviously, he'd overestimated himself. With anyone else under such circumstances, he would never have barged in with the steamroller routine. But with her, all he'd wanted to do was get in, get the information he wanted, and get out. All the way across town, he'd reminded himself that whatever it was they'd once shared had ceased to matter the day she'd run off without so much as a goodbye, good luck or go to hell. The visit today was strictly business.

He reminded himself of that again, wanting to believe it this time, and watched her cross her arms. The bright slash of red scarf tangled from elbow to wrist.

"Eve," he said, his tone quiet. "Why isn't he talking to you?"

He spoke her name the same way she remembered his saying it when he knew something was on her mind. As if he was prepared to patiently drag it out of her if he had to.

He'd never had to try very hard.

"He's upset because Mom named me the executor of her estate instead of him. We haven't agreed on much of anything since we found her will." She paused, just short of adding that she thought Hal's feelings were hurt.

"So he's punishing you by not giving you information?"

It sounded so juvenile when he put it that way.

"Grief affects people in many different ways," she said defensively, thinking that someone who covered the trials and traumas of life for a living should certainly know that. Her older brother's pain was as deep as her own. "But it's not like Mom cut Hal out of the will. All she did was change her executor."

"When did she do this?"

"Just a few months ago. Her attorney said he was talking to her about some other matters and she brought it up, almost as an afterthought."

"She never hinted she was thinking about it?"

"She never said a word to me. I keep thinking that she planned to mention it and just didn't get the chance. There was always so much going on with her, and with Hal's wedding and everything, it just wasn't a priority."

She pushed her hand through her hair, the motion as unsteady as she looked. "She left so much undone, Rio. Every time I turn around, I find some other project she was in the middle of. If it's not something for the Children's Center, it's the women's shelter. And I'm trying to tie up all those loose ends by guessing how she would have wanted things handled. In the meantime, I'm on the fringes as far as the investigation is concerned. It's hard not knowing anything.''

It shouldn't have been so easy to admit all that to him. Nor should it have seemed so natural to stand there letting him see the frustrations she was so careful to shield from everyone else. But then, no one else had ever known her like he had. Even when she hadn't felt like talking, he'd always been able to draw her out. And he'd always listened.

The knowledge was not only seductive, it was dangerous. And she had to be seriously addled to be going on as she was with Molly en route even as they spoke. Her little girl would be barreling up the steps in a matter of minutes.

''You know, Eve, it's possible that you know more than you realize.''

''I really don't think so.''

''Are you willing to talk to me to find out?''

She didn't even hesitate. ''I'll do whatever I can to find out who did this to Mom. And I'll answer your questions.'' Praying the bus wouldn't be early, she glanced nervously toward the door. ''I just can't do it now.''

''Are you expecting someone?''

The man was observant to a fault.

She told him she was and started across the room. ''This isn't a good time to talk.''

''Then, I'll come by later. Just give me a time.''

''No! No,'' she repeated, more quietly. ''I'll meet you tomorrow. In the morning. Is that okay?''

More curious about her reaction than about whoever she was expecting, he lifted his shoulder in a deceptively casual shrug. ''Sure. When?''

''Is nine all right?''

She was already at the door. Rio was right behind her, wondering what had put the sudden tension in her slender shoulders. She was definitely more agitated than she'd been a moment ago, and far more evasive. He'd already noticed how she tended to avoid his eyes. But he wanted to think that was only because she was feeling a little guilty about the way she'd dumped him. Anxious as she was to get rid of him now, however, he couldn't help thinking she was hiding something.

Whatever it was, he told himself, unless it had to do with Olivia Stuart's murder, he didn't care about it.

She opened the door, standing back so he could pass. He didn't move, though. The doorway was blocked.

"You have company," he quietly said, and watched with interest as the color drained from her face in the instant before she whirled around.

"You'd think the incompetents at the *Herald* would hire people with a decent aim, wouldn't you?" A large woman with a headful of silver waves, silver-rimmed glasses and wearing a peacock blue pantsuit, held out a newspaper. "Yours was in the arborvitae. I found ours in my rosebushes. Yesterday, he missed the fountain by an inch."

"Millicent," Eve murmured, her hand leaving her throat to open the screen and reach for the paper the sprinkler had soaked. "Come in."

"I can't, dear." She cast a pleasant smile toward the darkly attractive man by Eve's shoulder, but just as she opened her mouth to continue, she recognized the reporter who'd interviewed most of the neighbors following Olivia's death. "Well, Mr. Redtree. I didn't realize you were here. How nice to see you again."

A surprisingly easy smile deepened the masculine creases in Rio's cheeks. "Mrs. Atwell," he replied, acknowledging her with a nod.

The light in his eyes had color creeping up Millicent's neck. "Oh, my. What I said about the paper, that doesn't reflect on you, of course. About the incompetents, I mean. I was talking about the kids who deliver the paper. But you must know that." Jeweled rings glittering, she waved the matter off, her curiosity overruling embarrassment. "Did I interrupt an interview?"

"I was just leaving."

"Well, I still won't keep you." She turned to Eve. "I'm on my way to a hair appointment and I'm already late. I just wanted to let you know that the cleaning service I use can do the house for you if you'd like. I know your mother wasn't very happy with the one she'd been using, so you might have better luck with this new company. Should I have someone come over to give you an estimate?"

Looking rushed, yet trying not to, Eve cast a cautious glance toward Rio. He seemed in no rush at all.

"That's awfully nice of you," Eve told the woman, wishing Millicent had waited thirty seconds more to show up. That was all the time she and Rio needed to settle where they'd meet and he could leave. "But I'm going to take care of the house myself. If you know of anyone who does exterior windows, though, I'd appreciate his name."

It was apparent from the slow arch of Millicent's carefully plucked eyebrows that she regarded Eve's decision to clean the house herself as somewhat extraordinary. In their social circle, it probably was. But Eve didn't offer an explanation about why she couldn't leave the task to strangers. Nor did she mention that she'd done her own cleaning for years. She simply waited for Millicent to tell her she would be happy to give her the name of a man she could call, while the knots in her stomach cloned themselves.

"I really must go," the woman finally said, casting one more glance at the man watching Eve. "I don't want to lose my appointment."

Eve didn't want her to, either. As good a neighbor as Millicent had always been to her family and as kind as she'd been to her and Molly lately, Eve just wanted her to leave. So she thanked her again, then watched the sides of her blue silk jacket flutter behind her as she hurried down the steps.

Rio paid little attention to her departing neighbor. Trying

to do the same with Eve, he pulled his keys from his pocket, then skimmed a glance over the delicate contours of her face. She looked tired. And edgy. He could appreciate the latter. Standing close enough to breathe the decidedly provocative perfume she wore had tightened every single muscle in his body.

"Nine's fine," he told her, taking up where they'd been interrupted. "Where?"

Eve didn't miss a beat. "The miner's memorial in Vanderbilt Park?"

He gave her nod as tight as the muscle in his jaw and trotted down the steps, his long, powerful strides carrying him to the black Bronco at the curb. He didn't care where they met so long as he got what he was after. If he was anything like he used to be, all he cared about was reaching his goal.

Eve was trembling when she stepped out onto the porch behind him and watched him pull away. The relief she felt that the bus hadn't yet arrived was enormous. But she didn't feel any sense of reprieve. As she lifted her face to the warm breeze and tried to calm her mind, she felt only a growing sense of apprehension—and a vague sense of loss that made no sense at all, considering how long it had been since she'd seen him. But then, her relationship with Rio Redtree hadn't been based on common sense, anyway.

She had no trouble at all recalling the very first time she'd laid eyes on him and she still couldn't help but think that he never should have noticed her at all. She'd been a lowly freshman with a nose for art books and an outstanding ability to blend in with the scenery. Ever since she'd skipped fifth grade, she'd been the youngest kid in her class, and the smallest, and that first day at Grand Springs University, among all the older college students, she'd felt totally out of place. But whether or not a heart-stoppingly handsome, slightly dangerous-looking upperclassman with a long black ponytail should have noticed her, Rio had singled her out of a hundred Spanish class students and sat down behind her. She could still remember the hair on her neck standing straight up when he'd leaned forward to whisper in her ear.

His voice had mesmerized her as surely as his words. Low, husky and as soothing as the sound of wind deep in a forest, his voice had seemed to flow over her, through her. He'd told her to not look so scared, that the first week was always the hardest. She would be fine.

She'd turned around and met his beautiful black eyes. He hadn't smiled at her. He'd merely given her a nod to affirm what he'd said and slid back in his chair. Rio had somehow known exactly what she'd needed to hear that day. He'd seemed to possess some indefinable sixth sense for knowing when someone was feeling lost, or when they were vulnerable, or when they needed help. But she'd soon discovered a reticence about him that held him back from those very situations. It was as if he didn't want to get involved at all. Yet, when no else did what needed to be done, he always stepped in.

That he'd so selflessly put her at ease was what had drawn her to him from that very first day. In a matter of weeks, she'd been drawn by other things, as well. His patience. His insights. His persistence. He could always get her to open up, even when she didn't think she wanted to, and once she started talking, he listened as if every word she said actually mattered to him.

As isolated as she'd felt at that time, having someone she could share her thoughts and feelings with had meant the world to her. The kids her own age had still been in high school, and because she had looked as young as she was and still lived at home, she never meshed with the college crowd. She hadn't fit in much of anywhere that year. When she told Rio that, he told her he didn't fit anywhere, either.

She never understood why he felt that way. When she asked him, he changed the subject and never answered. What he would talk about, though, was what was going on around them, because he was curious about everything, and about his dreams, his plans. And by the end of that term, not a school day passed that they weren't together. He had become her friend, her confidant. He'd even been the first person she'd wanted to tell when one of her drawings had placed in a school competition. She remembered running all the way across campus in the pouring rain, and when she'd flung herself into his arms, laughing, his eyes had gone from smiling to smoldering in the time it took him to lower her to the ground. He'd kissed her then. That first time. And after he'd done it again, he asked her if she had any idea what she did to him and what would happen if they didn't stop.

She'd already been in love with him. Madly. And she still remembered exactly what she'd said. She told him she thought she did, but since she wasn't positive, he'd have to teach her.

So he had. But not until she discovered she was pregnant did she realize that, at seventeen, she wasn't ready for a commitment he wouldn't want, anyway. By then, she'd learned that his plans didn't include children. Ever. But not until she tried to contact him after Molly was born did she realize how much she *didn't* know about him.

A bright white bus turned the corner, its windows reflecting patterns of sunlight and trees on its way to where she stood on the sidewalk. As it stopped in front of her to open its doors with a whoosh of air, she didn't know which unnerved her more. The fact that she had known so little about Rio when she'd left six years ago. Or that she knew so much less about him now.

Two

Vanderbilt Park was a rectangular oasis of evergreens and rustling aspens, meandering paths and flowering gardens. The hospital complex fronted it on one side. Businesses, the courthouse and a chain of parked cars lined the rest of it.

Rio wedged his Bronco between a city waterworks barricade and a landscaper's pickup truck, did a slam dunk with the last of his coffee, then pitched the plastic cup through his window into a green City of Grand Springs trash barrel. Seconds later, with the bang of a door that had birds scattering, he was on his way to the miners memorial. It was five minutes to nine, and probably the first time in a month that he'd been on time for anything.

He could see the huge bronze of a battered miner leading a mule well before he reached it. The bench near it was empty. Rolling up his shirtsleeves, he glanced past the small mountain of fir branches and uprooted trees one of the local organizations had collected during the ongoing storm cleanup, and checked out the path leading in the opposite direction.

It took him all of ten seconds to decide nothing of interest was taking place among the teenagers near the fountain, or the young mothers watching their children in the play area. He wasn't looking for diversion, anyway. He wasn't even looking for a story. Between his regular police and fire beats, a staff meeting and follow-ups on yesterday's stories, he had plenty to keep himself out of trouble today. Any spare time he could scrape up, he'd spend on the cabin he was building near Two Falls Lake. He just wanted to make sure he hadn't missed Eve. She was the final name on his list of people known to have been in contact with Olivia Stuart that last day. If he couldn't get a lead out of her, he had no idea where to go.

Stifling his frustration on that score, he scowled at his watch. After the hurry Eve had been in to get rid of him yesterday, he had to wonder if she'd show up at all. Just because she'd seemed willing to talk didn't mean anything. He'd misjudged her before. He'd once believed she was different from the other people he'd let himself care about. He'd believed that he could trust her, count on her. But he'd never been more wrong.

He hadn't been wrong about her reaction when she'd opened the door to him yesterday, though. There hadn't been a hint of welcome in her expression. Not that he'd expected it. He'd seen caution. He'd sensed wariness. He'd even caught a fairly satisfying jolt of anxiety. What he would liked to have seen was regret.

One must never wish for another, what he would not wish twofold for himself.

Unexpected, unwanted, the elders' ancient teaching reared from the depths of his memory. Rio gave a snort, dismissing it, then closed his eyes against the automatic rebellion. He'd abandoned so many of the old teachings over the years that tossing out one more shouldn't matter.

The thought had scarcely nudged his conscience when his head came up. Eve was there. He knew it even before he saw her walking toward him. Though the reminder wasn't particularly welcome, he'd always had an odd, almost feral awareness where she was concerned.

The gentle morning breeze lifted her hair away from her face, the bright sunlight turning pale gold to platinum. Small gold earrings flashed with the turn of her head. Another discreet flash caught her watch when she lifted her hand to shield her eyes from the sun. The motion drew the short, sleeveless shift she wore higher, drawing attention to her slender legs, until she lowered her hand and his glance moved upward once again. The crisp white fabric that skimmed her hips and small breasts didn't define her shape. Rather, it gave subtle, intriguing hints of the enticing, feminine curves hidden beneath.

Sweetness and seduction, he thought, pushing his hands into his pockets as he watched her move closer. Innocence and sophistication. The combination was as appealing as it was dangerous.

She stopped an arm's length away. Eyes the clear, hypnotic blue of a summer sky met his.

"Before you say anything," she said, "I need to apologize. I'm sorry I was such a basket case yesterday. You caught me at a bad time."

He'd been well aware of that. He'd also spent half the night trying to forget everything else he'd noticed about her after he'd made it past the wariness and anxiety. The sadness in her eyes. Her bewilderment. The brave little smile that had caught him like a punch in the gut.

The way she'd practically pushed him out the door.

"Don't worry about it."

There was a hint of nerves behind the expression, but she smiled now at the reassurance. "So," she began, sounding as if she were determined to get things off to a better start this time. "When did you go to work for the *Herald?*"

"Checking my credentials?"

Her slender shoulder lifted in a tight little shrug. "Curious. I thought you would have moved to a bigger city. You always talked about working for a big paper."

"Still plan to." Determined to be objective, he motioned toward the gray concrete bench and pulled a small recorder from his pocket. "Do you mind if I tape this?"

She wasn't interested in him or his plans. He was sure of that. She was just trying to be civil by making conversation. All he wanted was to get this over with.

She got the hint. Her smile dying, she pulled her glance from his.

"You can tape it if you want," she told him, leaving three feet of space between them when she sat down. "But I don't know what I can tell you that I haven't already told the police. And that wasn't very much. I wasn't there when it happened."

He knew that. He'd read her statements.

He punched a button on the small silver recorder he'd set between them and angled himself to face her. He would remain objective if it killed him. "Some of this might be hard for you," he told her, refusing to deny her the understanding he would give anyone else under the circumstances. "We can stop anytime. Okay?"

That seemed to make her relax a little. "Okay."

"Just tell me when you last saw your mother."

The wind had blown a bit of twig onto the bench. He watched her pick it up, her attention following the motions of her fingers as she drew a deep breath, then quietly told him that the last time she'd seen her had been about an hour before her brother's wedding had been scheduled to start.

"We'd gone ahead to Squaw Creek," she explained, speaking of the ski lodge where her brother's wedding was to have been held. "I hadn't seen Hal yet and I wanted to wish him well before the ceremony. But Mom couldn't find one of the earrings she wanted to wear. She told us to go on and that she'd be right behind us."

"Who's us?" Rio watched Eve's hands, wondering if she had any idea how they gave her away. Though she appeared outwardly calm, when she was nervous or upset she couldn't keep her hands still. Yesterday, it had been the scarf she'd pulled, twisted and strangled. Now it was the twig. The motions were small, barely noticeable, but she was methodically annihilating the bit of broken branch. "You and your daughter?"

He saw those lovely hands go still.

"Several people mentioned her being with you," he explained, since she seemed surprised by his knowledge of the child. *Darling girl,* one of them had said. *So exotic,* claimed another. *And tiny, like her mother. Poor thing was scared to death when the lights went out.* "Is that who you mean?"

Eve cleared her throat. "Yes, it is."

"What's her name?"

"Molly. But she doesn't know anything that would be of help," she added hurriedly. "She was with me the whole time."

"How old is she?"

The question was automatic. Person at scene. Get name, age, occupation. The presence of Eve's daughter had just been one of those extraneous details he'd picked up during his interviews, along with dozens of others. Like the fact that the woman in charge of catering at the lodge was the minister's cousin. And that Eve didn't have a husband.

Not caring to consider why that latter detail should matter to him, he dismissed it. What he couldn't dismiss was how Eve pushed past the subject.

"She's too young to be interviewed," she replied, sounding as if she figured that was what he was after. "Really, Rio, she won't be any help at all. What else did you want to know about that night?"

He might have thought she was just being protective. Mothers of small children tended to be that way, after all. But there was something about the way Eve's glance faltered before she started in again on the twig that seemed vaguely familiar. She almost seemed as uneasy now as she had yesterday when she'd been in such a rush to get rid of him.

Or maybe, he considered, she was just in a rush to get this over with. That being the case, he reiterated that she'd last seen Olivia at home, then asked when Eve had realized something had happened to her.

Not until she'd returned to the house, she told him, still

seeming tense. Since it had been storming so badly and the streets were such a mess, it had taken them a while to get back to the house. The ambulance had been pulling out as they arrived. Confirming what he'd already learned from 911 dispatch, she told him Josie Reynolds had called it.

There didn't seem to be much she remembered after that. In the quiet tones of someone who has told the story before and learned to numb herself to the memories, she went on to explain that Millicent had taken Molly home with her. Eve had then gotten back in her car and followed the ambulance to the hospital. The rest of that night was apparently a blur. She had no answer for any other questions he asked about the evening. Though she tried, she couldn't recall seeing anyone acting suspicious. Nor did she remember anyone who'd seemed out of place. Once her daughter had been taken care of, her sole focus had been her mother.

Rio rested his elbow on the back of the bench. With his thumb hooked under his chin, he absently rubbed the cleft in his top lip while he studied Eve's profile. She wanted to help. More than that, she seemed to need to help, something he understood far better than he wanted to admit. But not a word she'd said had done him any good at all.

Still looking for suspect and motive, he tried a different tack and asked if there had been a man in the picture. Other than for business, no one could recall seeing Olivia in a man's company. But just because her personal life had seemed nonexistent, that didn't mean it had been. Or so Rio was thinking before the slow but certain shake of Eve's head cut off that particular avenue.

"Mom's life was this town. She didn't have time to have a boyfriend. We used to talk to each other on the phone every Sunday about what had gone on during the week. If there had been a man in her life, she'd have said something about him."

Faced with that dead end, he tried another route and asked about disagreements, or if she knew of anyone her mother had upset in any way. Eve's response didn't promise any more hope there, either—until she mentioned that Olivia had been getting a ton of grief from the miners union and the mining company about her position on a mining operation. When Eve had expressed concern about it, her mom had said that sort of disagreement came with the territory and reminded her that a person in political office couldn't possibly please everyone.

Rio's glance sharpened. It was common knowledge that Olivia's environmentalist leanings adversely affected renewal of the mine's land lease. It was no secret, either, that the last word to leave her dying lips had been "coal."

"Did she mention any names? Any person in particular she was arguing with?"

"If she did, I don't remember."

"Did she say if anyone from the union ever threatened her physically?"

"Never." Eve finally looked up from her twig. "Do you think someone from the union did it?"

"I'm not implying that."

"The police asked me these same questions, Rio. You know something, don't you?"

"It doesn't matter if I do or not. My deal with the police is that I keep what information I have between them and me until this thing breaks."

Holding his glance, her eyes narrowed.

"So that means everybody knows more than I do. Hal. The police. Now you. It's their investigation. They're his contacts. It's your story. Damn it, Rio. She was my mother."

For a moment, Rio said nothing. She hadn't raised her voice. But her tone echoed what flashed in her eyes. Not annoyance. It was something far more subtle. Yet potentially more volatile. It was more like fury that had been refined and suppressed. Or, more likely, quietly denied.

Rio understood why it was there. He even knew how it felt, though her reasons for fighting the suffocating feelings were far more tangible than his own. She was an unacknowledged victim of a murder, a survivor with no answers, struggling to deal with her grief.

That her brother was keeping her in the dark surprised Rio. That he wanted to go for her brother's throat because of it, surprised him, too.

He glanced at the tape recorder, then decided to leave it running.

"The union keeps coming up," he finally admitted, though he kept the confidential aspects of that fact to himself. "A couple of potential suspects have been identified in its membership, but the police haven't been able to get anything specific on them. That's why it could be important for you to recall anything she said to you about anyone connected with the lease renewal."

He could see her frustration slowly give way as she processed what he'd told her. It made no difference that he didn't want to consider how overwhelmed she might feel by all that had taken place. He was considering it, anyway. And he was beginning to sense an inner strength in Eve that the girl he'd known hadn't yet grown to possess. That strength had been evident even yesterday, despite her bewilderment over her mother's decisions and the stresses straining her relationship with her brother. She was doing what needed to be done and expecting no one to come to her rescue.

He had to admire that. He'd met too many people who expected others to bail them out when life got rough, or who took out their pain and frustration on everyone around them when something went wrong. Yet, despite her willingness to fight her own battles, to deal with her own pain, there was a vulnerability about her that was playing havoc with his more protective instincts.

His protective instincts weren't the ones he was concerned about at the moment, however. What he felt when Eve tipped her head back and blew out a breath was considerably more basic.

Already more aware of her than he wanted to be, he let

his glance slide down the long line of her throat, along her delicate collarbone and over the gentle swell of her breasts. They were fuller than he remembered, and he couldn't help wondering how they would fill his hands.

At the thought, heat spiked through his gut. He knew how it felt to lie with her. How perfectly she had once fit his harder, tougher body. She had been a virgin the first time they'd made love, totally inexperienced, but so trusting. So innocently willing. With no effort at all, he could recall far more about that night than was wanted or wise, and since seeing her yesterday, he could swear nearly every detail of that first afternoon had been resurrected. She'd had news she'd wanted to share, and she'd come to his apartment. It had been raining and she'd been laughing, and when she'd launched herself into his arms, the feel of her soft, supple body pressed to his had nearly brought him to his knees.

The muscles in his jaw jerked as he sought to banish the memory. What he needed to remember about Eve Stuart was that she had left without a word. Somewhere along the line, she'd gone on to another man, made love with him as they had done, borne a child. The past was over and done with. At least, it was about to be.

"I honestly can't think of anything else, Rio."

"Then, answer one last question." He'd told himself he didn't need to know. That her reasons couldn't possibly matter now. No longer willing to lie to himself, he turned off the tape recorder with a quiet click and looked up to meet her eyes. "Why did you leave without talking to me?"

Rio's glance never wavered. He simply sat there, solid and unyielding as granite while the color drained from her face.

He knew she hadn't expected the question. Not then. Not while she was dealing with the too-fresh memories of the night her mother had been killed. Not while she was struggling to remember something, anything, that would help the police.

"Do we have to talk about this now?"

"Seems to me it's as good a time as any."

"Because you decided so? I tried to talk to you about something other than this investigation a few minutes ago but you didn't want any part of it. And yesterday, you acted as if we'd never known each other at all."

He wasn't swayed by her logic. "It's been six years, Eve. How much longer do you need?"

Far more than you're giving me, she thought, catching the adversarial glint in his eyes. She honestly didn't think he would want anything to do with Molly. But if he did, she needed to know the man he had become, and what sort of influence he would be in her daughter's life. In her own life. She had so little to go on now.

Rio didn't seem to expect an answer. Despite the faint edge in his words, his deep voice remained as cool and matter-of-fact as his expression.

"Did you know that I tried for weeks to find out where you'd gone, Eve? Weeks," he repeated, the edge hardening. "But all I could find out was that you'd decided to finish school in California and that you were staying with relatives. Your mother refused to tell me anything else. So I went to the registrar's office at the college. I thought I could find out where your records had been sent. But they wouldn't give me a thing, so I tried your mom again. Only that time I asked her if she'd sent you away because of me."

"Rio—"

"She claimed it hadn't been her idea for you to leave," he said, cutting her off. "Apparently, you were the one who didn't want me to know where you were. But she said she'd ask you to call me. Did she ever ask you that, Eve?"

More than once. They'd even argued about it. "Yes," she quietly replied.

That wasn't the response Rio wanted. He'd wanted Eve to deny that Olivia ever gave her his message. He'd wanted her to tell him that her disappearance had been her mother's idea all along, and that Olivia really hadn't been as accepting of him as she'd seemed to be. It would have salved his pride enormously to know that Eve had been coerced into leaving. But all she'd done was confirm that it had, indeed, been her decision to leave without a word of explanation.

He slipped the recorder into his pocket, then leaned forward to let his clasped hands dangle between his knees. For so many years, none of this had mattered. He'd gone on, done what he'd wanted to do. Forgotten. Or so he'd thought. He'd forgotten nothing. He'd simply buried the feelings of hurt, confusion and anger along with a sense of loss that had stunned him. Seeing her again had been like entering a forbidden burial ground. All manner of ghosts had risen up to haunt him.

"Just tell me what I'd done that you couldn't at least talk to me before you took off."

"It wasn't like that, Rio. It wasn't a matter of who did what to whom. It was the circumstances."

"Like the circumstance that you're white and you decided you didn't want to be involved with an Indian? Was that it?"

Eve's startled "No!" was little more than a gasp as she grabbed his arm to keep him from moving away. Race had never been an issue. Not for her.

She wasn't sure Rio believed that. Seeing his dark eyes turn to flint, jarred by the unexpected accusation, she wasn't sure of anything at the moment. It was incomprehensible that her leaving so long ago would matter to him now. Just as unfathomable was how deeply he'd dug looking for the reason she'd gone. As for his heritage, he'd scarcely mentioned his family at all when they'd been together, and it was never a factor in their relationship.

The tension in the hard muscles beneath Eve's hand finally registered. Reaching for him had been instinctive. But touching him had been a mistake.

His glance fell to her hand, pale and slender against his

darker skin. In the space of a heartbeat, it moved to her lips, lingering long enough to seal the air in her lungs before shifting to meet her eyes once more.

He was a beautiful man. Solid as the earth. As mysterious as the craggy mountains rising all around them. She'd always thought him so. But there was an edge to him now, a kind of raw energy that surrounded him, an invisible force field that made him even more unreachable than he'd once been.

That thought caused a ball of nerves to knot in her stomach. Or maybe what she felt was the heat of his glance pooling the warmth low in her belly. He was a much harder man than she remembered. So much more cynical.

And so very…male.

Totally unnerved, her hand slipped from his arm. As it did, the rising cry of an ambulance siren sliced through the heavy silence. The sound had just started its downward arc when it was joined by an electronic beep.

Rio swore. With his jaw clenched tightly enough to crush bone, he reached for the pager on his belt and turned it off. "I've got to go."

Eve couldn't hide her relief at the reprieve. Still, desperate to keep the lines of communication open between them, for Molly's sake, she started to reach for him again.

Like a child who's just remembered the burner was hot, she pulled back and curled her fingers into her palm. "I don't want us to be like this, Rio. Please. We don't have to be enemies."

Rio was already on his feet, towering over where she remained seated on the bench. With her head tipped back as she looked up at him, she reminded him of a frightened doe with her throat exposed to a predator. She wasn't even trying to protect herself.

The beeper went off again, the sound as impatient as he was beginning to feel. "We'll have to talk later."

"Can I call you tomorrow?"

Her reluctant question caught him as he turned. Not at all sure what to make of her, he told her to suit herself and cut across the grass to where he'd left his Bronco parked at the curb.

The ambulance that had just left the hospital went screaming by as he picked up his cell phone to call the news desk. Thirty seconds later, he pulled onto the tree-lined street and was on his way to the other end of town to cover an accident involving a semi and a motorcycle. It didn't take a rocket scientist to figure out which vehicle had lost. He just wished whatever was going on with Eve was as obvious.

She clearly didn't want to talk about why she'd left. Yet she wasn't making any effort to avoid him, either. That alone made him curious. He hated unanswered questions.

He was even less enthralled with the unexpected feelings that had crawled out of nowhere.

He could usually separate his feelings from a situation, act only on those that were necessary. As a child, he'd been taught that judgment was impaired when the mind was not clear. Man must rule emotion, not the other way around. As a reporter, the talent was invaluable. As a man, he found it protective. So all he had to do was clear his mind. Focus. And put the entire encounter with Eve into perspective.

The task took a block and a half. Following the ambulance through a red light, he told himself he'd be a fool to let injured pride stand in the way of an investigation. Eve was a valuable source. If she'd talked to Olivia as often as she'd indicated, she probably knew more than anyone realized. He could use her to corroborate information and pick her brain about possible suspects. The rest, he would ignore. After all, he had no problem with balancing acts. Having walked the line between rebellion and conformity for as long as he could remember, he was actually pretty good at it by now.

The ambulance rolled to a stop mid-intersection, blocking the blinking lights of a patrol car. After pulling past a no-parking zone so he wouldn't be in the way of the paramedics, Rio headed at a trot toward the man who appeared to be the driver of the semi. Even as he mentally winced at the teenager sprawled near the mangled motorcycle, he reminded himself to ask Eve if Olivia had kept any sort of a diary.

The pages of the calendar her mom kept by the phone in her study reminded Eve of her own. Notes, phone numbers and artistic doodles showing a flair for spirals and curves lined the margins. Most of the grids were filled in with birthdays or anniversaries of friends and professional commitments of one sort or another.

Eve was on the phone, adding a few doodles of her own while making arrangements to cover one of those commitments, when three and a half feet of nightgowned and pigtailed little girl came tearing into the comfortable, book-lined room.

"Mommy," she whispered loudly, as if whispering didn't count as an interruption. "There's a man at the door. A big one. I didn't open it," she added, well versed in the perils of "stranger-danger," "but I saw him through the window. I waved."

Excusing herself to Betty Dodd, the intimidatingly efficient executive chairperson of the Children's Center, Eve put her hand over the mouthpiece. "Is it Uncle Hal?"

Molly gave an exaggerated shrug. "I don't know who he is. Want me to ask?"

Eve had already changed into her nightclothes. Buttoning the long white cotton robe she'd thrown on over her chemise, she told her little girl that she'd take care of it and to go back to her movie, then told the woman who'd asked her to speak in Olivia's place at a charity luncheon that she'd have to call her back. Eve wasn't expecting anyone this evening. Especially not at this hour. It was after nine o'clock.

The robe was fastened from mid-thigh to lace yoke when she hurried through the foyer. Passing the wide archway to the living room, she saw Molly sprawled in front of the television once more, watching *Aladdin* for the hundred and umpteenth time. Hoping the child would stay put, and pretty certain she would since her favorite part of the video was coming up, Eve glanced through the pattern of leaded glass on the door.

Rio stood in the blue-white glow of the porch light.

She opened the door but not the ornate metal screen.

A frown of uncertainty slashed Rio's chiseled features when his appraising glance slid from her neck to her knees. "You weren't in bed, were you?"

"Not yet." Watching his frown settle between her breasts, she reached for the button at her throat. "I was on the phone."

"I know," he muttered. "Your line's been busy all evening."

She meant to keep him on the porch. Overriding her intention to join him out there, he pulled open the screen the moment she unlatched it. Or maybe, she thought, seeing his mouth pinch when she shivered, it was the fact that she was getting cold that made him decide to step inside.

His rationale made no difference. Either way, Eve had to back up to avoid getting run over, but she refused to move any farther than the entry table. She wasn't concerned about how Rio's presence dominated the space, or even about his purely male interest when his glance strayed again to the sheer lace exposing glimpses of skin above her breasts. He could strip her naked for all she cared at the moment. What left her so unnerved was the fact that he was here, and so was Molly.

Exercising the only control he'd left her, short of pushing him back out the door, she turned her back to the wide oak staircase so he wouldn't be facing the living room.

"This isn't a good time, Rio. I know we need to talk, but maybe we could do it tomorrow. You can come back in the morning. Or I'll meet you."

"Relax, Eve. This isn't about us." He pushed his hands into his pockets, his sigh heavy. "I just want to know if Olivia kept any sort of a diary here."

Relaxing was impossible. Not with him standing thirty feet from the daughter he didn't know he had. Seeing him frown at her crossed arms, she did what she could to accommodate him and let them fall to her sides. "I don't know that she kept one at all. At least, I haven't come across one. I'll look again and let you know."

And ask you later why you want it, she added to herself as she started for the door.

He wasn't going to be dismissed that easily.

"What about a personal phone book? The kind that has family friends in it. Is that here, or did the police take it?"

"It's here. So is her personal calendar," she conceded, but she didn't get a chance to ask if his questions could wait. The chatter of animated voices drifting from the living room had given way to the strains of violins. Right on cue, Molly's clear, sweet voice joined the cartoon characters on the screen serenading the world from a magic carpet. Dynamite couldn't blast her away from this part of the show.

A bubble of panic lodged in Eve's chest when she saw Rio's dark head turn to the living room.

Molly was sitting up now, her back to them as she sang along with her favorite song. The child definitely had his attention, but with Molly glued to the television, all he could see of her was the back of her pink nightgown and two long, dark pigtails.

"That's your daughter?" he asked, without taking his eyes from the slender little back.

Protectiveness joined panic. "Yes. And she doesn't know anything that would be of any help."

His eyebrow arched at the easy way she'd read him. "People tend to underestimate kids. You never know what a child sees."

Had it not felt so imperative to put some distance between him and that particular child, Eve might have wondered how someone who'd wanted so little to do with children had come by such an insight. But with her nerves stretched thinner by the second, and unprepared for him to discover exactly who Molly was, creating that distance between father and child was her only interest.

"Mom's address book is in the study," she said, snagging his attention once more. "If you'll come with me, I'll get it."

With one last glance toward the little girl now holding her arms wide as she belted out an amazingly clear high C, Rio stifled a smile and followed Eve down the hall.

"How long have you been divorced?" he asked from behind her.

Her heart gave an unhealthy jerk. "I'm not divorced."

That gave him pause. Or maybe, Eve thought, he was just silent because they'd entered the study and he was looking around. At her mother's collection of law books, perhaps. Or the prints of wildflowers that saved the space from being too masculine. She honestly didn't know what he was doing when she headed for the antique mahogany desk that bisected the narrow room. Nor did she care. She just wanted him out of there.

"Are you widowed?" he asked, a little more quietly.

Just as quietly, she responded with a soft "No."

Another moment passed. Eve could have sworn she heard wheels turning.

"I heard that you didn't have a husband."

With her attention on the drawer she opened, she murmured, "It's nice to know the local grapevine is so accurate." She held up the small brown address book, determined to keep his focus on his investigation for now. "What do you want with this?"

Rio had come to a halt near the hunter green wing chair. His frown matched hers, but she couldn't tell if it was because he now knew she'd never been married, or because she was holding what he wanted and she didn't appear willing to give it up.

"I'm looking for names of people Olivia knew so I can talk to them. Until you came back, I couldn't get to any of her personal things."

It was on the tip of her tongue to ask him what made him think he could have access now. But that was her independence asserting itself. She couldn't afford to irritate him. For a number of reasons.

"Look," he began, seeming to realize he'd assumed more than he should. "Your mother routinely confided in you. And you said yourself that you aren't getting much information out of your brother. If you'll help me with my investigation, I'll see that you don't have to rely on him to keep up with what's going on, or worry about bothering the detectives. I'll tell my contact at the department that we have an arrangement, and keep you informed about anything that develops myself."

Eve felt the faintest trace of tension ease from her shoulders. She already knew she'd do whatever she could to help find her mother's killer, and to have access to the investigation through Rio would be a godsend. Not only would she know what was going on, she also would have the chance she needed to get to know him.

"I need some of the numbers in here," she said, thinking that he hadn't changed in at least one respect. He still seemed as driven as ever. She knew he'd been working since at least nine o'clock this morning. Twelve hours later, he was still at it. "The police made a copy of this and her calendar. I'll make photocopies of them and bring them by your office. Maybe I could buy you lunch?"

She didn't know if he was interested in her offer. Only that he was either surprised or intrigued by it. His eyebrow had barely arched when his attention was diverted by the little girl whose curiosity about their visitor had kicked in the moment her song was over.

Three

Molly stood in the study doorway, her long pink night-gown falling off one shoulder and puddling on the tops of her bare toes. Ted, her battered, blue teddy bear, dangled from one hand.

Eve didn't move. She wasn't sure she even breathed.

The address book had lost Rio's attention. Turning to the door, an easy, wholly unexpected smile stole over his face.

"Well, hi there," he said, that same smile entering his deep voice. "Is your show over?"

"The good part is." Molly's eyes, blue like her mother's, moved up his frame. As small as she was, he must have looked like a mountain to her. "I'm Molly Stuart. Who are you?"

"Rio Redtree." Yanking at the knees of his khakis, he crouched down in front of the curious child and held out his hand. "Nice to meet you, Molly."

Molly grinned and, doing what she thought people did when they went through this routine, laid her small hand in his broad palm.

As long as her mom was around, no person was a stranger. So it wasn't her daughter's behavior that gave Eve pause—even when Molly screwed up her nose at his last name and said she didn't know people could be named after colored trees. It was Rio's manner that was so unexpected.

It had been her experience that men, unless they were already familiar with children, tended to treat any human in the three-feet-tall range with either ambivalence, suspicion or a combination of both. Certainly, she'd never suspected Rio would seem so comfortable around a child. Not given how certain he'd been about never wanting any of his own.

Confusion joined trepidation as Molly, noticing the ring he wore, took his hand in both of hers and turned it over. Rio didn't seem to mind her interest. Nor did he seem in any particular hurry to get back to what he'd been so interested in just moments ago. As he explained the shapes etched in the heavy silver of the ring, Rio seemed as intent on the child as the child was on him.

"The symbol here is Cheyenne. And this one is Arapaho. The feather is important for lots of reasons, and the three blue circles," he explained, scanning her delicate features after he'd pointed out what he was talking about, "are a symbol of the Arapaho people."

"What's Cheyenne and Rapa...what is it?"

"Arapaho. They're the Indian tribes of my parents." His glance moved over her pigtails, taking in her hair's deep sable color. "Arapaho men used to tattoo the circles on their chests, and the women would tattoo a single circle right there." He touched his index finger to the center of her forehead.

Molly giggled. "What's a tattoo?"

"Come on, Molly," Eve cut in, curving a protective hand over one small shoulder. "You know who's here now, so go back to your movie."

The little girl looked up at her mom, her head tipping backward. "But I want to know what a tattoo is."

"It's like a drawing on your skin," Rio continued, never taking his glance from the little girl.

"Mommy won't let me draw on myself."

The way Molly's cupid's bow mouth drew up in one corner when she frowned made Rio smile again. He couldn't help it. The kid was a charmer.

He sat back on his haunches, watching the child's somber expression turn animated once more when he agreed that moms could sometimes ruin the really fun stuff. The women at the wedding had been right. Eve's daughter was, indeed, a tiny little thing. Delicate, dainty. Dainty, that was, except for the chokehold she had on her cyanotic stuffed bear. She had her mother's azure eyes and the same engaging smile. But there was a familiarity to the rest of her features that had him feeling as if something heavy was sitting on his chest.

That familiarity wasn't there because of her mother. As Eve was so fair, he didn't think it likely that Molly's dusky skin and nearly black hair had come from her gene pool. He had no idea what Eve's father had looked like, but the surname Stuart did not conjure up an image of a swarthy man. As for Olivia, the woman had been pale as milk. If it weren't for all the time Eve's brother, Hal, had spent on the slopes last winter and by his pool this summer perfecting his tan, he would have looked the same. What Rio recognized in the apple-cheeked child was the resemblance she bore to his youngest nieces. And to him. She had the same defined cleft above her upper lip and dimple in her chin.

He was thinking she might as well have a sky blue circle tattooed on her forehead when Eve finally snagged the little girl's attention long enough to tell her she needed to say good-night to him and finish her movie.

"Don't sit too close to the television," Eve called as Molly, having done what she was told with little more than an exaggerated sigh, disappeared around the corner.

Casting a furtive glance in Rio's direction, Eve hoped to heaven she wouldn't sound as nervous as she felt.

"Once she starts with questions, it's hard to get her stopped. You wouldn't believe the questions she was asking the gardener yesterday. Now, where were we? Oh, yes," she said, hurrying on, easing the death grip she had on the address book. "I'll bring a copy of this to you tomorrow. Okay?"

She was speaking to stone. Rio's attention was still fixed on the doorway, his stance rigid. Though she could see only his profile, it didn't appear that what she'd said registered at all.

"Will that be all right?" she asked, trying again.

Seconds passed with the tick of the clock on the desk. Muffled music filtered down the hall from the television. When he finally turned to face her, his eyes settled hard on hers.

"She's a cute kid."

Ambivalence sliced through her. "Yes. She is."

"I don't suppose you adopted her."

The statement wasn't unreasonable. Not given the disparity in looks between mother and daughter. It was Rio's phrasing that made Eve's heart kick her ribs. To anyone else, the question might have sounded like simple curiosity. To Eve, it sounded like a process of elimination.

"No," she quietly returned. "I didn't."

"Did you have another Indian boyfriend?"

"No."

"How old is she?"

"Rio, we need…"

"It's a simple question." His tone was mild. Deceptively so. "How *old* is she?"

The edge of the address book bit into her palm. "Five."

A muscle in his jaw constricted, tightening the cords in his strong neck and turning his tone utterly flat.

"I was careful, Eve. We always used protection. Always," he repeated, as if she were going to dispute the fact.

Eve had no intention of doing any such thing. She had no intention, either, of pointing out that protection obviously didn't always work. Rio was doing a fine job of drawing his own conclusions.

"She's mine, isn't she."

She wished she could read him. She wished something about that frustratingly impenetrable facade would let her know what was going on inside his head. But he kept his thoughts too hidden. Just as he always had.

The Fates, she decided, were truly perverse. Of all the things that had changed in the past six weeks—the past six years, for that matter—Rio's ability to suppress his reactions seemed the one thing that had remained the same.

"Yes," she admitted, not sure if she should be relieved or worried by his apparent calm. "She is."

"How much longer before she goes to bed?"

"She should be there now. Why?"

It was hard enough to gauge his reaction with him facing her; it was impossible for her to comprehend what she was up against when he turned to the night-blackened window.

"Go take care of her. I'll wait."

Molly's movie wasn't over, but it really was past her bedtime and she had day camp in the morning. Since Molly loved camp, she offered only a token protest, then, on the way to the stairs, reminded Eve of her promise to leave on the hall light so the monster under her bed wouldn't get her.

The monster nightmare was new. Hating the thought of her little girl being scared, Eve promised not only to leave the light on, but that she would personally check to make sure the only things under the bed were dust bunnies. When that didn't completely alleviate Molly's fear, Eve caved in and tucked the child into her own bed.

Her little girl's eyes were already closing when, prayers, hugs and kisses dispensed, Eve left the room, leaving the light on as promised.

Rio was right where she'd left him in the study.

He still stood in front of the window, his hands on his hips and his shoulders rigid. Eve didn't know what he saw beyond the dark glass. Or even if he noticed anything at all. In the reflection, it looked as if his eyes were closed.

Feeling as if she were shutting the gate on a cage, she closed the door behind her with a quiet click and leaned against it.

He didn't move. "Why didn't you tell me?"

"I couldn't."

"Couldn't? Was someone physically restraining you?"

"Of course not. What I meant—"

"What you meant," he interrupted, wheeling around, "is you wouldn't." He kept his voice deliberately low. "All you had to do was say, Rio, I'm pregnant."

He made it sound as simple as commenting on the weather.

"And what would you have done?" she retorted, regarding his attitude as highly unfair. "Helped me put her up for adoption? Paid for an abortion? You didn't want children," she pointed out as something fierce flashed in his eyes. "You told me so yourself when you talked about what you wanted to do with your life. Even if you had wanted them, it's not as if marriage had been an option. I didn't know that much about you. Until you mentioned it to Molly a few minutes ago, I didn't even know what tribes you came from."

"There'd have been no abortion."

There was as much possessiveness as moral conviction in his curt pronouncement. She should have found that telling. All she considered was that he'd responded to the only thing that had never been an issue.

"I never even considered one," she muttered, amazed by how he'd completely missed the point.

Determined to be reasonable, she reiterated what he'd conveniently overlooked. "You didn't want children," she repeated. "I asked you once how you felt about them and you made it perfectly clear that they were fine for other people, but not for you. Kids hold a person back, you said, and nothing was going to stop you from getting where you were going. You were positively driven, Rio. You had to graduate and get a job on a paper and work your way up to the city desk. For all I knew, you had plans for a Pulitzer and a move to the *New York Times*. If it didn't have to do with your career, it wasn't in the equation."

Rio didn't deny a word she said. As implacable as ever,

he planted his hands on his hips and stared at the nap in the carpet while he wore down the enamel on his back teeth. She'd never known him to let anything stand in his way. From the moment she'd met him, he'd known exactly what he was going to do, and when; what he wanted for himself—and what he didn't want. That confidence was one of the things she'd admired most about him. Especially when back then, she'd had so little confidence in herself.

When she'd first met him, she'd been a slightly overwhelmed, seventeen-year-old college freshman. Rio had already finished three years of college in two and was cramming his senior year into six months. She didn't doubt he'd finished right on his schedule, either. According to her mom, he'd been the youngest intern ever hired onto the *Herald*'s staff.

"You knew what you wanted," she repeated, thinking of how quickly a person could learn to stand on her own when she had to. "But I didn't. I was seventeen, Rio. I hardly knew what I wanted to major in, much less what I wanted to do with the rest of my life. The way I saw it, we were in a situation that wouldn't work for any of us. It was best to go away and give the baby up for adoption."

She'd been seventeen.

Rio wasn't sure why that made him wince. Grappling with the knowledge that he had a child, he didn't try to figure it out. He was a reasonable man. He prided himself on his objectivity, his ability to see both sides of a story—and he knew for a fact that he'd done everything in his power to remain objective about Eve. But any sense of perspective he'd had was forever gone. She hadn't believed he would do right by her. She'd doubted his integrity. Rather than trust him to work the problem out with her, she'd chosen to run away from him. At the moment, her distrust and deceit were all he could think about.

Tension vibrated from him like sound waves from a tuning fork.

"That's very compelling, Eve. Except you didn't *give* her up."

"I didn't plan to keep her. I didn't," she repeated, because he so clearly didn't believe her. "But when I saw her, I couldn't bear to part with her." She didn't know how to describe to him what she'd felt. Or even if it would matter. "I even thought you might change your mind about children if you saw her yourself."

Had there been any room for Eve to back up, she would have done so by then. As it was, with her back pressed to the door, there was nowhere for her to go. Hating the position she found herself in, resenting him for putting her there, she deliberately tipped up her chin.

She didn't understand the accusation in his eyes, or the anger he held so tightly in check. Those were things a man who'd felt cheated would feel. She would have understood if he'd been indifferent to what he'd just discovered. Or if he'd felt threatened or skeptical. She wouldn't have been surprised had he told her he wanted nothing to do with their little girl. Or if he'd become wary and wanted to know what she expected from him. But she'd never expected him to act as if she'd betrayed him by keeping the child from him.

Unable to bear his accusation any longer, she hugged her arms to her chest and moved to pace between the desk and the door.

"I tried to call you after she was born," she said, her voice strained. "You have no idea how much courage it took to finally make that call. I think I picked up the phone twenty times before I actually pressed all the numbers.

"It had been between semesters," she recalled, wanting him to know this even if it didn't matter to him. Now that he knew about Molly, she wanted everything out in the open. It was the only way they could get over the past and do what was best for Molly. "I'd tried to call you at your apartment, but after a couple of days of getting no answer, I figured you'd gone home for the break."

She hadn't been sure where "home" was exactly, other

than on the reservation northwest of Grand Springs, but she finally got a number for his mother. Only, when she had asked for him and his mother had asked who she was, any thought Eve had of sharing the news of their daughter died right there.

"Your mom said she didn't want me to talk to you anymore. It seemed you had a new girlfriend."

I must ask you to leave my son alone, Eve Stuart. You are not of our people, and Rio knows his obligations. My son has a nice Indian girlfriend now.

Hesitation washed over Rio's expression. Jaw working, he pulled a deep breath. Seconds later, his thoughts seeming dark and distant, his displeasure expanded. "She never told me you called."

That didn't surprise Eve. What did, was that she could still remember how hurt she'd been. Focusing on the bookshelf, she told herself she'd had no business feeling that way. She had left him. He'd had every right to move on to someone else. But the fact that Rio hadn't denied the truth to what his mother had said somehow made the hurt seem fresh all over again.

That made no sense at all, she told herself, and concentrated on what had been truly important about her conversation with Rio's mother, for it had revealed an obstacle she hadn't even realized existed.

"I didn't think she had," she quietly concluded. "But what your mother said made it pretty obvious she wouldn't take kindly to the idea of a half-breed for a granddaughter. It seemed to me that if you understood the obligations she mentioned, you might not have been too thrilled, either."

Eve hugged herself tighter. "I remember picking up Molly after I'd hung up the phone and trying to pretend I'd never seen her before. I knew she was darker than I was, but to me, she was just my precious baby and everything about her was beautiful. I hadn't thought about the color of her eyes or her hair or her skin. All that had mattered was that she had ten fingers and ten toes and she was healthy.''

She'd been blind to so much, she thought, aware of his shadow covering her. Too much. ''Your mother made me realize that you probably wouldn't have seen her the way I did, and that you had responsibilities to what she'd called 'your people.' That was when I realized how little I truly knew about you.''

He'd come up behind her. She could feel him. But she wasn't prepared for the feel of his hand on her shoulder, or the heat in his eyes when he turned her to face him.

''My mother was out of line saying what she did. And she had no business keeping your call from me. But you never should have left to begin with. You knew all that mattered.'' Defense marked his tone. Bridled anger etched his features. ''My heritage is important to me. So is my family. But I decided a long time ago that neither the tribe nor my family was going to dictate my life.''

''You never told *me* that. You rarely talked about your family, and you never mentioned your heritage at all. How was I supposed to know how you felt if you never told me?''

''You knew how I felt,'' he insisted. ''I cared about you.'' His heated glance swept her face, the source of his anger eluding her completely. ''I don't know how I could have made that any clearer.''

Nothing she said was getting through to him. Upset as she was, that was her only thought before she felt his hands clench her shoulders. His thumb swept downward, edging lightly along her collarbone, and his hard gaze dropped to her mouth.

He was close enough that she could feel the heat and tension radiating from him. Close enough that she could almost feel his body pressing against hers. But it was the motion of his thumbs that destroyed her attempt to make him understand, and left her feeling completely exposed.

He'd once had the habit of tracing her collarbone when

he'd been about to kiss her. He'd be trying to make a point, or telling her about something that had happened that day, and his thumbs would do what they were doing now. Inevitably, his hands would slide up into her hair and he'd settle his mouth over hers, turning her knees weak and her blood to steam. He would kiss her hard. Or sometimes he was so gentle she'd want to cry. But, always, she never wanted him to stop.

The memory shouldn't have tugged so deeply. The weight of his hands shouldn't have felt so familiar. But what should have been bore scant resemblance to what was.

"I think we both need some time," she said, not caring how unsteady she sounded. "This is..." Dangerous. Foolish. Irrational.

"Yeah," Rio muttered, seeming to understand what she couldn't articulate. "This isn't good."

He stepped back, disquiet etched in his angular features as his hands slipped away. He pushed one through his hair, backing up another step. "I think I'd better go. We'll talk about this...about Molly," he amended, "later."

Eve started toward the door.

Not trusting himself around her any longer, Rio held up his hand. As jarred as he felt, he was surprised it wasn't shaking. "I can find my way out."

He didn't remember what Eve said, or if she said anything at all before he walked through the brightly lit foyer, past the long entry table with its matching vases and out the front door. He wasn't sure he recalled getting in his Bronco and starting it, either—though he'd obviously done both because, within the minute, he was driving into darkness, heading nowhere in particular except away from the Stuart house.

He felt as if he'd just taken a gut punch. Only, at the moment, he wasn't sure which was more accountable for the sensation. The white heat he'd felt rip through him at the thought of kissing her, the fact that he'd almost done something like kiss her in anger, or the realization that he had a child.

A child.

He was a father.

The night air rushing in his open window smelled of pine and dew. He sucked in a lungful of it, seeking to calm the thoughts careening through his mind. But calm wasn't going to come easily to him. It never did. Had it been daylight, he'd have headed for his lot and exhausted himself hauling wood or hammering a few pounds of nails. But it wasn't light, and though he would have preferred physical activity for the escape it offered, he'd have to settle for being still.

He found himself heading for his lot, anyway, seeking solace in the only place he ever found it anymore.

Two Falls Lake was fifteen minutes out of town and a million miles from civilization. There were several lakes in the area, but this one was too small and too inaccessible to be popular. At night, even Rio didn't attempt the hike down to it, so he left his truck in the clearing near the skeletal frame of his cabin and made his way to the outcropping of rock overlooking the still, black water.

The moon trailed a wide band of light across the glassy surface of the lake. Walls of enormous firs rose up like solemn black sentinels, dwarfing everything below them. There was nothing to be heard here but the sigh of the wind, the occasional yelp of coyotes and the inner voices a man couldn't silence.

He shoved his fingers through his hair, too agitated to appreciate the stillness. Any other time, he could have forced himself to concentrate on the night sounds. Not now. All he could think about now was that Eve had been pregnant when she'd left years ago.

The thought that had made him wince earlier came rushing back to him. The fact that the protection they'd used had failed was a moot point. So was his mother's interference, and to indulge his anger with her would only dredge up resentments he never allowed himself to think about, anyway. There was no changing what was done. But what bothered him most was that Eve hadn't only been pregnant—she'd been seventeen and pregnant. Had he ever given any thought to her age when he'd known her?

He couldn't have, Rio decided, or he'd have considered just how dangerous sleeping with her could be. To him, she'd just been Eve; the person who'd never questioned his goals, who'd looked up to him. The one person who had finally allowed him to believe in himself. Looking back now, he'd been light-years older than she was—even though he'd only been nineteen at the time. But, then, Stone Richardson, his detective friend, had once told him he'd probably been born old.

Rio drew his hand down his face and blew out a breath. Dear God, he thought, she'd been jailbait. On top of that, her mother had been the mayor, as close to "society" as people came in Grand Springs. His home had been a trailer on the reservation, and he'd possessed nothing but a determination to escape the specter of his father and a fire in his belly for a dream no one wanted him to pursue. It was a miracle Olivia hadn't had his sorry hide thrown in jail.

There were spirits to be thanked for that, he was sure. He just wasn't sure which ones handled that sort of thing. Anyway, he was more concerned with what had happened than with what hadn't. He hadn't wanted a child. Not then. Not now. The problem was figuring out what to do about the daughter he'd just discovered he had.

It was late afternoon the next day before Eve heard from Rio. As it was, she didn't actually talk to him. She was at the women's shelter dropping off boxes of clothing when he called, but he'd left a message on her mom's answering machine. It was the only message on the tape.

"Eve, it's Rio. I'm tied up for the next few days. If you wouldn't mind dropping the photocopies of your mom's address book and calendar off at the newspaper, I'd appre-

ciate it. Stick them in an envelope with my name on it and
leave it at the desk inside the main door.'' There was a
pause, a long one that seemed to indicate there was something else he needed to add. Something about his daughter,
perhaps. But ''Thanks'' was all he finally said.

Eve listened to the tape rewind and glanced at the photocopies and the address book she'd just placed beside the
photo of Molly that Olivia kept on the corner of her desk.
Eve and Molly had made the copies while they'd been out.

He'd be tied up for a few days, he'd said.

If she were to give him the benefit of the doubt, she had
to admit he might need a little time to come to grips with
what he'd learned last night. Anyone would. A man didn't
wake up one morning realizing he was the father of a child
he'd known nothing about without feeling a little shell-
shocked. But his message hadn't said a word about
Molly....

Eve pulled a manila envelope from the desk drawer and
wrote Rio's name on it. It was obvious what his priority
was.

Hers was to forget what she'd felt when he touched her.

By the following Monday, any uneasiness Eve felt about
her reaction to Rio was buried under a healthy dose of
frustration with her brother. Hal had come up with every
excuse short of having to do his nails to avoid checking
over the inventory she'd prepared for the attorney. He
seemed to be avoiding everything that had anything to do
with settling their mother's affairs, and that was making
her tasks as executor far harder than they needed to be.

She was hoping Rio wasn't going to follow suit when
she walked into Clancy's Grill, the publike restaurant where
he'd asked her to meet him, and saw him slide from the
booth at the back of the long, uncrowded room. Well-worn
jeans hugged his lean hips, and the sleeves of his chambray
shirt were rolled to his elbows, revealing strong, sinewy
forearms. The wide silver band of his watch caught the light

as he planted his hands on his hips, his dark head dipping in a tight, acknowledging nod at her approach.

He looked impatient and rugged and far more sure of himself than she felt at the moment. Seeing him, all she wanted to do was turn around and walk right back out.

"I'd have called sooner," he prefaced the moment she reached him. "But I just got back in town last night. I was in Denver," he added, reseating himself across from her when she slid into the high-backed booth, "so I spent the weekend looking up the people in the Denver area who were listed in Olivia's address book. Those I hadn't already talked to from the wedding, I mean. By the way, thanks for the photocopies."

If it was his intention to throw her off balance, he succeeded beautifully. She hadn't considered that the reason she hadn't heard from him was because he'd been away. She'd thought his silence meant he was either trying to figure out what he wanted to do about Molly, or that he had already decided and was ignoring them both.

With an ease that was becoming all too familiar, the source of her anxiety immediately switched focus. "Did you learn anything?"

"Nothing that helps."

Giving her a look that said "that's the way it goes," he pulled a menu from between a napkin holder and the salt and pepper shakers and held it out to her. As he did, a young girl in a tight Clancy's T-shirt and even tighter jeans set glasses of water in front of them.

Rio ordered a hamburger. Eve didn't care what she ate, so she ordered the same. She doubted she'd taste it, anyway. The issues that had been raised the other night sat between them like an invisible time bomb, ticking away as surely as if the timer had been tripped and killing any trace of an appetite. By the time the waitress returned with their iced tea and departed again, Eve was wondering why she'd ordered at all.

"Have you said anything to Molly?" he asked, just when

Eve had decided to put herself out of her misery and bring up the issue herself. "About who I am?"

She bit back a sigh. He really hadn't understood what she'd said the other night. "I don't *know* who you are, Rio. I meant that when I said it. There was so much I didn't know about you six years ago. I know you even less now." Her lack of knowledge about him was as much her fault as his, she supposed. She'd never asked about his family, his home, what it was that had shaped him. But then, she hadn't thought of him as being any different from herself. How incredibly naive she'd been. How incredibly innocent. "After all this time, we might as well be strangers. That's what makes this all so awkward."

He didn't seem to share her concern with how disconcerting she found their situation. His relief was almost as tangible as the tension tightening his jaw. "Then you didn't tell her."

"I didn't think that would be fair," she explained, unconsciously rolling the corner of her napkin under her knife and fork. "To her or to you. And I do want to be fair to you, Rio. But Molly is my first concern. Until you've decided how involved you want to be with her, or if you want to be involved with her at all, I think it would be better if nothing was said. I don't want her hurt."

Velvet over steel. Rio had heard the expression before, but he'd never realized how impressive the combination was until that moment. Her voice was as gentle as spring rain, but the determination in her impossibly angelic features was unmistakable.

Just because he admired the spirit didn't mean he appreciated the warning. The last thing he intended to do was hurt an innocent child. He knew all too well how far-reaching the actions of a parent could be.

The waitress appeared in record time. Leaning back while she slid their plates onto the table, he wondered at how very little Eve must think of him. The thought only heightened the sense of betrayal he already felt.

He couldn't believe she'd said she hadn't known that much about him. He'd shared with her everything that had mattered to him. He'd never allowed anyone to get as close as he had her. Not before and not since. And he wouldn't have felt so tremendously let down by her had he not once thought she believed in him. But he knew now that when that belief had been put to the test, she'd actually had no more faith in him than had anyone else.

With a ruthlessness he reserved only for himself, he jammed down the resentment he wanted to feel, only to be hit again with the reality of having a child. Every time he thought about it, his stomach tightened. He'd get used to the idea, though. He had to. There were those who would swear he possessed no principles at all, but his sense of honor made denying his responsibility impossible.

Pushing his plate aside the moment the waitress left, he crossed his arms on the table. Eve wasn't the only one who could feel protective. She might as well learn that about him right now.

"I don't regard my involvement as a choice. You're right about my not wanting to have kids, but I've got one now and I'll do what needs to be done for her."

Mirroring his position, Eve leaned forward, her voice just as low, just as certain. "It would do her more harm than good to have a father who regards her only as an obligation. I'd rather she didn't—"

"She's more than an obligation," he growled, his eyes flashing. "She's a child. I'm not going to do to her what my father did to me."

Eve went still.

Aware of heads turning in their direction, Rio pulled a deep breath and lowered his head. Though he doubted anyone had heard what they were saying, it was apparent to anyone with a functioning brain that they weren't discussing the weather.

"What did your father do?" Eve whispered.

"He left. It happens," he muttered, dismissing the impact of that long-ago event to focus on his daughter. "But I won't abandon Molly." He met Eve's eyes, bracing himself against the quick, unguarded empathy he saw there. "As for how involved I get, we'll just have to play that by ear. How long before you go back to California?"

For a moment, Eve said nothing. She simply studied the strong, sculpted features that betrayed nothing but the tension she'd noticed the moment she'd seen him. Whatever Rio was dealing with where his father was concerned was buried. But she now realized that his reasons for not wanting a family of his own were far more complicated than she'd thought. *He* was more complicated than she'd thought. But while she found his conviction to do right by his daughter admirable, she also found it threatening.

"I don't want to go back until the house is sold," she told him, amazed by how rational she sounded when another piece of her life was slipping from her control. "Or before the police finish their investigation. But school starts in September, so I'll have to be back by then."

"What about your job? I understand you're an interior designer. It was on the police report," he added, since she looked as if she didn't know where he'd come by the information.

"I'm on a leave of absence."

"So you'll be around for a couple of months."

"Probably."

"How much support do you want?"

Her brow creased. "Support?"

"Money."

"Is that what you think?" The furrows in her forehead increased in direct proportion to his. "That this is about money?"

"Isn't that part of it?" he muttered, not sure why her back was up. "I figure it's something we need to talk about. I'm new at this, Eve. I've never had a kid pop out of the blue before, so forgive me if I don't know the right place to start or how to approach this in a logical order."

He didn't want to argue with her. From the way she closed her eyes and rubbed the middle of her forehead, it appeared that she didn't, either. It was just that, knowing she was supporting the child alone, his concerns had immediately gone to the practical.

What Eve wanted was something more complicated than that.

"If you truly want to be part of her life, then all I want right now is for her to get used to you, and for you to get to know her. We'll start out slow and see what happens. This changes my life as much as it does yours, Rio. Let's not make it any harder than it has to be."

She didn't hide how wary she was about the situation. He doubted she could if she tried. But now he noticed the weariness that shadowed her eyes and put the faint plea in her voice.

"We'll do it your way," he conceded, though it wasn't much of a concession, considering he had no definite concept of where else to start. "It's probably best for Molly to ease into the idea of having a father. I could use a little more time to adjust to the idea myself.

"As for what you keep implying about you and me being strangers," he added, his voice skimming her nerves like the low rumble of distant thunder, "I wouldn't go quite that far. We've slept together. We created a child together. At one point, I even thought we were friends."

The recrimination in his words was subtle. But it was there. It was there, too, in the ebony eyes that so steadily held hers.

He didn't seem to expect a response. There was none she could give him, anyway. Despite the doubt he'd expressed, they had been friends. They had shared their bodies with each other. Molly existed. But there was something about facing their intimacy head-on that removed any possibility of pretense at that moment. He had taught her how to make love, how to respond to him, to his touch. That was how close they had been.

Try as she might, she couldn't help the way her pulse picked up speed at the thought. From the way Rio's eyes darkened as he quietly watched her now, he seemed to be remembering that, too.

The memories shimmered between them, enlivening nerves and making the air feel too thick to breathe. But those memories were surrounded by the walls the years had built. Far too much had happened for them to ever regain the innocence of their beginning. And as he deliberately looked away, Eve knew the trust they'd once shared could never be the same.

Four

It had taken some doing, and more than another week, but Eve finally coerced her brother into looking over the inventory she'd prepared of their mother's earthly possessions. The message she'd left on his answering machine had finally done the trick. She'd made it clear that it wasn't his help she was after. Or his approval. She didn't need either. She wanted him to review what she'd prepared only because she didn't want to leave him out of anything. But if he wasn't interested in what was going on with the estate, she'd have the attorney file the inventory as it was. Tomorrow. Before the first of August.

She'd left the message that morning. Hal himself had arrived a few minutes ago, just as she and Molly were finishing the lasagna Millicent had brought over. He'd promptly declined her offer of a drink or something to eat and, with little more than a perfunctory "Where is it?" proceeded to pace the dining room while he studied the long yellow pad she'd handed him.

Eve couldn't see him from where she stood at the sink, surrounded by copper pots and the wildflower-patterned plates visible through the glass doors of the cabinets. But every minute or so she could hear the sharp crackle of a page being quickly turned. The sound was as agitated as Hal himself.

Had she thought it would do any good, she'd have gone in there with him. She knew he hadn't been inside the house since the funeral, so his being here had to be difficult for him. There were so many memories a person had to sort through when faced with a loss, and being eight years older than she, he had eight more years of memories to deal with than she did. But he didn't seem to want whatever support she could have offered. He just wanted to get the job done so he could leave.

She turned the water off at the sink and reached for the towel. As she did, she became aware of voices drifting through the foyer from the front porch. The low tones were definitely male. The higher ones were Molly's giggle.

The male voice didn't belong to Hal, either.

Since Molly and her teddy bear were outside playing with her dolls, Eve had left the front door open. The little girl liked the big railed porch with its wicker chairs and potted geraniums better than the backyard because, out front, she could watch the big kids play.

Eve could hear the boys now, the three preteens from two doors down. The new dentist's sons, Millicent had told her. They were playing hacky sack on the sidewalk. Even with them out there, Eve still didn't want her daughter talking to strange men.

She was past the narrow entry table in the foyer when some of the urgency left her stride. Rio sat on the top step next to Molly. A black shirt covered his broad back and one back pocket of his faded jeans was worn white around his wallet. She couldn't see much of his face, though. Molly was on her knees beside him, grinding dirt into her pink overalls as she scooted as close as she could get to see what he held in his hands. With her dark little head bent toward his, one of her beribboned pigtails had draped across his shoulder. There wasn't a shade's worth of difference in the color of their hair.

Eve started to open the screen, only to be stopped by what she could hear Rio saying.

"It does look like a spiderweb," he quietly said, sounding as if he were confirming an observation. "It's supposed to. Have you ever seen a bug caught in one?"

The smaller head bobbed vigorously.

"Do you know why they can't get out?"

Molly's head went just as vigorously the other way.

"It's because a real web is sticky. The more the bug struggles, the more it gets caught. That's why the bad dreams can't get out of a dream catcher, either. When you go to sleep, the good dreams know the way through the hole right here in the center. Then they slide down the feather so they can come back to you and you can dream them again. But the bad dreams don't know the way out. They get caught in the web, and when the sun rises the next morning, they disappear."

The two heads became two profiles as Rio and Molly looked at each other.

"Really?"

"It worked for me," he said, looking as honest as a Boy Scout. "I had one when I was little, and I sure don't remember having dreams about monsters under my bed." He nodded toward the hoop of twig and crystal-clear filament Molly held in her hands. "Maybe it'll work for you, too. I'll hang that above your bed if you want."

As Molly skeptically studied the talisman, Eve realized that Rio must have heard Molly mention the monster the other night on her way upstairs. That was the only reason she could think of why he had brought the child such a gift.

In light of everything he'd learned that night, the fact that he'd remembered something so seemingly insignificant was definitely telling. So was the concern he'd shown by wanting to alleviate a child's fears.

Rio was still sitting on the step, but he'd noticed her standing in the doorway. He lifted his chin to acknowledge her, then returned his attention to the child.

"So what do you think?" he asked. "Should we ask your mom if we can hang it?"

As gifts went, Molly was more accustomed to girl-stuff. Spiders and twigs were definitely in the boy category. Still, she must have been impressed either by Rio's story, or with

Rio himself. After another moment of consideration, she gave him a nod, remembered to say "Thank you," and before Rio knew what was coming, she threw her arms around his neck.

He clearly wasn't prepared for the impulsive response. The instant Molly's wiry little body pressed to his chest, he went stock-still. Seconds later, looking as if he feared the child might break, he swallowed hard, closed his eyes—and hugged her back.

The breath Eve drew caught in her throat. Rio had never held his daughter before, and the moment left him totally exposed. Fear, wonder, apprehension and joy were all wound up in an expression that bordered on pain. The feelings were familiar. She had experienced them herself the very first time Molly had been placed in her arms. She still felt them sometimes just watching Molly sleep. But Rio was revealing far more of himself in this unguarded moment than he could possibly realize. No man who did not truly care for children could possibly be so moved by nothing more than an exuberant hug.

She realized something else, too. She was very probably going to lose a piece of her daughter's heart.

Molly's narrow little body had all but disappeared in his strong arms. But as quickly as she had flung herself at him, she just as quickly pulled back.

Seeing her mom, she turned her grin to her and held up the saucer-size hoop. Its gray feather swayed from a beaded leather thong.

"See what he brought me, Mommy." She frowned at the man rising beside her. "What is it called? Oh, yeah!" Remembering, she turned back before he could answer. "It's a dream catcher. It's going to catch the monster under the bed and make it disappear."

"So I heard," Eve returned, her soft smile masking the quick surge of annoyance she felt with the bearer of the gift. "Do you want to play out here for a while longer, or come inside?"

"Stay out here."

Eve's glance slid to Rio.

Taking the hint, his air of control firmly in place, he stepped inside with her. Following her far enough into the foyer to escape inquisitive little ears, he matched her frown.

"What's the matter?"

"You shouldn't tell her things like that. If she has a bad dream now, she's not going to believe anything else you say."

"I didn't promise she wouldn't have bad dreams," he said, defending himself. "You heard what I said. I said maybe it would work. And it will, if she believes it."

"But it's deceptive."

"Deceptive? You've never told her about Santa Claus? Or the tooth fairy?" He eyed her evenly, his expression turning shrewd. "Does it bother you that I brought her something?"

What bothered her was that he might be able to calm a fear of Molly's that Eve hadn't been able to do anything about herself. Not sure if she was feeling jealous or inadequate, suspecting more of the former, she made herself back down.

"Maybe. A little," she amended, wishing he couldn't read her so easily.

"Would you prefer that I checked with you before I brought her anything?"

There was enough challenge in the question to make it clear that he was testing his ground where Molly was concerned. Or maybe he was testing her. The more she was around him, the more apparent it became that they couldn't go longer than a few minutes without stepping on each other's toes. Before, they'd never argued about anything.

"Only if it will ruin a meal, or needs to be fed." They definitely had to set a few more rules. But now wasn't the time. Not with Hal and Molly around. "As for what you just brought," she had to add, because she truly was touched by what he'd done, "it was a very thoughtful gift."

Her last words were underscored by the faint squeak of the back screen door. Hal must have heard their voices, she thought, and headed out for a cigarette. Considering that he didn't want to be there to begin with, it was a sure bet he wasn't up to meeting anyone dropping by.

"My brother's here," she said, since Rio had heard the door, too. "Did you come just to see Molly?"

A faint frown pinched Rio's forehead as he glanced over her shoulder. Seeming a little distracted when he looked back at her, he pushed his hands into his pockets. "I just met a friend not too far from here, so I thought I'd drop the dream catcher off for her."

"A friend?"

"Stone Richardson. You've met him."

The skirmish of moments ago was all but forgotten as the image of a big, square-jawed cop formed in her mind. Detective Richardson was on the team investigating her mother's death. "Several times," she confirmed, thinking there was precious little Rio didn't seem to know about her. "He's the one who told me about the woman from the ski lodge. The one who had the visions about Mom."

The strange visions plaguing Jessica Hanson in the days following Olivia's death were what had turned the pain of losing her mother into an ongoing nightmare. Until the coroner had requested the autopsy based on what the soft-spoken and shy young woman had "seen," everyone accepted that Olivia had died of natural causes.

"Has she offered any new information?" she asked, speaking of Jessica.

Rio pulled a breath, hating how susceptible he was to her when they talked about the investigation. Every time she asked a question, her eyes would fill with hope. And every time he saw that hope, it never failed to get to him.

"There's no new information. Stone accepts that Jessica can see things that have happened in the past. But it seems she's had a couple of premonitions about things that haven't happened yet, and that's got him a little nervous. He knows I believe in psychics."

"You do?"

His glance never wavered. "Why not? There's all kinds of energy out there." The songs and chants he'd learned as a child taught that people and nature were all inexorably joined in the sacred circle of life. At its most basic level, Rio figured a cursory study of the food chain bore that claim out easily enough. The elders also taught that nature was energy. The movement of the wind. The beat of a bird wing. The firing of a neuron in a human brain. "Who's to say it can't be transmitted telepathically? Or that the energy patterns forming to make an event happen can't be picked up by a receptive source? But Jessica hasn't had any new visions concerning your mom," he had to tell her, hating how the hope dimmed in her eyes. "I already asked."

Hope might have been dimmed, but it hadn't been defeated. "But she thinks a woman attacked Mom, right? When Detective Richardson explained what had led them to do the autopsy, what it was Jessica was seeing, I mean, he alluded to the attacker being female. Did anyone ever have her look at mug shots of women? Maybe if she did, that would trigger something."

Caution made Rio hesitate. It wasn't unusual in an investigation for the police to withhold information from the public. Most often, the press didn't know what that information was. In this case, it did. Rio did, anyway. But he was no more interested in jeopardizing the case than he was in breaking his word to his friend about what he'd overheard. That was why the paper had never reported all of what Jessica Hanson claimed to have seen in her vision of the attack. That she'd had no sense of a whole person. What she remembered was an impression of the attacker being female, an image of that person's hands, a hypodermic syringe—and the overpowering scent of gardenias.

The public didn't have that particular information. But Rio knew that Hal Stuart, with his connections to the department, certainly would. He'd apparently refrained from sharing any of it with his sister, though. And Rio wasn't in a position to say anything himself.

Unwilling to let her think some avenue wasn't being explored, the best he could do was remind her of what had been reported. "Stone would agree with you. So would I. But Jessica never had an impression of a face." Once more, Rio heard a door closing in the back of the house. "What she visualized could have just as easily been a man in a wig."

The sound of footsteps drew his attention from the disappointment adding to the shadows in Eve's eyes. The slim figure of a man was moving past the doorway leading to the kitchen.

Hal Stuart seemed to catch himself mid-stride. In the time it took for the reporter's commanding presence to register, Hal's eyebrows had slammed together.

"What are you doing here?"

At her brother's surprisingly inhospitable demand, Eve whirled around, her hand flattening over the pearl at her throat.

"Hal? What's the matter with you? This is Rio. Redtree," she added, though she was sure her brother, being a public official, must have met the reporter on any number of occasions.

Hal kept coming, the sound of his polished Italian loafers going from impatient to muffled when he moved from hardwood to Aubusson carpet. He'd loosened his red silk "power" tie from the collar of his tailored white shirt. With his hands planted at the waist of his perfectly pleated slacks, and his meticulously cut, dark blond hair silvering prematurely at his temples, he looked like a poster boy for a high-fashion executive ad. Or he would have, had he been smiling.

The fact that he wasn't puzzled Eve far more than she let on. Her brother usually treated everyone as if they were his best buddy.

"I know who he is," Hal muttered.

Rio was no slouch when it came to being personable himself. Eve had seen his quiet charm at work on Millicent the day he'd shown up on her porch, his gentle patience with Molly only minutes ago. What Eve witnessed now was his absolute self-possession. With her brother staring at him as if he'd like to see him trussed and on a spit, Rio simply inclined his head in acknowledgment and, keeping his hands at his side since the other man had his hands planted on his hips, regarded him evenly.

"How are things going, Hal?"

"You never answered my question."

Eve's glance bounced from the dark and compelling man at her side to her fair-haired brother. At a loss to explain his behavior, she reached for his arm to draw his attention.

"Rio's investigating Mom's death," she told him, catching the scent of tobacco clinging to his shirt. "We were just talking about the woman who had those visions. Apparently she won't be of much more help."

"I know all that. What I want to know is where he gets off following me here. He's been hounding me all day."

"I've only called you twice," Rio countered, his tone as reasonable as Hal's was not. "I don't believe that qualifies as hounding. And just for the record, I didn't know you were here. The only car out front—" Cutting himself off, his glance sliced toward the front door and the vehicle parked at the curb. "I thought you drove a Lexus. Is that your Mercedes out there? The silver SL?"

"Am I going to see that on the front page tomorrow? Acting Mayor Buys New Car?"

Hal's scowl removed the natural affability from his even features. Rio was amazed by the man's defensiveness. Hal Stuart usually covered himself better than this. The city's acting mayor was a master at public relations. In the five years Rio had been on the paper, he'd seen the politician portray sincerity, outrage, sympathy and enthusiasm with the skill of an Oscar-winning actor. But the man wasn't acting now. Noting the pallor beneath his tan, Rio couldn't help thinking that Hal looked far too tense to make the effort. To him, he looked very much like a man who'd been stretched about as far as he could go and was about to snap.

It also appeared that he wasn't going to be real cooperative.

"Since you are here," Rio continued, too practical to waste the opportunity, "you could save me another phone call in the morning. All I want is your statement about the stock you owned in the mining company Olivia was fighting on its lease renewal. As it stands right now, the article that will appear in the morning paper says you couldn't be reached for comment." It could easily be changed to "refused to comment," but he didn't care to pose that subtle threat. Not with Eve uneasily watching them both. "I can still get your remark in before the paper goes to press tonight."

Closing his eyes, Hal raked his fingers through his hair, his expression moving from defensive to beleaguered.

"The police have already questioned me about this. I did own stock, but it was a poor choice of investments and I've already unloaded it. It's no secret Mom and I had philosophical differences over the impact of that mine on the environment and the economy here, but it's ludicrous for anyone to think I'd want her harmed because of it. I wish to hell that someone in this town would use a little logic. Why would I be pushing the investigation of anyone involved with the mine if I was illegally involved myself?

"Look," Hal muttered, overlooking the fact that he'd revealed more to his sibling in the past minute than he had in the past month. "I'm as convinced as anyone in this town that someone connected with that mining operation is responsible for my mother's death. Our mother," he amended, belatedly including his sister. "I just wish the police would get some evidence on whoever it is so this would all be over with." He paused, looking as if he didn't know why Rio wasn't writing any of this down. "You've got your statement, Redtree. You can leave now."

Rio said nothing to Hal. He merely looked at Eve, who at that moment had no idea which of the two men she knew the least. Two minutes ago, she'd have bet her sanity she knew far less about Rio. "Hal," she began, "Rio didn't come to get a statement from you. He said he didn't even know you were here, remember? He came to see Molly."

Incomprehension flashed over her brother's features. But any confusion he suffered lasted only long enough for his glance to slide in the general direction of the front porch. Molly had her back to them all, involved as she was with her bear and her dolls.

Hal apparently didn't need a side-by-side comparison, anyway. His narrowed eyes jerked to the man at Eve's side, then back to her.

It was obvious to most people that her child's father was of ethnic blood, but Rio was hardly the only Native American man in town. There had been talk among their family friends since Eve had returned, and speculation, she was sure, about who Molly's father might be. There always was when an unmarried woman had a child. But her mother, fiercely independent herself, had understood that cutting all ties with the father was sometimes the only way a woman could move on with her life, so Eve's secret had been safe. Until now.

"I see."

Without another word, Hal turned on his heel and disappeared through the kitchen. A moment later, having made the loop through the dining and living rooms, he emerged at the opposite end of the foyer near the front door.

His jacket dangled by the middle from his fist.

"I got about halfway through what you wanted me to look at," he told her, refusing to meet her eyes as he fished his cigarettes out of his shirt pocket. "I don't know why you're in such a damn rush to get this done, but if you insist on taking everything to the attorney tomorrow, go ahead.''

The screen opened with a whine, causing Molly to look up from her play. Her sweet ''Bye, Uncle Hal'' drifted in on the early evening breeze, but whether or not Hal answered back, Eve couldn't tell. He didn't break stride until he reached his shiny new car. And not until he reached his car did Eve give up the impulse to go after him, whip him around and make him listen while she explained that she was hardly in a damn rush. She'd already been there for nearly three weeks, and she was simply trying to do what needed to be done. The house couldn't sit there forever. She had other obligations—another *life*—waiting for her a thousand miles away. Though, as removed from it as she felt, it might as well be a million.

Willing herself to calm down, she turned back to Rio, her glance skimming his chin to settle on the middle button of his black rayon shirt. His chest looked so solid, his arms so strong. And she really hated that what she wanted right then was to feel those arms around her.

She was saved having to wonder where that impossible thought had come from by Rio's quiet observation.

''I take it he didn't know.''

''No one did. Other than Mom,'' she added, just as the telephone rang.

Eve closed her eyes and rubbed her temple. Telling herself she could deal with all of this just fine if she'd take things one at a time, she set aside her frustration with her brother, put her concern over the police questioning him on hold and excused herself to the man who was in the process of slowly upending her life. Tomorrow, if she had time, she was going to have a nervous breakdown.

Straightening her shoulders, she headed into the living room.

Rio stayed back, watching her pick up the phone by the deeply tufted royal blue sofa. She seemed rattled and worried, and he was pretty sure from the paleness of her delicate skin that she hadn't slept any better last night than she had the nights before. He was also dead certain she attributed her brother's abrupt departure to what he'd just put together about the two of them.

He didn't think she was right, though. He had been watching Olivia's son for a while now, and he'd bet his Bronco that the man had been more concerned just then with how he had embarrassed himself than with the paternity of his niece. Rio had to admit a little ambivalence on that matter, however. Though it would have been his own hide the guy would have gone for, he'd have thought a lot more of Hal had the man shown a little protectiveness toward his sister. Or even a little interest. As it was, when it came to Hal's treatment of Eve, he was truly beginning to dislike the man.

It appeared that Eve's conversation was going to take a minute. From what he could make of her end of it, the call had to do with a women's shelter auction. With her attention occupied, Rio moved into the elegantly understated room, with its rich colors and gleaming mahogany. He'd never been inside this house until last week. The campus or his apartment had been his and Eve's world. Even when he'd asked Olivia that last time where Eve had gone, he'd done the asking in her mother's office downtown. But this had been Eve's world, too, and it was light-years from the near poverty he'd grown up with.

Had he been the sort of man who craved wealth or possessions, he might have felt resentful or bitter about the disparity. He certainly knew those who would have. Indian and white. But the lure for him had never been material things. He had no need now for anything he didn't already own. So all he considered as he moved through the room, aware of the fresh flowers Eve had added and the potpourri scenting the air with roses and spice, was that Olivia had done very well for herself.

According to what he'd dug up in the archives, Olivia was a self-made woman. Her husband had died twenty-one years earlier, and she'd managed to put herself through law school, work her way into private practice and then into politics, all while raising her family alone.

His glance skimmed Eve's slender frame, her crisp white slacks, the navy blouse, the sleekly fashionable haircut. As he moved into the dining room, he listened to her voice, the certainty and sincerity in it. The sweetness. No one would ever have described Olivia Stuart as "sweet." Tenacious and passionate. Dedicated, definitely. And, in many of those same ways, Eve was definitely her mother's daughter. The one thing she didn't have, however, was her mother's thick skin. When something bothered Eve, it showed.

At least it did to him.

The long mahogany dining table gleamed beneath an ornate brass chandelier. The papers spread over one end caught his attention.

"I'm happy to help," he heard Eve say, listening unashamedly to her conversation as he picked up a long yellow tablet.

He held the tablet toward Eve, lifting it as he raised his eyebrows in silent question to see if she minded his taking a look at it.

Her response was the slight pinch of her brow, but she didn't shake her head no, so he turned his attention to the exhaustingly extensive list.

Thinking that these had to be the papers Hal had referred to before he'd split, Rio cast a quick glance across the rest of the documents. Those nearest a vase filled with yellow roses were formal pleadings that Wendall Norton, a local attorney, had prepared for filing with the probate court. Beyond them was the calling card of a real estate agent and an unsigned agreement to list the house for sale. What Rio held appeared to be a list of every item of value in the place. Everything from the crystal sparkling in the china cabinet behind him to every teaspoon, book and trowel in the house, garage and garden shed.

He pulled a breath and slowly released it. He didn't have to try very hard to remember the day he'd come barging in here with all the finesse of a tank wanting his interview. Eve had been sorting through her mother's clothes when he'd arrived, and the task had torn her apart. It seemed that she'd since had to go through the entire house.

"If you're sure that's what she wanted to donate, I'll pick one up and drop it by the center this week. No, that's fine. I can do it myself. I'm sure the electronics store on Juniper has plenty of VCRs. It's no problem at all."

She watched him from across the room as she spoke. Hanging up a few moments later, she looked from him to the list he held. The consternation she'd masked during her call reasserted itself.

"That's private."

It wouldn't be once it was filed with the court, but he didn't mention that. He wasn't looking for a story. Though he didn't want to admit it, he just wanted to know what all she was dealing with.

He also wanted to know why she was looking at him as if he'd just pulled the wings off a butterfly.

He set the tablet back on the table. "I didn't think you minded. I was just looking."

"Like you were just asking my brother about his car and his stock?"

The accusation in her voice threw him. "What?"

"You heard me."

"Eve, I was doing my job. He's the one who assumed I'd come here looking for him. I wouldn't have brought any of that up, if he hadn't."

"It doesn't matter who brought it up." Crossing her arms, she moved toward him, stopping a cautious arm's length away. "I just want to know what that was all about. Why would the police treat Hal like a suspect?"

She was truly bewildered. That was easy enough to see. He could also tell, despite the way she'd deliberately lowered her voice, or maybe because of it, that she was more upset than she wanted to let on.

"The police are looking into anything that appears even remotely out of line, Eve. No one is exempt."

"But he's family!"

She spoke as if the relationship provided automatic immunity. Hal was family, therefore he was incapable of harming any of its members. While Rio admired her loyalty and idealism, he couldn't help wondering at her naiveté.

"I take it you don't catch much of the evening news or crime shows," he muttered, not particularly proud of how jaded his own thinking had become.

"I have a five-year-old. At our house it's Pony Princess and reruns of 'Mr. Ed.' But I don't see what that has to do with anything."

"It has to do with motive. That's the key to any investigation. The members of the victim's family are usually the first people the police check out in a murder case. Especially when one of those members isn't being terribly cooperative. Your brother didn't even want them to do the autopsy that revealed what had happened to your mother. Remember?"

Of course she remembered. The fact that she hadn't sided with Hal on that issue hadn't helped his attitude toward her at all.

"Did it occur to anyone to consider the stress he was under at the time? If he was less than cooperative, it was because it seemed so unnecessary to him to have that awful procedure done on her. If you think he's not as cooperative as he should be now, maybe it's because he's as frustrated as I am with the lack of progress in the investigation. Instead of wasting time looking into his affairs, the police should be out looking for whoever killed our mother. It's been nearly two months."

Molly was on the porch. For her daughter's sake, Eve tried to calm herself. She didn't want Molly to know she was upset. The little girl never slept well when she knew her mommy was troubled.

"Losing Mom has been hard on him," she continued, her tone lower even if her level of anger and frustration was not. "Aside from that, I don't think he's heard a word from his fiancée since she left. I don't know if he's hurt or worried or what he's dealing with there, but being dumped two minutes before the ceremony would certainly impact a person's mood. When you add all that to the fact that he's trying to handle his city council work along with doing Mom's job, it doesn't take a degree in psychology to figure out that the stress might be getting to him."

Her thick bangs slipped down to brush the corner of her eye and the top of her cheek. She started to push them back, but when she lifted her hand it was trembling. Not wanting him to notice, she lowered her hand before it reached her chin and recrossed her arms.

That small show of control got to him.

Had it not been for that effort, he could have stepped back, considered himself chastised and let it go at that. But he knew the stress of all she was dealing with was getting to her, too. It was obvious to anyone who cared to look closely enough. But instead of thinking of her own needs the way her brother seemed to do, she reached beyond herself, graciously handling all that needed to be done and protecting the people she cared about. Her daughter. Her brother.

He didn't want another connection to her. Sharing a child and needing her as a source were about two too many strings as it was. But Rio understood all too well the need to keep feelings in check. And to protect. Like it or not, that was how he felt toward her. He must have. Otherwise, he'd have put the questions he had about her brother to her long before now.

"I understand things aren't easy for him," he said, his objectivity firmly in place. The guy really had been dumped on lately, and, despite his thoughts about the way he was treating Eve, Rio kept his mind truly open where Hal was concerned. The chips could fall either way. "It's just that he raises more questions than he answers, Eve. Take that car he's driving." He lifted his hand toward the door, then threaded his fingers through his own hair to keep from pushing her bangs back from her eyes. "How can he afford a new Mercedes on a public servant's salary? That car's worth sixty thousand bucks, easy. The Lexus hadn't been cheap, either. Thirty, at least. Is he spending his inheritance already?"

She shot him a disgusted look.

Taking that for a no, he tried again.

"He mentioned investments. Is that how he makes his money?"

She didn't know. And when Eve admitted that, she also had to admit that yet another facet of her life was no longer what it had once been. She and her brother had never been close, but now it seemed she knew precious little about him. Except for one thing.

"I love my brother, Rio. And he loved Mom as much as I did. He can't possibly know anything about her murder."

She spoke with conviction, but what Rio heard was a plea. She wanted him to believe as she believed. Or maybe, he thought, lifting his hand toward her face, she was just trying to find a belief she could hold on to herself.

With the tip of his finger, he drew her bangs away from her eyebrows. Her skin was warm to his touch, and so soft that it almost felt like air.

His fingers lingered at her temple, his palm curving near the side of her face. "For your sake, I hope not," he said. Feeling her head move almost imperceptibly toward his hand, he pulled away.

From the way he stepped back, his jaw working as he shoved his hands in his pockets, it was apparent that his action had caught him off guard. But while Rio looked as if he wished he'd kept his hands to himself, Eve couldn't deny the oddly calming effect the gesture seemed to have on her. Maybe it was because it had so abruptly shifted her focus. Or maybe it had been the gentleness of the contact itself. As big as he was, as strong as he was, he'd always been amazingly gentle with her.

The bang of the screen door was followed by a bellowed "Mommy? There's nobody else playing outside. Do I have to come in now?"

Grateful for the distraction, Eve stepped back. "Yes, you do." That was the rule. Molly could be on the porch only as long as other children were outside. "Bring in your dolls."

Molly walked into the living room, her arms already laden with two Barbies and a bear. From her right fist dangled the dream catcher.

"I already got my dolls. Can he hang my catcher up for me now?"

He. Twice now, Eve had heard her little girl refer to Rio that way.

With anyone else, she would have pointed out that the man had a name and encouraged her to use it. But since this particular man's name happened to be Daddy, and Eve was nowhere near ready to bring that particular subject up tonight, she let it go.

"Can he?" Molly repeated when her mother hadn't answered.

Eve slid a hesitant glance toward Rio. He was waiting for an answer, too.

Five

Hanging the dream catcher didn't require any special skill. It didn't even require a hammer. Molly could have done it herself. But Rio had brought the child the gift, and since he'd offered to hang it earlier, Eve knew it was something he wanted to do. What made her feel like the Grinch was the fact that Molly wanted him to do it.

Jealousy was new to her. Hating it, but afraid to focus on the other feelings churning inside her, Eve stood in the doorway of the room that had once been her own and watched her inquisitive five-year-old direct the placement of the talisman. All the way up the stairs Molly had chattered away, wanting to know if the catcher Rio'd had when he was little was just like hers and if he had brothers and sisters.

The non sequitur was typical Molly. Her facile mind often took enormous, logic-defying leaps. But Rio took the jump in stride, seeming to have no trouble at all tracking her thoughts. No, the dream catcher wasn't exactly the same, he'd told her, but it was close enough to do the job. And yes, he had a brother and a sister. He also had a mom and more nieces, nephews, aunts and uncles than he could count, he told her, then asked if she wanted him to hang her catcher high or low.

That's what they were trying to decide now.

Molly sat on the edge of the bed, hugging Ted and contemplating the underside of the white eyelet canopy. Rio was stretched at an angle as he reached across the bed to secure his gift in the corner of the canopy frame, looking totally out of place in the overtly feminine room. Corded muscle shifted beneath his black shirt when he pulled back, his dark head reappearing from under the filmy white fabric.

"How's that?" he asked the child.

Molly looked to her mom.

"How about there, Mommy?"

"It's up to you, honey. If you like it there, it's fine."

"But I want you to see."

Eve couldn't see where "there" was from the doorway. Forcing back her reluctance, she stepped into the room, picked up a coloring book from the floor on her way and dropped it on the French provincial dresser by the old rocking chair.

"You know, Molly," Rio said when Eve stopped next to the child. "Even without the dream catcher, you don't need to be afraid when you sleep. I don't imagine your mom is very far away."

"She sleeps in there." A small index finger pointed to a door kitty-corner across the hall. "It's where she used to study. This is where she slept when she was little."

The room, like its former occupant, had grown up over the years. But other than the bright art prints on the wall, there was nothing to reveal much about the woman herself. The storybooks and dolls all belonged to her daughter.

Rio seemed to sense that there was little here of the girl he'd once known. And all that was visible in the room across the hall was the corner of the rose-print coverlet on the daybed. So he didn't bother to look around as he might have, searching for clues as to who Eve had become. He simply held her glance, watching her as if her eyes told him all he needed to know—that his presence here wasn't as welcome as she let it seem.

He didn't know quite what to make of her. For reasons he didn't care to explore, it made him feel better to know she felt that way about him, too.

"She keeps the door open," Molly added, ever so helpfully. "'Cept sometimes when I wake up at night, she's not there. That's when I get scared."

Eve saw Rio's wide brow lower just before she smoothed her hand over the little girl's shoulder. "I always leave the light on for you," she reminded Molly, more concerned with what the child had just revealed than with what Rio might think of it. "And you know I'm never far away. I'm usually right downstairs."

Molly's little mouth screwed up in one corner. "I know. But how come you always get up after you go to bed?"

She didn't always get up. She distinctly remembered several nights where she'd simply lain awake staring at the shadows in the room instead of getting up to pace it. That had been before Rio had shown up, though. Since he'd reappeared in her life, she'd found herself too restless and worried to lie in the dark waiting for the oblivion of sleep. It was easier to numb her mind with late-night TV and fall asleep on the sofa. She couldn't even concentrate to sketch or draw anymore. That had always been her escape before.

"I guess I have trouble sleeping sometimes, too," she told the child, though she really wished she hadn't had to admit that in front of Rio. To ease her child's concern, she gave her a smile. "If your dream catcher works, maybe I'll get one for me."

Molly brightened. "He could bring you one."

Molly was pointing again. As a reminder that the gesture wasn't polite, Eve curved her hand over her daughter's. She was about to tell her, too, that it wasn't polite to take a person's generosity for granted when Rio crouched down by the bed and clasped his big hands between his knees.

"You know, Molly, these things don't always work for big people."

"They're just for kids?"

"Yeah. Pretty much. But if your mom knows you're sleeping all right, then she'll probably sleep a little better, too."

Molly contemplated his little revelation, looking quite

serious when she told him she was glad she was a kid so it would work for her. Rio told her he was glad she was a kid, too, his attention divided between the little imp smiling at him and the graceful curve of her mother's hand resting on her narrow little shoulder. Eve had beautiful hands, soft-looking, feminine. Her fingers were long and slender, and her perfectly manicured nails were painted a delicate shade of rose. He could well imagine the feel of those hands sliding up his chest.

Bracing his own hands on his knees, he straightened himself up and took a step back. He shouldn't have touched her before. That one small indulgence had him itching to do it again. Only he suspected he wouldn't be satisfied with a touch, and the thoughts of what he could do with Eve in bed to take her mind off whatever it was that kept her awake did nothing but guarantee another restless night for himself.

"I have to go," he said, sparing the child a wink. "I'll see you later. Okay?"

Molly gave him a nod and jumped off the bed, dragging Ted with her. She was already out the door when Eve turned to the stairway herself.

"I'll walk you down."

"Eve."

With her back still to him, she quietly asked, "What?"

She heard him move behind her. A moment later, something brushed her shoulder. At least, she thought she'd felt something. The touch had been so light, so fleeting, that she really couldn't be sure.

"We don't have to rush into anything here. I know we agreed to hold off telling her who I am until she gets used to me. But we won't say anything until you're comfortable with it. I know I'm not the only one who needs time here."

She thought she'd see hesitation in his expression. All she saw in the hard angles of his face was a grudging sort of understanding. It was almost as if he knew how hard it was for her to let him into their lives, but that he would overlook her unspoken unwillingness if it would help make the transition a little easier.

Given the turmoil she felt, there wasn't much for her to say just then that wouldn't unleash too much of what she was trying to hold in. She couldn't even tell him how nice it had been of him to say what he just had to Molly. So she settled for a quiet "Thank you," and led him down the stairs and to the front door.

He called out "'Night, Molly" just before he left, then walked away with both hands jammed in his pockets.

The dream catcher worked. That had been the first thing Molly had said when she'd come bounding down the stairs and screeched to a halt just before she reached the kitchen, because she knew she wasn't supposed to run in the house.

"It caught the monster!" was the actual proclamation, and the child had been so excited that she'd practically danced around the room. "The monster didn't wake me up at all!"

If she believes, it will be so.

Rio's words drifted through Eve's mind as she searched the breakfast area off the kitchen for her pearl studs between bites of yogurt. The phrase spoke volumes about the man, about the strength of his own beliefs, his own convictions. It also made her want very much to borrow that strength for a little while. She wouldn't be opposed to thanking him for making her daughter—their daughter—so happy this morning, either.

The breath she blew out feathered her bangs. She had no business thinking about any of this right now. She needed to find her earrings so she could leave. She had put Molly on the bus for day camp five minutes ago, which meant she had four hours and ten minutes to do the things that were easier to do without one particular five-year-old tagging along. Not that Molly was ever really in the way. There were just some things that were easier for Eve to do alone. There were also some places that weren't suitable for children.

Such as the attorney's office. She had a nine-thirty appointment.

She found one earring under the manila envelope on the dining room table. Remembering that she'd set them there so she could put the papers she'd needed to take with her into the envelope, she slipped the earring in and proceeded to check her mental list. After she left the attorney's office, she would run by an electronics store, then stop for groceries. Since she'd asked two of her mother's friends over to pick out mementos for themselves, she wouldn't have time to drop the video recorder off at the fund-raiser chairman's house today, but she could do it tomorrow before the real estate appraiser arrived. This afternoon, she'd promised Molly she'd take her to see the new Disney movie at the Northend Mall Multiplex.

The second earring had rolled off the table and was on the floor by a chair leg. Eve picked it up as the phone rang.

It was her brother.

"Eve," Hal began without preamble. "Come by my office this morning around ten. No, better make it ten-thirty. I need to talk to you."

She didn't know which she disliked more. The demand in his voice, or the demand itself. There were a couple of things about last night that she'd very much like to clear up, but nothing seemed so urgent that she should do his bidding at the drop of a hat. He'd put off her requests to see him for more than a week.

"I'd love to talk to you," she returned, suspecting he acted as he did because she'd refused to play the little sister role he'd apparently felt she should assume. Being a feminist's son, he should have known better. "But I don't have time to go to your office this morning. I can talk for about three minutes now, though. Are you all right?"

He didn't seem to expect her concern. Or her refusal.

"No, I'm not all right." He paused, seeming to regroup. "What's with you and Redtree?"

Considering what Hal had concluded last night, Eve figured he had every right to ask the question. Working on her earring, she sank into the wing chair.

"We were friends," she explained, deciding that was definition enough. "I never said anything to anyone but Mom about who Molly's father is because I didn't think it was anyone else's business. Rio didn't even know about her until last week. We're..."

"I mean with the investigation. Why was he talking to you about the Hanson woman?"

His impatience was as much a surprise as his dismissal of what she'd just admitted. "I'm answering questions for him about people Mom knew, and he's keeping me informed about what's going on. What's wrong with that?"

He hesitated. "What kind of questions?"

Far more generous with her information than he'd ever been with his, she told him what Rio had asked, starting with the questions he'd posed about the night Olivia died. When she got to those he'd asked last night, however, it was her turn to pause.

"He asked me about you, too," she finally said, feeling like a traitor but not at all sure why. She'd never told Rio she wouldn't say anything to Hal. He hadn't asked her not to, for that matter. "He wanted to know how you could afford that new car. I told him I didn't know where you got your money." She twisted the phone cord around her finger. "I don't know what a city councillor makes, but, Hal, Mom couldn't even afford to live where you do."

She hated the doubt in her voice. Hal was her brother. The only family she had left. She needed to believe in him. But after Rio had raised the questions, she couldn't help wondering herself how he could afford the expensive clothes he wore and the house her mom had said he'd bought last year. The Heights was the most exclusive area in Grand Springs. It cost a small fortune to live there.

From the other end of the line came the sound of breath being slowly expelled.

"Mom didn't believe in taking chances with her money," Hal finally muttered, sounding more than a little weary of defending himself. "You know from dealing with the bank on her estate that all she ever invested in were a few long-term CDs and a nice, safe little money market account. I took a few big risks when the market was down a couple of years back, and they paid off well. I've been playing the stocks ever since. That's where my money comes from."

"I thought it must be something like that."

"Sure you did."

"Hal, don't. I know you're upset about a lot of things right now, but I'm on your side. Stop trying to punish me because Mom made me executor instead of you."

"I don't give a damn about that."

"Sure you don't."

Hal didn't seem to know what to say to that. So, like the good politician he was, he simply sidestepped it.

"If you're on my side, stay away from Redtree. If you want more information, talk to me."

"I've tried, but you haven't told me anything."

"I've been busy."

"I know that," she replied, calling on the patience she often had to use with her daughter. "Rio is—"

"Rio is a reporter," he interrupted, cutting her off. "I can't believe how gullible you are where he's concerned. That man is positively ruthless, Eve. I know a lot of people around here are fooled by that quiet act of his, but he'll do anything for a headline. Including seducing you. Again. Can't you see he's using you?"

As indignant as Hal sounded, Eve almost expected him to say that he was going to tell Rio to stay away from the lot of them—something that, until last night, she would have thought completely out of character. Hal was a charmer, not a fighter. He picked the battles he could win on wit and diplomacy alone, and left the nastier skirmishes to those who didn't mind dirtying their hands. He'd been criticized for that in the past. On more than one occasion, their mom had alluded to his approach not being aggressive enough for some of his constituents. But Olivia had felt the world could use another pacifist. At least, Eve could recall her mother once feeling that way. Other than for the pleasure Olivia had expressed at Hal's engagement and her disappointment in him for opposing her on the mining issue, her mom hadn't said very much about him in the past year.

Eve didn't know whether Hal had started to change long ago or if the current pressures on him were forcing the metamorphosis. What she did know was that this was the first time he had ever come to her defense.

She couldn't help being touched by that brotherly show of support, misinformed though it was.

"I know what I'm doing where Rio is concerned," she gamely assured him. Seduction was not on the man's mind. It was as clear as her Mom's best crystal that he didn't trust either her or whatever attraction he felt. "He's been completely up-front with me from the beginning. He wants Mom's murderer found as badly as we do. If I can help him, I'll do it. I have to," she stressed, certain he would understand. "As for Molly, he and I will just have to work that one out together."

She checked her watch and grimaced. "I've got to go, Hal. I'm meeting the attorney and I'm late already. He thinks we should be ready to file for probate by the end of next week. Do you have any questions you want me to ask him?"

Hal's pause was brief, just enough time passing for Eve to wonder if he wasn't considering one last shot at Rio. He must have decided he'd be wasting his breath.

"No questions," he finally said. "You're doing a good job, Eve."

As grudging and unexpected as it was, the compliment pleased her. Not because her brother seemed surprised that she could handle the responsibilities she'd inherited, but because it meant she wasn't bungling the tasks as badly as she sometimes felt she was. She was flying blind with just about everything in her life right now, and praying hard that she wouldn't crash and burn somewhere along the way. The confident front her mother insisted all women needed was just that. A front.

Whether or not she was a woman of substance didn't matter at the moment. She was a woman with a child who'd be home in three hours and fifty minutes. That meant she didn't have time to worry about whether Rio, her brother or anyone else knew that she would give just about anything to lean on somebody else for a while.

Parking along Main Street had been at a premium ever since the storm. For the past two months, construction and repairs had turned something that had once been taken for granted into a true challenge. This particular morning the city had one stretch of curb blocked off for sewer work, and the flower shop was finally getting its new roof. The semi delivering the trusses took up most of the block.

Rio was on his way into the newspaper office with a double espresso to kick-start his brain when he noticed Eve attempting to parallel park in front of the Irvine Building. She had the concept down to a science. She just wasn't cranking the wheel hard enough. Each of the two tries she'd made had left half of her little red Altima hanging out in the street.

When she pulled out for a third attempt, Rio figured he should put her out of her misery and go park it for her, but a car on the opposite side of the street backed out just then. Before he'd done much more than make the decision to help, she'd shot across both lanes and into the angled space. Seconds later, she was trotting across the street in a beige suit and high heels and smiling sweetly at the driver of an oncoming van who'd slammed on its brakes to avoid spreading her out on the pavement.

He had to hand it to her. He'd bet that more than one person had made the mistake of assuming that Eve, petite and pretty as she was, was as fragile as a hothouse flower. He'd have thought so himself if he hadn't come up close and personal with her tenacity lately. He knew people twice her age who would have crumbled under her circumstances. Yet she seemed to be handling it all. And handling it alone.

Not wanting to consider why that kept bothering him, Rio turned on his heel and headed through the *Herald*'s front doors. She was going to see the attorney. He was sure of it. He'd noticed last night that the firm handling her mother's probate was in the Irvine Building. And, just now, she'd had a large manila envelope in her hand—an envelope similar to the one he'd seen on her dining room table. It didn't take much to piece the two together.

By way of greeting, Rio lifted his paper cup toward Wendy, the bespectacled, brunette receptionist. A dozen steps later, he was behind the counter that separated the public from the peons and sucking in the perfume of newsprint and scorched coffee drifting up from the basement. He liked taking insignificant little bits of information and fitting them together. That's what made him good at his job. He also liked to figure out what motivated people, how they felt, what they thought. If he hadn't been a reporter, he might have been a detective. Stone had told him more than once that he ought to can the newspaper business and become a cop.

If he hadn't hated guns, he might have done just that. In the meantime, he relied on the adage of the pen being mightier than the sword. Not that he was out to fight any battles. He just had a talent for presenting situations and people as they were. And he'd always been intrigued by puzzles. Even as a kid, he was happiest trying to figure out how or why something did or didn't work. But as much as he liked fitting pieces of a puzzle together, loose bits that didn't seem to fit anywhere drove him crazy. There was a stray bit nagging at him now.

Setting his cup by his computer terminal, he flipped through his phone file for the number of the Bank of Grand Springs. No reporter worth his byline was without contacts, and he had one at the bank that he was about to hit up for anything he could learn about Eve's brother. Rio could buy what she had said about Hal's objections to the autopsy. And Hal's own comment about pushing the investigation of the miners did seem to remove suspicion from him on that score. He could even appreciate that the guy's stress levels were making him paranoid. But that new Mercedes had put Rio's curiosity about the man's finances right over the top.

He had the information he was after by ten-thirty the following morning. But having to cover a hostage situation that developed minutes later prevented him from doing anything about it just then.

Detective Stone Richardson had been off duty Friday morning when he'd stopped at the main branch of the Bank of Grand Springs to cash a check—and walked into the nightmare Jessica Hanson had warned him about. Thirty-six hours later, having saved the lives of thirteen people at the peril of his own, he was resting somewhat uncomfortably in Jessica's bed with a bandage over the bullet hole in his shoulder.

Being the good friend he was, Rio had suggested Stone can cop work and become a journalist. The word Stone used in reply hadn't been fit to print.

That had been roughly twelve hours ago. Because the Sunday edition of the *Herald* was larger than the daily, it was put to bed early Saturday afternoon and on the stands by six. A later edition of the front page went to press at midnight, and that was what landed on subscribers' doorsteps Sunday morning. The text Rio had phoned in from behind a squad car at the bank for the early edition had been sketchy, given the lack of information coming from inside the cordoned-off bank building. But the story his

editor held the presses for at midnight contained details of
a tense negotiating session that had broken down completely before the situation had ended in a struggle between
police and suspects.

After grabbing a few hours' sleep, Rio was back at the
police station for the official version of the incident and to
scrape up what he could on the robbers. All four had served
time before and were in holding cells waiting for their
court-appointed attorney. It seemed their speciality was hitting small-town banks, and they'd considered Grand
Springs an easy target. After a few more interviews, with
the bank president and the two tellers he'd missed last
night, Rio had Monday's story ready to go.

He was halfway out of the building when he remembered
what his contact at the bank had faxed him two days ago.
Since he'd already abandoned the idea of spending his day
off working on his cabin because there was a little girl he
needed to get to know, he took the copies of Hal Stuart's
bank statements to his apartment, thinking he'd look them
over later.

Curiosity got the better of him, however. When he got
to his modest apartment, what started as nothing more than
a cursory glance at the statements ended with his coffee
table cluttered with calculator and charts.

Though he'd told Eve he'd be there by one, it was three
o'clock that afternoon before he pulled up in front of Olivia
Stuart's house.

Eve stood at the window in Molly's bedroom, watching
Rio's powerful, long-legged strides carry him up the walk.
He'd actually called before showing up this time. Twice.
The last time he'd called, apologizing because he was late,
he'd added that he had something he wanted to talk to her
about. The first time, he'd said only that he wanted to spend
a little time with Molly, if Eve didn't mind.

She figured that what he wanted to talk to her about was
their daughter. She also figured she should have appreciated

the calls. But all the warning had done was give her a head start on the apprehension knotting her stomach. Every time she saw him, he added a new element of worry to her ever-growing list.

He'll do anything for a headline. Including seducing you. Can't you see he's using you?

She gave her head a shake, willing away the odd little ache that had come with her brother's words. Hal honestly didn't know what he was talking about where Rio was concerned. Rio was about as likely to seduce her as he was to dip himself in purple paint and run screaming through Vanderbilt Park. What he wanted from her had nothing to do with sex.

Returning her attention to the canopied bed, she stripped off the bottom sheet and pad, then scooped the rest of the bedding from the floor. Molly knew she wasn't supposed to bring juice upstairs.

"Mommy's in a bad mood."

Eve had just reached the top of the stairs when she heard her not-so-angelic little girl make the pronouncement. Arms laden, she turned sideways so she could watch where she was going, and saw Molly unlock the screen for the big man on the other side.

The screen groaned as Molly pushed it open. "Will you fix my bike? The training wheel came off and Mommy can't put it back on."

The perplexed little girl moved back as Rio stepped inside, tipping her head so far back that the end of her long French braid reached the lace on the hem of her purple shorts set.

Standing over her, Rio slipped his sunglasses into the pocket of his white polo shirt and hitched at the knees of his well-worn jeans. He crouched in front of the child, drawing the fabric tight over his thighs.

"Tell me why your mom's in a bad mood, then we'll talk about the bike."

"I dunno why she is." Molly gave an exaggerated shrug. "She's just grumpy."

"Grumpy, huh?"

"Yep."

"And you have no idea why?"

She held her arms wide and shrugged again. "Maybe she has MPS."

Rio hesitated. "You mean PMS?"

Since Molly's back was to her, Eve couldn't see her daughter's face. She could see Rio's, though, along with the glance he shot toward the stairs. Though he saw her, he did nothing to acknowledge her. He simply returned his attention to his chatty little daughter.

Before Molly could share anything else, Eve headed down the steps.

"I don't have PMS," she said defensively, exasperation diluting the claim. "Nor am I in a particularly bad mood. I'll fix your bike when I find something to tighten the nuts with. Did you rinse off Ted and put him on the washer?"

No longer looking quite as innocent as she had a moment ago, Molly turned contrite blue eyes to her mom. "Uh-huh. And the pillow."

"Good. You can take these into the laundry room, too."

Eve had reached the bottom of the stairs. Two more steps and she was on the richly patterned entry carpet. So was the armload of pastel pink bedding.

Picking out the top and bottom twin sheets, she loaded Molly up with them and tucked the fabric under her chin so she could see. "Put them on the floor in the laundry room, then come back and get the blanket."

"Are you going to wash the bedspread, too?"

"No. That goes to the cleaners."

"Oh."

Arms full, neck stretched and head high, Molly marched through the foyer, into the kitchen, then made a left toward the laundry room.

Like a monolith rising from the earth, Rio stood to tower beside Eve. "What happened?"

"She and Ted had a tea party. With juice."

A smile, quick and wholly unexpected, flashed in his dark eyes. Quashing the one that threatened at the corner of his mouth, he crossed his arms over his broad chest and muttered, "I see."

The look Eve shot him wasn't nearly as disapproving as it could have been. She wasn't all that upset. Not with Molly, anyway. Spilled juice was an inconvenience. Not a problem. By the way the smile lingered in his eyes, he seemed to know that.

"I take it she can be a real handful sometimes."

"She can when she wants to be."

For one unguarded and too revealing moment, Eve found that shared realization about their daughter far more comfortable than threatening. Maybe it was because she knew he cared about the child. Or maybe parents just had an automatic connection where their children were concerned. On the other hand, she thought, liking the feeling a little too much, it could have simply been because she was tired and her defenses were down.

"How's Detective Richardson? Is he going to be all right?"

Rio accepted the change of subject for the diversion it was. He knew Eve didn't know Stone all that well, but he'd bet she'd held her breath right along with the rest of the town while the hostage situation at the bank had played out. What intrigued him, though, was that the concern etched in her delicate features was as genuine as it would have been for a friend.

"He took a bullet in the shoulder. But he's sure he'll be fine."

"That's what I read." She nodded toward the coffee table. The newspaper was still spread out on one end, a coloring book on the other. "In your article, I mean. I just wondered if he was hurt worse than you said."

''He's okay. Honest.''

Eve lifted her chin, letting herself feel relieved as she hugged her arms to herself. She was glad the detective was okay. She really was, but her relief wasn't as great as it could have been. The *Herald* was beginning to look just like the papers in Santa Barbara. Robberies. Domestic violence. Crimes related to a surge in drug traffic. Grand Springs never even *had* a drug problem until a couple of years ago. Then there was what had happened to her mother.

Taking a deep breath, she cut off the thought. She spent enough time on this sort of thing at night.

''How's the sleep situation?''

She couldn't tell if he was speaking about hers or Molly's. Not believing that the concern in his expression might actually be for her, she tipped her head toward the child emerging for another load of bedding. ''I'm sure she'll be glad to tell you, right after she takes the rest of this to the laundry room.''

All Molly heard was that she had to make another trip. ''Can he help?''

''He wasn't the one who took the juice upstairs,'' Eve pointed out, overriding whatever it was Rio had been about to say. Doing with the blanket what she'd done with the sheets, she loaded Molly up again, turned her by the shoulders and gave her a gentle nudge toward the door. ''Wait for me. I'll be there in a minute and we'll put the sheets in.''

It looked to Eve as if Rio was suppressing another smile. He must have realized that having Molly do her own sheets was hardly punishment, especially with her mom doing ninety percent of the work. Molly loved to ''help.''

''I've got some tools in the car. Tell me where her bike is and I'll fix it while we talk.'' The light faded from his eyes, but the concern remained. ''I've come across something interesting about your brother.''

Six

Eve thought she'd made her feelings about her brother clear to Rio. Apparently, she hadn't. She didn't want to talk about Hal. She especially didn't want to hear anything bad about him, which could only be what "something interesting" meant. She wasn't in a position, however, to explain that to Rio at the moment. Molly was tugging on her arm to come get the soap.

One thing at a time, she reminded herself, repeating the phrase like a mantra while she helped Molly stuff sheets into the washing machine and listened to the animated child tell Rio that the catcher had made the monster disappear. Then, not wanting Molly to get grease on herself should she decide to help Rio, Eve left the washer chugging away when Rio produced the wrench he'd retrieved from his Bronco and he and Molly set to work in the driveway.

The task wouldn't have taken him but a minute, but Rio wanted to make sure both training wheels on the little purple bike were secure. As long as he was at it, he checked the chain and adjusted the seat, patiently explaining to Molly that the bike was safer to ride if she could reach the pedals. Molly, fascinated, watched and questioned every move he made.

So did Eve. She watched, anyway.

She stood a few feet behind them in the sun-dappled driveway, her arms crossed over her sleeveless blue tank top, while she made herself admit that it hadn't been the thought of having to degrease flowered denim shorts that had prompted her to follow them out. It wasn't even the threat he posed to the peace of her little family unit, though that particular feeling was never far away. As she watched Rio's capable hands, she experienced an unexpected sort of reassurance. The kind that came with knowing someone else worried about her little girl's safety, too.

"Lookit, Mom. He fixed it!"

Molly didn't require a reply. With a damp Ted, rescued from the top of the washer and propped in the metal basket, and lavender-and-purple streamers flying from the ends of the handlebars, she took off past Millicent's redbrick two-story and headed for the corner of the aspen-lined street.

From her spot near the lilac bushes at the edge of the drive, Eve saw Rio slip the wrench into the back pocket of his jeans. He stood for a moment, at an angle to her, his attention on the child now waving back at them. The white of his shirt accentuated the bronze skin of his sinewy arms, the soft cotton stretching across muscular shoulders and a lean, strong back. His dark hair, swept back from his striking, angular features, gleamed like a raven's wing in the late afternoon sun.

She knew she was staring. But something about his stance made it impossible for her to look away; the way his long legs were planted slightly apart, his head up, meeting the gentle breeze straight on. Watching him, aware of him now in ways she'd once been too naive to appreciate, she could see him as she'd never imagined him before—as the son of people persecuted and proud. Of indomitable spirit. Of nobility in the truest sense of the word. There was a sense of protectiveness about him, and of possession. Those, she'd noticed before. Yet she'd never considered how he had come by them.

She'd once realized how little she'd known about him, but, by then, she'd been left with nothing to do but try to forget him. And she had tried. Desperately. Because of that she had never before considered how truly diverse his worlds must be—the one she knew, and the one from which he'd come. She knew nothing of his struggles.

Those were what she wanted to understand, she realized, watching him give one last glance toward Molly before he turned around. But she didn't have time to add "for Molly's sake" before he had walked over to stand beside her.

"That chain could use some oil," he advised, still following the little girl's progress down the street. "Is there any in the garage?"

"There's a can in the garden shed. I'll get it."

She started to turn, only to find her progress canceled by Rio's hand closing around her upper arm. The contact was unexpected. So was the jolt of warmth racing inward from his gentle grip.

There were calluses at the base of his fingers; she felt them when he let his hand slide away. Her glance darted to his. He was a journalist, yet his hand was that of a man well accustomed to physical labor.

"I don't need it right now." Rio was aware of the curiosity in her expression, more aware of how soft her skin felt, how small-boned she was. He preferred to ignore both. "I'd rather talk while she's occupied."

He saw her nod, then wondered at the way she crossed her arms when she turned back to watch her daughter. Though she managed a smile before she told him that was probably a good idea, since Molly's attention span could be rather short, her body language was definitely self-protective.

Molly's was just the opposite. Turning the corner, the child waved madly and started back, legs pumping. Rio wasn't sure why, but just looking at that kid could make him smile. Which was a little odd, considering that she also scared him half to death.

"How are things with you and Hal?"

"We're doing all right." She hesitated, seeming torn between reluctance and interest. "You said you discovered something interesting about him."

Suspicious would have been a better word, Rio thought, but he didn't want to say anything that would jeopardize his source. Since he couldn't tell Eve how he'd obtained the information, he couldn't mention that he'd researched her brother's checking account. From the sudden coolness in her voice, it didn't appear that she'd take too kindly to the information, anyway.

What Rio had actually discovered was that Hal had three accounts, none of which was particularly remarkable until they were put together. In addition to his twice monthly paycheck from the city, several deposits had been made over the past year from various local businesses; specifically, two laundromats, a restaurant, a couple of bars and an auto repair shop. There had also been significant deposits of cash.

Legitimate business earnings, however oddly managed, could be one explanation. "Has he bought into any of the businesses around here?" Rio asked.

"I have no idea. You'll have to check with him." The curiosity remained, but the coolness grew. "Why do want to know?"

"Because he seems to be tied in with several local establishments."

Considering other options, such as the possibility that those businesses could be buying political favors, he overlooked the narrowing of Eve's eyes.

"What about running for office?" Maybe the guy was collecting contributions already and diverting them to his personal accounts. Tapping campaign funds would be one way to support his life-style. "His seat on the city council isn't up for two years, but his position as acting mayor is only temporary. Has he said anything about a political campaign?"

"Rio," she began, her voice as flat as the bug Molly had rolled over in the driveway. "I have no idea what you're getting at here. I said I'd answer any questions I could to help you with your investigation about Mom. But I'm not going to help you with an article that could hurt my brother.''

"What makes you think I'm working on an article about him?"

"Why else would you be interested in any of this?"

"I'm just trying to figure out where his money's coming from.''

"That has nothing to do with what I agreed to help you with. If you want to know what Hal's political plans are, or what he owns or doesn't own, or whatever it is you're getting at, you'll have to ask him.''

Eve had that mother cat look about her; the one that he'd encountered when he'd hung the dream catcher for Molly and which, at the moment, he should have found more annoying than admirable. Something wasn't right with Hal Stuart, and because his instincts wouldn't let him drop it, Rio wanted answers. She was just the wrong person to provide them. As she kept reminding him, Hal was her brother.

More empathetic to her situation than she realized, Rio muttered a terse "I will." He understood family ties all too well. Though his kin would dispute his own loyalty, he knew a person could still love, defend and respect family without agreeing with their philosophies or actions. Some bonds simply defied logic.

"One more question and I won't mention him again."

"Rio..."

"I just want to know if there were any repercussions from my being here the other night."

The warning in Eve's eyes turned to hesitation.

"He told you to stay away from me, didn't he?"

She didn't need to answer. The way her glance flickered from his said it all.

"You know, Eve, you should never play poker. You'd have to fold after the first hand. How is he with Molly?" he continued before she could chafe at the observation.

"Now that he knows she's mine, does he have a problem with it?"

He could understand that the man would want his sister to stay away from him for professional reasons. Even as fair as Rio tried to be, as a reporter, he was a threat to Hal right now. But this was personal.

Molly wheeled into the driveway, waved and cut an arc toward the corner again. Eve uncrossed her arms long enough to wave back.

"If he does, he didn't mention it. Molly is still his niece, no matter who her father is. Or what race he is," she added, slanting him a glance. "I think he's concerned with other things."

"I'm not being defensive, Eve. I just want her to be accepted."

There truly was no defense in his tone. A hint of impatience, maybe. But Eve supposed that was understandable. He was new to the concerns parents face with their offspring, so she could appreciate his need for reassurance. It was just that his concerns were so different from what her own had always been. Her worries had been about making sure Molly got her vitamins and that she was developing at the right pace. That she learned to share with her little friends and that she received enough hugs. But with her glance locked on Rio's, she realized that her concerns had just expanded to include his. Only it wasn't her side of the family she was worried about. Because of what his mother had said to her years ago, it was his. And, because of that, though the last thing she needed was something else to worry about, she was now worried about Rio.

"So what are you going to do?" he asked, before she could question the direction of her concern. "Are you going to listen to Hal and stay away from me?"

She wasn't fooled by the mild tone of the question.

"We have an agreement. And we have Molly to consider. What anyone else thinks I should do doesn't matter."

"I'm hungry," the child under discussion announced, rolling into the driveway. "When can we have dinner?"

Pulling her glance from Rio's, far too aware of the tension in his body, Eve managed a smile for her daughter. "You can help me start it right after you put your bike in the garage."

Rio watched Molly slide off the seat of her bike and pushed his hands into his pockets. He smiled at her, too, something he couldn't seem to avoid, since the child was grinning at him. But Eve couldn't help notice that the smile was gone long before he glanced back at her.

"Look, Eve, I don't want to interrupt your routine. I just wanted to see her." And to let her get to know me, he could have added, but she might point out that it would take more than a ten-minute visit to accomplish that and he already felt guilty about being late. "Let me help her put her bike away, and I'll leave."

"You don't need to do that." She paused. "Leave, I mean."

Her self-protective instincts must have been at an all-time low. When she saw the question slip into his eyes, she hesitated only long enough to tell herself that she was doing this for her daughter. "We're not having much. I promised Molly hamburgers. If there's enough gas for the grill," she had to add, since she hadn't yet checked it. "But you're welcome to stay."

There wasn't enough propane. Eve shrugged the detail off and said a frying pan would work just as well, but Rio, being practical, pointed out that she still needed the tank filled if she planned to use it later. Unless she wanted to wrestle with it herself and haul it to the truck stop on the highway, since that was the nearest place that sold propane, they might as well do it now. If they all went together, they could grab hamburgers while they were out.

Molly thought that was a fine idea. Especially if they could go to the Burger Palace, because they gave prizes with their kiddie meals. So that was where they wound up after the tank had been filled. Eve wasn't quite so sure how Rio and Molly talked her into feeding the ducks at the park, though. But she didn't worry about it. All she let herself consider as late afternoon faded into evening was that Molly was having a wonderful time.

The child was clearly drawn to Rio, if for no other reason than the patient way he answered her endless questions. Molly wanted to know why so many trees around the pond had fallen over, so, as they walked, Rio explained that the wind from the storm had done it. When Molly couldn't understand how wind, something she couldn't see, could move anything, Rio stuck a fir twig in the dirt and had her blow it over. Two minutes later, having found a duck's nest in the rocks and low rushes, she wanted to know why ducks didn't build nests high up like robins did.

When Rio began explaining that it was because ducks weren't built like robins, Eve caught her best glimpse of the man she'd once known. Rio seemed so indomitable to her now, and as impenetrable as any person she'd ever encountered. Yet, with Molly, his guard and reserve were scarcely evident at all. He seemed so much more accessible, so open, and as he and Molly talked, Eve couldn't help but notice how intently he watched the child. Quietly, unobtrusively, he simply took in what others probably wouldn't notice at all. Little things, such as how Molly was more drawn to pink flowers than to red ones. How she tipped her head when she listened. How her mouth hitched to one side when she was thinking.

Yet, as interested as he clearly was in his daughter, Eve couldn't help but notice that he didn't ask any questions about his little girl. He didn't want to know what Molly had been like when she was younger. Nor did he seek out the milestones he'd missed. He seemed to be getting to know her his own way, and in his own time.

The fact that he wasn't pushing to accelerate the process actually allowed Eve to relax a little—until she began to suspect that the reason he wasn't asking her about Molly was because he figured she'd just get all defensive on him. Every single time he'd been around, her insecurities about his presence in Molly's life had surfaced in one way or another.

By the time they got back to the house, the stars had come out, Molly had fallen asleep in the back seat and Eve was struggling between protectiveness and practicality. There was no doubt that Rio intended to have a real relationship with his daughter. And even though Eve worried about how that would affect Molly if Molly became attached to him, since they would ultimately be leaving Grand Springs, she knew the situation was going to take more than token cooperation on her part to make it work. At the very least, she needed to let Rio know he was free to ask anything he needed to know about his little girl. As soon as she got Molly into bed, she planned to tell him that.

It was with that thought in mind that Eve unlocked the front door by the glow of the porch light, while Rio, carrying Molly, stood behind her with their child's head resting on his shoulder. Anyone driving by would think they looked very much like a family coming home for the evening. For reasons Eve didn't trust herself to consider, she refused to carry the fleeting thought any further than that. She would cooperate with Rio, and she would hope she was doing the right thing for Molly, but she would not tease herself with dead dreams.

Entering the dark foyer, she switched on the entry table lamp and turned to ask Rio if he'd mind taking Molly upstairs. The request wasn't necessary. He was already heading there, looking very much as if he'd carried his little girl to bed a hundred times before.

"Her bed isn't made," Eve whispered, preferring to focus on the sheets she'd left in the washer, rather than how natural he looked with a sleeping child in his arms. "Put her in mine. Okay?"

He gave her a nod and continued on before she could tell him where her room was. She didn't have to do that, either. Molly had pointed it out when he'd been up there the other day, and he headed straight for it, stopping outside the door so Eve could go ahead of him and turn down the blankets.

They moved silently around each other in the dim room, she pulling back the sheets on the daybed and Rio coming up behind her to take the extra pillows. Neither said a word, until she started to take Molly from him.

In the shadows, she saw him shake his head. "I can do it," he said, his voice low. "Just get her shoes."

Thinking only to get the task done, Eve reached for a dangling foot. The smell of fresh air clung to Molly. It clung to Rio, too, along with the clean scent of his soap and something indefinably male. Trying to ignore how the tension in her body changed quality when she breathed in that scent, she carefully pulled off little white sneakers and lace-trimmed socks. She slipped off Molly's dusty shorts, too, and when Rio bent to settle the sleeping child on the bed, Eve bent with him to pull the sheet from under Molly's legs. But when she felt his arm pressed the length of hers and glanced over to find his mouth inches away, she pulled back to let him finish on his own.

Her heart was beating faster than she liked as she watched Rio pull the sheet to the middle of Molly's chest, his big hands amazingly gentle. He didn't kiss the child as Eve thought he might. After the exhausted little girl curled up on her side, then settled down again, all Rio did was touch his fingers to her hair. A moment later, he stepped away, looking as if he wasn't sure he should have indulged himself even that much.

Or maybe, Eve made herself consider, it was her presence that held him back.

Prodded by the possibility, she tightened her fingers around Molly's bear. A moment later, she held it out. "She needs Ted."

His face seemed harder, hungrier, in the dim gray light. The shadows sharpened the angles and planes, and made his dark eyes glitter as he glanced from the stuffed animal and back to her. "Where do I put him?"

His uncertainty caused something inside her to soften, weakening the reluctance she still fought. "Just tuck him in beside her."

It was a moment before he pulled his glance from the encouragement in hers. But when he did, he took the toy for the concession it was and placed the stuffed bear in the crook of Molly's elbow.

"Like that?" he whispered.   •

He was actually looking to her for reassurance. More touched than she would have believed possible by his unprotected need to get it right, she gave him a tenuous nod, then bent to kiss her sleeping child's forehead before he could do anything else to complicate her feelings about him. Her feelings were confused enough as it was.

When she straightened, it was to find him quietly watching her.

Eve had no idea what was going through his mind. But she didn't think it wise to stand so close to him while she tried to figure it out. Ducking her head, she started for the door, thinking to wait for him there. Rio was right behind her, closing the door halfway as they stepped into the hall.

"I'll bring the tank around back."

The propane tank was still in his Bronco. She'd forgotten all about it.

"I'll get the garage door for you."

"I'll get it. I only need a few minutes to hook it up."

Rio was halfway down the steps when she realized that all he wanted just then was to get away from her. She wasn't sure what she'd said or done, but there was no mistaking his desire for distance when she saw his dark head disappear at the landing and heard the front door open.

So much for trying to cooperate. Desperate for distraction herself, she grabbed an extra set of sheets from the linen closet and headed for Molly's unmade bed.

Ten minutes later, the bed was made, the sheets from the washer were in the dryer, the blanket on presoak, and she was wondering how to get past Rio's insulating wall when she found him in the kitchen. He was washing up at the sink.

He must have caught her reflection in the window. Like a wolf on a scent, his head came up as she moved toward him. He was turning off the water when she caught sight of the furrows between his eyebrows.

She held out a towel. "Thank you," she said, because she really did need to let him know she appreciated all he'd done. "For taking care of the tank. And for the evening. Molly had a great time."

Seeming distracted, he took the towel from her. "No thanks necessary."

She would have liked to tell him that she'd had a nice time, too. As caught up as she'd been with the interaction between him and their daughter, she hadn't given a single thought to the pending estate sale, her brother or the investigation. But she doubted he'd be interested in knowing that, so she kept the thought to herself. His interest was in his daughter. And there was something else she had to say to him, anyway.

"I'm sure you have questions, Rio. You can ask me anything you want about her."

"No need."

Eve's eyebrows arched at the laconic response.

"Molly is what she is. An innocent, curious five-year-old. I can see that for myself." He handed the towel back to her, the reason for his preoccupation coming into focus. "I'd be more interested in hearing about you."

The smoothly delivered statement caught her as she looped the yellow terry cloth halfway through the handle of the fridge. "Me?" she returned, confused. "Why?"

She would have to ask, Rio thought, hoping he could

explain what he wanted without offending her. Awkward as it seemed at times, and as resistant as she had to feel, Eve was truly trying to let him know his child. And while no one could be more amazed than he was himself, the little imp was definitely getting under his skin. But ever since they'd spoken about the conversation she'd had with her brother, a new concern had nagged at him with the consistency of a toothache. Despite Eve's reassurance that she wasn't going to avoid him, should she change her mind, a little more information could come in mighty handy.

"Because you're her mother, and you were right. We don't know much about each other. I know where you work, but I know nothing of what you do in Santa Barbara other than that. I don't know what part of the city you live in. What you do in your spare time. I don't even know if you have a boyfriend."

Her expression remained encouraging—until he added that last one.

"Does that matter?"

"The boyfriend?"

She gave him a nod.

"You're concerned about the influence I can have on her," he pointed out. "If some guy is part of Molly's life, then yes, I think it does. Who you associate with affects her, doesn't it?"

There was no challenge in his tone, no interest beyond whatever influence some nebulous male might have over his daughter. She couldn't even detect the offense Rio surely must have felt when she'd all but said she knew little now about his character.

Looping the towel the rest of the way through the handle, Eve supposed his questions were every bit as reasonable as he made them sound. As adamant as she had been about needing to know him before telling Molly who he was, she could hardly deny him equal knowledge about the person raising his daughter.

When she turned back, Rio had leaned against the

counter. With his arms crossed over his chest and his legs stretched out and crossed at the ankles, he appeared fully prepared to stay put until he got what he was after.

He wouldn't have to stay long, she thought, twirling a piece of lint from the towel as she leaned against the opposite counter herself. The story was as short as it was uninspiring.

It took her all of a minute to detail a life that included little other than work, an occasional class toward a necessary design certification, and the demands of a preschooler. She had a friend, a designer, too, who was raising two children by herself, and they would take the kids places together. And a couple of times a month, she and Molly would go to her aunt and uncle's house for dinner. Before Molly was born, she'd stayed with her mother's older brother and his wife, her mom's only relatives. Between preschool and day care, and tumbling class or T-ball on Saturdays, as well as the requisite weekend chores, there was little money, and less time, for anything else.

"As for a boyfriend," she concluded, thinking how boring her life must sound to him, "I've never had one. And while we're at it," she continued, thinking now as good a time as any to get off that subject and to satisfy her own curiosity, "what happened to the girl your mother told me about?"

Rio's eyes were hooded, his expression thoughtful as he scanned her face. She was beginning to feel distinctly disadvantaged whenever he looked at her that way. Mostly because she never knew what he was looking for. She always had the feeling, too, that whatever it was, he found it.

"Fawn was my mother's idea. She was a nice girl. She still is," he added easily, wondering if Eve realized what she'd just revealed. "I'm sure she makes my brother an excellent wife. But I wasn't interested in her, or in marriage. My mother knew that."

"She married your brother?"

He nodded, unfolding himself. "They have three children. Two girls and a boy."

"Isn't that awkward?"

"Having three children?"

She shot him a bland look as he slowly crossed toward her. "Your brother being married to someone who wanted to marry you."

"I don't know that she was especially interested in me." She'd seemed to be, but all Rio had cared about that summer was that Fawn wasn't Eve, and that Eve had been nowhere to be found. He'd even returned early to college to keep his mother from pushing the poor girl at him—then stayed away for nearly three years for reasons that went far beyond that single incident. "But that has nothing to do with what we were discussing."

Eve was still leaning against the beige counter, her back to the glass-faced dish cabinets. Rio had stopped in front of her.

They were talking about matters that affected Molly, Eve reminded herself. Not about what had happened between the two of them. Tipping her head to meet his eyes, she supposed she could point out that his mother's interference was hardly irrelevant to their present circumstances. But that little fact didn't change what Eve had done in the first place, or what they'd been left to deal with now. That was clearly all that mattered to Rio.

"I don't know what else to tell you," she said. "Except that I'll do whatever I have to do to see that Molly is taken care of. I always have."

"And you've always done that alone?"

Eve wasn't sure why she didn't trust the question. Maybe it was the mild way he posed it. Or maybe it was just because Rio was close enough that she could feel the latent tension in his body. The curious way he was watching her made her feel as if he thought there was something she wasn't telling him. Or that he didn't believe something she had already said. Whatever it was, it suddenly felt very necessary to make it clear he would never have reason to worry about how she took care of their daughter.

"There's something you need to understand," she began, her deliberate calm an indication of how badly she wanted to preserve the ground they'd gained this evening. "When I told Mom I was keeping Molly, she didn't try to change my mind. But she did make sure I understood what keeping her meant. It meant trading the freedom I would have had to go on with my life for the responsibility of raising her.

"I was luckier than most girls would have been in my circumstances," she continued, all too aware of how differently her life could have turned out had it not been for her mother. "Mom was both willing and able to help me financially. After I told her what had happened with your mother, she told me she'd pay for college or a trade school and help me support the baby until I graduated. But she also made me promise that Molly would always be my first priority. Molly would be my first priority even if I hadn't made that promise. She is and always has been. You don't need to worry about her."

It was apparent to Rio that Eve hadn't understood why he'd asked what he had. It had never occurred to him to question her commitment to Molly. Time and again, as he'd watched her with the child, he'd been drawn by the strength of the bond between them. Even tonight, especially tonight, he'd been conscious of the interaction between mother and daughter. Though he and Molly had spent most of the time talking, it had been Eve who Molly had turned to when she'd wanted a hand to hold, and when she'd grown tired. Just before they'd left the park, Molly had crawled onto the bench where her mother had sat watching them and laid her head in Eve's lap. He'd been aware of how Eve had automatically begun to stroke the child's hair, and how Molly's eyes had immediately closed. He'd been aware, too, that the gesture had seemed to give as much comfort to Eve as to the child.

He didn't think it at all unusual that he should notice

such things. Not when he was so aware of her in every other way. What had surprised him was the comfort he'd felt, too, just being with them. Being with her. But as he absorbed what she'd said just now, it wasn't those few fragile moments of peace he considered. Or how long it had been since he'd felt such calm. It was how indebted Eve felt to her mother—and what she may have denied herself to keep his child.

"I've never doubted how good a mother you are. That's not what I was questioning at all. You said a minute ago that you never had a boyfriend," he added, explaining the direction his thoughts had taken. "I was just wondering if you meant that the way it sounded. That's why I'd asked if you'd always taken care of her by yourself."

Caution replaced defense. "I don't know what you mean."

"*Never* is an absolute." His tone became amazingly innocent. "Didn't I count?"

"Of course you did. I meant there'd been no one…"

Rio thought she flushed when she cut herself off. He couldn't be sure because she ducked her head, suddenly developing a fascination with the piece of lint she'd rolled into a little ball. All he could see was the pale shades of gold gleaming in her hair.

He should let it go. But what he should do didn't matter all that much to him at the moment. A need buried deep inside demanded an answer.

He lifted his hand, hesitating long enough to be certain that he couldn't change his mind before slipping his fingers beneath her chin. Ignoring the way she went still at the contact, he tipped her head up with his thumb.

"There'd been no one…what?"

He wasn't being fair. Eve might have told him that, too, had the feel of his fingers stroking her throat not paralyzed her vocal chords. She wasn't even sure he knew he was doing it, not as intently as he was watching her.

"There's been no one since me?" he cautiously suggested.

"Relationships take time."

"And you've never had any time to spare."

Considering what she'd just told him, that would have been the most obvious conclusion. Not sure he was going to believe that was her only reason, praying he would, she started to shake her head, but the motion threatened to move his thumb to the corner of her mouth. Instead, she simply whispered, "No."

She knew what she was admitting; that he was the only man she'd ever been with. Why that mattered to him, she had no idea. Or even if it did. She only knew that the knowledge did something disturbing to his dark, fathomless eyes.

That disturbing gaze held hers, probing, questioning, making the air seem too thin to breathe. Then his glance slowly slipped to her mouth. An unsteady heartbeat later, she felt his fingers drift down her throat.

She swallowed, the motion causing the delicate chords in her neck to convulse. Rio's eyes met hers again. Only this time, she didn't see questions. What she saw was something primal and fierce and far too edgy for the smooth tones of his deep voice.

"Relationships do take time." He skimmed the hollow at the base of her throat. Beneath his finger, her pulse leapt. "Sex is the easy part."

She couldn't argue his conclusion. It took time to get to know someone; to build trust. Or rebuild it. The latter was much harder, really. But the thought had scarcely occurred to Eve when she felt Rio's hand move along her collarbone.

"We had a relationship once." His eyes glittered over her face, frustration charged with heat. "The trouble is, I don't know where to go with it now. Do I take up where we left off, start over or forget I ever laid eyes on you again? If it weren't for Molly..."

He cut himself off, looking like a man torn as he followed the motion of his fingers.

"If it weren't for Molly," Eve concluded, her pulse skittering, "you wouldn't be here right now."

A muscle in his jaw jerked. "We don't know that for certain, do we?"

They couldn't know what would have happened had the past been any different. All they had to work with was the present, and the present was getting more complicated by the second.

Rio's fingers sank into her hair. Drawing her forward, he tipped her head up. "Unfortunately, forgetting you doesn't seem to be an option."

His last words were spoken as his head descended, the rasp of his voice seeming to vibrate through her when his mouth touched hers. The contact was little more than the brush of skin and breath against her lips before he pulled back far enough to see the questions in her eyes. He did it again, seeming to test either her resolve or his own willpower before she whispered his name.

She didn't know who leaned forward first. One moment his name was on her lips. The next his mouth crushed hers, and she forgot to breathe.

His mouth felt hot and hard. So did his body when he pulled her up against him, molding her hips to his, her breasts to his chest. Beyond that, beyond him, her senses failed. She was aware of nothing but the feel of his lips softening against hers, the groan deep in his chest when her tongue touched his, and the heady feel of his hands sliding down her back. She could taste frustration, but she could taste hunger, too, and passion. And a kind of pent-up longing that seemed to fuel it all.

Her heart recognized that longing. Her body recognized him. Aching for what was once familiar, she curved her arms around his neck, seeking his lean, hard contours. But he was bigger than she remembered, more overwhelming, and the familiarity she'd sought wasn't there at all. Instead, she discovered the rocklike strength she craved.

In the space of a heartbeat, long-buried yearnings careened to the surface. It had been six years since she'd been held like this. Six years since his arms had been around her. At the thought, something like a sob caught in her throat.

Hearing it, Rio went still.

He lifted his head, recrimination warring with desire as he searched her eyes. He looked like a man in pain when he brushed his thumb over her bottom lip.

"I wasn't going to do that," he said, his breathing as erratic as her own.

Pulling her hands from his shoulders, he held them between his. But whatever else he'd been about to say was cut off by the ring of the telephone. Eve couldn't remember the last time she'd been so grateful for an interruption. Exposed as she felt at that moment, she didn't think she'd be able to stand it if he apologized.

Rio's hands slipped from hers as he stepped back. Shoving his fingers through his hair, he picked up the receiver from the phone beneath the cabinet and held it out to her.

"I'm leaving," he said, his voice low. "Think about us taking Molly to the park again after work Wednesday, and I'll call you later."

"Wait!"

Looking from him to the phone, she took the call long enough to discover Millicent on the other end of the line and to ask her to hang on a minute before covering the mouthpiece with her palm.

"Wednesday won't be good," she told him, determined to sound as unaffected as he did about what had just happened. "A man is coming by about seven-thirty to look at Mom's car. He might buy it."

"Somebody you know?"

"Not personally," she returned, unsure why he wanted

to know. "He's a friend of the gardener's neighbor's cousin."

"Now, there's a recommendation." His brow knitted, his thoughts in conflict once again. "Can you handle that? I mean, you won't let him lowball you on the price?"

She hadn't thought about it. That was apparent from her hesitation.

Rio's mental struggle lasted another half-dozen seconds before resignation slipped over the hard angles of his face. "If I don't talk to you before, I'll be here Wednesday. Before seven-thirty." He pointed to the phone to remind her she had a caller waiting. Looking sorely tempted to do what he'd done just moments ago, seeming just as determined not to do it again, he stuffed his hands in his pockets and headed for the front door.

Seven

The potential buyer of Olivia's two-year-old sedan arrived right on time. Rio did not. Eve told herself she wasn't worried, though. She could handle this. She just wished the wiry, middle-aged man who'd introduced himself as a mechanic wouldn't wink at her every time he caught her eye.

Standing in the driveway, she watched him hitch up his jeans as he walked around the car. After poking his head under the hood, he got in and started it up. A moment later, he got out, opened the hood again, winked once more and started frowning and humming to himself.

Her confidence faltered. He was going to want to take the car for a drive. She didn't know why she hadn't considered that before, but she did know she didn't want to give a virtual stranger the keys and let him go off alone. There was no way, however, that she would put herself and Molly in the car with that man, either.

That bit of certainty was met with undeniable relief when she saw Rio's Bronco round the corner and pull to a stop at the curb.

The mechanic must have thought he had competition for the car. Rio had no sooner come up beside Eve than the man at the hood motioned her over and told her what he'd give her for it. The offer wasn't for very much, but he said he couldn't do any better than that because the car needed extensive work on its turbo.

The make of car in question didn't have a turbo, something Eve wouldn't have known had Rio not quietly pointed it out when the self-proclaimed mechanic got back inside the car to rev the engine again. She wouldn't have cared about the lack, either, had the guy not been trying to do exactly what Rio had suspected he might.

The man had already known that the vehicle was being sold by a young woman, but he'd taken one look at Eve and assumed she'd be a pushover. Eve realized that the moment he called out, "So what'll it be, little lady?" About the time he added that he'd be happy to take this burden off of her hands, she also realized that there was more to selling a car than getting the value of the vehicle from a book at the bank and expecting people to be fair with their offers.

She understood negotiating. She did it all the time with furniture and fabric buyers. She was even getting pretty good at it. But when it came to her mother's possessions, she just couldn't stomach the haggling.

The fact that Rio suspected as much was obvious when he bent his head to hers.

"Do you want me to handle this?" he asked, his voice little more than a whisper of air near her ear.

She pulled back, aware of the smaller man watching them, though he couldn't hear anything Rio had said.

"It's Mom's car," she returned, just as quietly. "I should do it."

Should, she'd said, which Rio knew explained a lot about why she'd refused, however graciously, to accept anyone else's help with all she had to do. This was an obligation, a responsibility. And she was repaying a debt.

"You won't be neglecting a duty, Eve. Honest."

He turned from the gratitude she couldn't hide, introducing himself to the suddenly wary mechanic and suggesting that perhaps he'd confused the make of the car with something else when he'd assessed its condition. It was immediately apparent that Rio knew what he was doing. It was apparent, too, that he wasn't going to let anyone take advantage of the "little lady."

Within the minute the man lost interest in bargaining.

Since he wasn't going to walk away with a steal, he also lost interest in the car. That meant Eve still had a car to sell. So Rio suggested she put an ad in the paper for the following weekend, then told her he would handle the people who came by to look at it. A minute later, having waved to Molly, who was watching from the front window, he was on his way to an interview. In the past week, he told Eve, three students had been arrested in drug-related incidents, and he was meeting with the high school principal to find out why the problem was getting worse.

What he didn't say was that he'd come by only to help her with the car. And what Eve didn't understand was why he'd done that.

Three days later, she was still wondering about it.

True to his word, Rio arrived Saturday morning to handle the half-dozen callers who'd responded to the ad. He and Molly handled them, that was. While Eve cleaned out storage cupboards in the garage, father and daughter talked and kicked tires with the prospective buyers. When it came time for a test drive, Rio sent Molly in to Eve or off for a ride on her bike. Then Molly would head right back to him immediately upon his return. The bond developing between them was obvious. Just as obvious to Eve was how careful Rio was to keep physical distance between her and himself.

She already knew that he regarded what had happened in the kitchen the other night as a mistake, something that would not be repeated. But she didn't understand why he'd decided to help her. When someone wasn't looking at the car, he helped her in the garage with the heavy stuff. And the next day, after the car had finally been sold, he stuck around to help her carry everything from the attic to the garage.

They worked amazingly well together, and by avoiding the subjects of their situation and her brother, the time he spent with them gave Eve the most peace she'd felt in two months. It was only when Molly wasn't right with them that the deliberate distance he kept between them became noticeable.

Rio seemed to ignore the strain. Eve tried, but she really wanted him to take her in his arms again. Just for a little while. None of the difficulties she was dealing with could intrude when he held her.

The thought was as appealing as it was dangerous. It also resurrected all manner of impossible dreams. Watching him with the child who was clearly coming to adore him, those dreams begged to be indulged. She couldn't allow herself to do that, though. She had no idea how to reach past the emotional armor he wore so well; how to reach the man she wanted so badly to understand. The only person who seemed able to do that was Molly—and he had yet to bring up anything specific about the role he would play in her life.

Had Eve not been so reluctant to upset the fragile truce they were operating under, she would have raised the issue herself. She didn't want to be bumping shoulders with Rio while they jockeyed for their respective positions in Molly's life. Whatever he wanted to do would only mean more changes for her, though, and sharing Molly could get very difficult—even though the sharing had started happening all by itself.

"So how was the fishing, Rio?" Lettie Meyers, the *Herald*'s soon-to-retire assistant editor, leaned a heavy hip on the edge of Rio's desk and straightened the bow over the gap in her blouse. "If it's any good, I might dig out a pole myself."

"I didn't go fishing."

"You must have worked on your cabin, then."

"I didn't do that, either."

Penciled auburn eyebrows merged. "You're kidding. You took the weekend off. What else would you have done?"

There was no insult in the question. Not coming from

Lettie. She was the only person Rio knew who, like him, divided her life into two modes: work and relax. The fact that it was usually a ninety-ten split was something they both overlooked.

"I was helping a friend."

"That's what I like about you, Rio. You don't waste time bending an ear. How's the Stuart investigation coming?"

"Not."

"Did you get stats for that highway development article?"

"Done."

Rio snapped up the lid on his double espresso. The scent of roasted caffeine was teasing his nostrils when Lettie hoisted herself from his desk and patted his shoulder.

"Good. I always know I can count on you. Don't forget to check your E-mail. You've got a meeting with Kleinfelter at one."

Kleinfelter was the editor-in-chief. "What about?"

Lettie's heavily made-up brown eyes shifted first left, then right, to see who else was around at seven-thirty on a Monday morning. Finding no one as dedicated—or as unencumbered—as they were, she took a step forward. They were alone, but she lowered her voice, anyway. Every reporter knew that walls had ears.

"He wants to talk to you about taking over my job. I told him you can't have it, though. Not until you tell me where that secret fishing hole of yours is." She gave him another pat on the shoulder, the motherly gesture a true sign of acceptance from a woman who had once hired him only to meet a minority quota.

"By the way, you'd better knock off that stuff," she added, pointing to the steaming cardboard cup. "You've got thirty plus years ahead of you in this business. You'll have ulcers enough without melting your stomach lining on purpose."

Patting at her short gray hair, she threaded her way through the maze of desks on her way to the fridge in the lounge. That was where she kept the milk she took her antacids with. The chocolate bars to kill the taste were kept in her bottom desk drawer.

Remembering, he spun back around. "Don't sit down without looking in your chair," he called after her. "Some kids were trying to raise money for baseball equipment. I thought of you."

"What kind did you bring me?"

"I think they're almond."

The wrinkles around her mouth deepened with her suppressed smile. "Are you trying to bribe me?"

"If I were trying to bribe you, I'd tell you where my fishing hole is."

Rio knew she didn't really want to know. It just bugged her that he was never specific about where he went when he felt the need to get away for a while. Until he'd decided to build himself a cabin, all he ever said was that he was going fishing. He'd never bothered to mention that he didn't own a single pole, reel or hook.

With a grin, he turned back to his desk. The smile was gone long before he reached for his coffee. From what Lettie had just said, it looked as if he was about to move another step closer to his goal. Assistant Editor would look very nice on his résumé. And that's all he was working for—to beef up the résumé that would get him onto a paper in some distant city.

Yet, as he checked his schedule of meetings and appointments for the day, he couldn't feel pleased about the potential move up. Not just because an editorial position would mean he'd no longer be out chasing stories. There was actually some appeal to that. His reluctance existed because to count on anything before it was a done deal was to make a date with disappointment. Rio had learned the hard way to take nothing for granted. Ever.

It was that hard-learned lesson that had him jogging up the steps of the library when it opened at ten o'clock.

Grand Springs' main library was on the hill near Grand Springs University. Because the university was small, it pooled its resources with the community to provide a facility that served the students and the public better than either could have been served alone. It even boasted a modest law library downstairs near the archives. Usually Rio utilized the archives, most often to dig up background from the state newspapers on microfiche for a current story. Today, he headed for the heavy tomes across the hall.

He needed to talk to Eve about Molly. Before he did, he needed to know his legal rights.

The murmur of voices drifted toward him as he moved between the high rows of books. Finding the volume he wanted, he pulled it from the shelf and headed for the tables near the fiche viewers. Terry Sanchez, one of the librarians, was leaning over the broad shoulder of a fair-haired man sitting at the machine. Very pretty, and very pregnant, she wiggled her fingers at Rio when she saw him, smiled and turned back to the man she was helping. The guy looked vaguely familiar, but, preoccupied, Rio didn't bother to wonder why.

Blocking their quiet voices, Rio pulled out a chair, loosened his tie and opened one of the thick volumes of Colorado statutes. He had friends at the courthouse who could have told him where to start. He could have called on the *Herald*'s attorney, for that matter. But he preferred to keep his business to himself. He wasn't sure how to explain his relationship with Eve to anyone, anyway. He wasn't so sure he could explain it to himself.

They were no longer friends. Not as they'd once been. But they weren't strangers to each other anymore, either. He wasn't even completely sure how he felt about her—though he was well aware of her ambivalence toward him. She wore every emotion on her sleeve. In the space of an hour he had seen her pout, laugh, tease and frown, all with the same intensity. He'd never known anyone like her, anyone so open and honest with her feelings. Or anyone so blindly accepting of people. Maybe that was why he'd felt such freedom with her before. Why, after six long years, he sometimes felt it with her now. But he didn't trust the feeling any more than he trusted the attraction that had him feeling as tense and twitchy as a caged bear.

He wanted her. He couldn't have denied that if he'd tried. He couldn't get within three feet of her without wanting to be inside her. Her scent, the sound of her voice, the way she moved, anything and everything about her seemed destined to drive him slowly out of his mind. If he ever got her near a bed without Molly around, he knew it would take every ounce of willpower he possessed not to back her onto it—which was precisely why he hadn't let himself be alone with her.

Concentrate, he muttered to himself, and forced his attention to the index.

Paper rustled lightly when he finally turned to the section he wanted. It might be getting harder all the time to keep his hands to himself, but he couldn't let physical need override his common sense. Eve had walked out on him once before. Though he didn't think she'd leave before she finished what she'd come here to do, there was really nothing to prevent her from walking away again.

But Molly was another matter. He wasn't about to let his daughter disappear from his life. That was why he needed to know what his legal rights were before he got serious about discussing joint custody with Eve. Just in case she opposed the idea.

Before he talked to Eve, though, he needed to talk to his family. Molly was part of his life, his family, and his mother needed to know she had another grandchild.

"Copies of the Denver papers might help," he heard Terry say just as he figured out that the first thing he needed to do was legally establish paternity. "Good luck."

Hating how cold and impersonal the legalities sounded, Rio finished up his notes and closed the heavy book. He wasn't sure he was ready for this. He knew Eve wasn't.

Abandoning the thought for now, since there were other matters to attend to first, anyway, he claimed the spot the friendly librarian had vacated and extended his hand to the man frowning at the print on the screen. "Martin Smith, right?"

Six feet three inches of lean muscle rose from the chair. The frown had disappeared, revealing little beyond curiosity in his intense blue eyes.

"I suppose," he replied, accepting Rio's handshake. A scar, faded from red to pink, slashed the right side of his forehead. Even without it, the man had a faintly dangerous air about him. "Do I know you?"

"We met at the hospital a couple of months ago. I'm Rio Redtree. A reporter with the *Herald*." Martin Smith wasn't the man's real name. That was just the name the hospital had stuck on him because the staff had needed to call him something other than "the amnesia case." The man had suffered a head injury the night of the storm and hadn't been able to remember anything since. When the hospital had tried to help him locate family, the newspaper had run a request for help identifying him.

"I didn't know you were still around."

"Don't know where else to go." His shrug might have appeared philosophical had it not been for the tension in it. "I thought looking through old newspapers might trigger something."

His tone was flat, as if he didn't expect anything to come from his efforts. But Rio sensed a quiet sort of desperation in him, masked though it was by a kind of ironclad control he knew all too well. The only thing a person truly had any power over was himself. When that control was threatened, as it certainly would be not knowing who he was, a man's hold over himself would became that much more imperative.

That Martin Smith appeared almost afraid to discover who he was prompted Rio to ignore his inclination to simply leave the man to his task. If he was afraid to discover who he was, might that be because he was afraid to discover what he'd done?

The man was a stranger. No one had ever seen him before the night of the storm—which also happened to be the night Olivia had been murdered. But the speculation had no sooner formed than Rio remembered that Stone had already talked to this guy—and that, at the time of Olivia's attack, "Martin" had been stuck on the side of a mountain. Two local citizens, Sean and Cassandra Frame, had seen him there. Aside from that, if there was any credence to Jessica Hanson's visions, there was no way on God's green earth that Martin Smith could ever be mistaken for a woman.

Every time Rio thought he had a lead, the trail evaporated before it even started to take off. Still, long after he had wished Martin luck and returned to the newspaper office, an idea nagged in the back of his mind. Mud slides had trapped the Frames on the mountain. Those same slides had made passage in or out of town impossible for days. Their little airport had been closed, too. So whoever had killed Olivia couldn't have left town. It was always possible that whoever had done it lived in town and was still right there. For the first few days, at least, the killer could well have been right under their noses.

He felt about as much hope of discovering anything of value pursuing the idea as Martin did poking around newspapers for a hint of his past, but when something started nagging at Rio, he couldn't let it go.

"I know it's late, but your lights were on."

He should have called first. Even before Eve stepped back to let him in, Rio could tell that his timing was lousy. She looked as pale as snow, and there was a telltale sheen to her eyes.

"If this isn't a good time…"

"It's fine." True to form, she straightened her shoulders and made herself smile. "Actually, I could use the break.

Some of the boxes we brought down from the attic were full of pictures,'' she said, self-consciously stuffing a tissue into the pocket of her short denim jumper. "I was just going through them.''

"By yourself?''

Eve lifted her shoulder in a dismissing shrug. She didn't know if he was aware of the concern behind his frown, but it was definitely undermining her efforts to maintain her composure. "Molly helped before she went to bed.''

"That's not what I mean.''

She knew that. She also knew that standing there wondering if he would ever put his arms around her again wasn't helping her effort, either. "I asked Hal if he wanted to go through them with me,'' she told him, heading into the dining room. "But he didn't have time. All I'm doing is dividing them up.'' She motioned to the clear plastic photo boxes on the table. "I'd forgotten how fanatical Mom was about getting every occasion on film.''

Shaking her head as if she'd just remembered something, she glanced back at him. "I'm sorry. Is there something you wanted?''

The light of the brass chandelier bounced off the crystal in the mahogany-and-glass china cupboard, the glint of pure white light reminding Rio of the telltale brightness in her eyes moments ago. He'd undoubtedly caught her fighting memories as she'd sorted through photographs of birthdays and holidays and whatever else her family had celebrated, but already she'd pulled herself together. Anyone seeing her now might think she only looked tired.

"There is. But this might not be a good time to talk about it.''

With anyone else, considering the seriousness of the matter, he would have forced himself past his natural reluctance to intrude on her pain. It was a battle he constantly fought when faced with certain types of stories, which was why he went after facts rather than what his editor euphemistically referred to as "human interest.'' He'd quit his job before he'd shove a recorder in a victim's face to ask how she felt while she watched her house burn. But he would ask if she knew how the fire had started.

That he was willing to wait for a better time to talk to Eve might have worried him a little, had she not suddenly looked so uneasy.

"You want to talk about Molly."

"No. No," he repeated. "Not now. We need to talk about her, but that can wait. I wanted to talk to you about the people you saw when you were here in June."

She didn't understand what he was getting at. She told him that, too, sinking onto a chair at the table and pushing aside the pictures someone had taken at an office party. "What about them?"

Since she expressed more interest than reluctance, Rio pulled out the chair next to her, sat down with his elbows on his knees and his hands clasped between them, and proceeded to explain his theory about the killer being in town for the first few days following her mom's death. He wanted to know if she'd seen anyone who'd appeared suspicious, or if anyone she hadn't recognized had come by the house. He'd asked her that question before about the people at the house and the hospital the night her mom had been taken there. But what about visitors afterward?

"There were so many," she told him, sounding bewildered at the task of sorting through all the faces. "Mom had friends and business acquaintances I'd never met." She pushed her fingers through her hair, trying to think. "It just seemed as if people were dropping off casseroles and flowers from the moment I got back from the hospital."

"Flowers?"

Not sure why he thought that extraordinary, her voice went flat. "People do that when someone dies, Rio. Send flowers, I mean."

His bland expression mirrored hers. "But how did they do that? There were power lines and trees down everywhere, remember? Emergency vehicles could barely get through. And the businesses that weren't damaged were closed because there was no electricity.''

In other words, of the half-dozen florists in town, none had been delivering that day.

''Maybe people were bringing them from their gardens,'' she suggested. ''I really don't remember there being many that first day. The only reason I remember any at all was because someone brought a huge bowl of gardenias. I had to put it on the patio table before we went to bed that night because the scent was so overpowering.''

Her words sent up an immediate red flag, but Rio kept his expression even. ''Did you see who brought them?''

Eve shook her head, trying to get through the haze that clouded those days. ''Millicent must have answered the door. Or maybe one of the women from the church. I just remember thinking that I'd never be able to stand the smell of gardenias again.''

''Do you know what happened to the bowl?''

Eve had been watching his clasped hands. Strong, steady, still. She envied him his calm. Now, puzzled by his question, she glanced up. ''It's out in the garage, in a box of old vases and things to be donated to the thrift shop. Why?''

''Was there a card with it?''

''I'm sure there wasn't. The florist cards all have the type of arrangement or plant written on the back of them. We did that when someone would bring something to the house, and the funeral home did it for arrangements that were sent there. I just finished the thank-you notes for all the remembrances last week, and I know I never came across anything for those flowers.'' She cocked her head. ''You didn't answer me,'' she reminded him. ''Why are you so interested in this?''

Rio figured that any fingerprints had probably already been obliterated. The bowl would have been handled by heaven only knew who by now, not to mention washed and wiped clean.

"It's a complete long shot," he told her, refusing to get her hopes up. "But I'm going to mention this to Stone. He might want to have that bowl picked up. Don't handle it anymore. Just leave it where it is." In the meantime, he was going to pay Millicent Atwell a visit.

"What's this all about, Rio?"

"Ask Stone. Okay?"

She could have pointed out that one of the reasons she was answering his questions was because he'd agreed to give her information so she wouldn't have to bother the police for it. But she had the feeling this was one of those details he'd promised his friend he wouldn't discuss, and she knew Rio would never break his word. His basic sense of integrity wouldn't allow it.

Because she respected him for that, she wouldn't ask any more questions. Except, maybe, one. "I know it frustrates you when I can't remember things about those days, but has anything I've told you been any help at all?"

She wouldn't have asked had she not been feeling so powerless just then. But she knew the second the words were out of her mouth that she was seeking reassurance Rio couldn't give.

"Never mind," she murmured, letting him off with a smile that didn't quite work. "I'll ask the detective. Would you hand me those pictures, please?"

It wasn't her request that had Rio hesitating. It was the thought of Stone or some other officer offering her the reassurance she so badly needed. Not that Stone would do anything other than talk to her.

The thought didn't help. Palming the stack of colorful photos, he slid them across the gleaming wood surface. He was battling enough where this woman was concerned without having to admit to jealousy.

He started to hand the pictures over, but when her fingers closed around the opposite ends, he didn't let go. "Do you want me to stay and help you with this?"

She looked down at their hands, thumbs grasping from

the top, fingers from below, contact separated by the smiling face of Hal at thirteen.

"Why would you want to?"

"It's not that big a deal, Eve."

She didn't buy the disclaimer. "It is to me," she insisted, no longer willing to speculate. "Why are you helping me the way you have been? Don't get me wrong," she hurried on, loath to let him misunderstand. "I appreciate everything you've done. But you don't have to help me so you can spend time with Molly. You have to know that."

"I do."

"Then, why?"

Because I know you need to do this for your mother, but I can't stand the thought of you doing it all alone. Because you haven't accepted anyone else's help, but you've accepted mine, and I like the way that makes me feel. "Because you're my daughter's mother." The faintest hint of a smile tugged at the corner of his mouth. "And it seemed the easiest way for us to get to know each other again."

She should have known he was just being practical. Still, she was grateful. For what he'd done, and for what he was doing now.

"You can put those in that big box over there," she quietly said, letting go of the snapshots. "That's the one for Hal." She turned to the pictures she'd been looking at when she'd heard Rio at the door. It was already easier with him here. "I really wanted him to do this with me."

"Then, why don't you put it off for a while? Maybe he'll have time later."

"Time isn't really his problem," she returned, pushing birthday party pictures toward him so he could divide them up. "He just doesn't want to go through these. It's too hard. But I'd hoped he'd come, anyway," she continued as Rio, seeming to know exactly what she'd wanted, started picking out similar poses and putting them into two separate piles. "With him being so much older, we weren't particularly close when we were growing up. I'd thought that going through these together might be good for us both."

She reached into the box at her elbow. "Hal could have told me more about our oldest brother," she said, laying a photo on the table between them and pointed to the oldest child. "Roy ran away from home when I was two, so I don't remember him at all. He was named after my father, so I guess he's really Roy, Jr."

Rio picked up the photo, a Polaroid that had been taken in someone's yard. Three blond kids faced the camera. The only one with a smile was the tiny little girl with huge blue eyes. The boys, one narrow-shouldered and thin, the other taller and beginning to show some muscle, looked as if they wanted only to get the shot over with.

Rio was already aware of Eve's older sibling. He'd come across a reference to him while searching the newspaper's archives for possible enemies of Olivia. She had spoken about her runaway son when she'd first announced her candidacy for office. Her own circumstances had prompted much of her interest in helping other women who were raising families on their own.

He mentioned the article to Eve and offered to get her a copy. She answered with a quiet "Thank you," and took the picture back to study it herself.

"Mom said he ran off after Dad died. That would be over twenty years ago now." She shook her head, her brow furrowing. "I don't know that she ever heard from him again. I remember asking about him once, but all she said was that he was a very brave and special boy. I never asked her about him after that," she added, setting the picture aside. "It was too hard for her to talk about him. But it wasn't long after she told me that, that I started picturing my missing oldest brother as the white knight my present big brother was not."

She made a face, the expression amazingly reminiscent of Molly. "Until I was about ten, Hal had no time and less patience for watching after his kid sister. The way he'd carry on about having to take me to the movies with him and his friends, you'd think I was his personal albatross.''

"What happened when you where ten?''

"He moved away to college. In Denver.''

At that, Rio smiled. It wasn't much of a smile. Just enough to let her know he understood that separation had salvaged what little she and Hal had of a relationship, and to relieve the pensiveness she'd fought. It also encouraged a question of her own.

"What about you?'' she quietly asked. "You have a brother and a sister. Did you get along when you were growing up?''

Rio had never said much about his siblings. With a glance that said he didn't care to talk much about them now, either, he said, "Well enough, I guess.''

He glanced from her as he spoke, clearly preparing to dismiss the subject.

"Do they have names?'' she asked before he could.

Rocking back in his chair, he reached for another envelope. "Dusty and Shana. Dusty's three years older. Shana's two younger.''

A middle child. She'd never known that before.

She tipped her head, studying his features in the buttery light of the chandelier. He looked relaxed enough. But even with his attention on another batch of pictures, she could swear she felt him tensing.

She wanted to know this man. Needed to know him. More important, she realized, she needed to understand what kept him from her.

Leaning forward, she placed her hand over the photos.

"Would you tell me what it was like, growing up on the reservation?''

His eyes met hers, steady and as unreadable to her as petroglyphs. For a moment, she thought he might evade her question, that he'd turn back to the pictures she'd just covered and change the subject. The tactic would have been so typical of the man she'd once known.

Instead, he pushed the stack aside.

"It's like growing up in a box."

She thought from his closed expression that he might mention the rampant unemployment and the alcohol and drug problems she remembered people talking about. At seventeen, she'd never associated him with any of that. Now she couldn't avoid it.

He said nothing of those matters, though.

"There's the res," he continued. "Then, there's what is off of it. On the res, you're supposed to think and feel and act like everyone else. If you don't, you're criticized for not being in harmony with the people." He paused, brow pinching. "Some people criticize you, anyway. The ones who say they care about you.

"I guess it's like living anywhere else," he finally said, checking the bitterness creeping into his tone. "You learn to adapt. Or you leave."

Caution entered Eve's expression. "Are you talking about the reservation, or your own home?"

The muscle in his jaw jumped. "It's the same thing."

For a moment, Eve said nothing. In less than a minute, he'd given her more insight to him than he had in all the time she'd known him. She could understand how the culture of a place would influence the people living in it, so she had no problem seeing how difficult it would be for him to divorce one from the other. But she was beginning to see that, while his heritage might have been the catalyst, it was his own family, or a member of it, that had instilled the unsettled need he'd felt to move beyond the bounds of the reservation.

Long ago, he'd told her he didn't belong anywhere. Recalling that now, she couldn't help but think that, somehow, he hadn't been accepted even in his own home. It was no wonder he'd felt in need of escape.

"You sound as if you were searching for something when you left."

If her insight was at all accurate, she couldn't tell from the quiet way he watched her. "Maybe I was."

"Did you ever find it?"

He held her eyes, his face devoid of expression. A second passed. Then, another.

Finally, his voice remote, he calmly said, "I have no idea what I'm looking for."

It was another moment before he looked way. But in those moments, Eve had the feeling she was only beginning to appreciate the enormity of his struggle.

Wanting to help, having no idea how, she focused on the one thing she felt certain was weighing on his mind.

"Have you told your family about Molly?"

A full ten seconds passed before he answered. When he did, it was with the resignation of a man who'd already been wrestling with the question and had just made up his mind. "I'm going up tomorrow."

Eight

In summer, the reservation where Rio grew up was a two-hour drive from Grand Springs. It could take twice as long in winter. Sometimes, if the wind blew hard enough and the snow got deep enough, the trip couldn't be made at all. When the temperature dropped to freezing and the wind-driven snow obliterated everything but miles of low flats and barren hills, this stretch of land could be the most desolate place on earth. Now the land was rich with crops of wheat and sugar beets; the mountains beyond alive with grazing elk. But even the thought of all the summers he'd spent exploring this rugged and beautiful place couldn't ease the tension knotting his insides.

The closer Rio got to the highway sign proclaiming entry onto tribal land, the more he wished the streaky white clouds overhead would gray up and dump about thirty inches of the icy white stuff. He could use the excuse to turn around. A person needed to be careful what he wished for, though. There were those who believed thought itself could make something happen. His mother was one of them.

Holding that thought at bay, he drove past clusters of old housing and new, a well-tended farm and another gone fallow. The wind was blowing cool when, fifteen miles in, he crossed a narrow bridge and pulled into the cluster of modest little houses and one large mobile home. The drop in temperature was an omen of his reception, Rio was sure.

The cries of "Uncle!" made him smile despite himself. After his initial three-year absence, he'd come home because his grandfather had taken ill. After that, he'd made it back three or four times a year, though he never stayed more than a day. The little ones remembered him, though. And he always remembered them—along with the other small children who showed up with his cherub-faced little nieces.

He was thinking how Molly would fit right in with this animated crowd of laughing, dark-haired children when a toddler on a Big Wheel came tearing across the patches of grass poking through the hard-packed dirt. Rio didn't recognize the little boy, someone his mother was baby-sitting probably, but like the rest of the kids, he got a piece of the red licorice Rio doled out to the lot.

"Something is wrong."

His mother's voice came from behind him. Maria Redtree stood in the door of the long, gray-and-white trailer, wiping her hands on her apron, her dark eyes trained on her son. Her hair, drawn back in a single thick braid was still black as coal, though Rio could see hints of silver threading through it as he moved closer. Her body was rounding, but the years were settling well on her. Her bronze skin was smooth, with only a trace of the wrinkles she should have had, considering the grief he seemed to have given her.

"Why is something wrong?" he asked, breathing in the scents of fry bread and wild herbs when he hugged her.

She stepped back, shooing a brown puppy from behind her long tiered skirt. "Because you never come without calling first. And never in the middle of the week."

The omission had been deliberate. So was the timing. Midweek, his brother and sister would be working. Dusty at the tribal government office. His sister at the reservation clinic.

He asked after them both, and about his uncles, and when Fawn, who tended the children with her mother-in-law while the others worked, walked in with her youngest on her hip, he asked after her family, too. A person didn't just pop up and open Pandora's box without first attending to amenities. Though his mother wore her concern like a shield, something she always did when he was around, she wouldn't have allowed it to be any other way.

Fawn was feeding the children, the five that belonged to the family and the two that didn't, when his mother decided they could talk best outside.

"You know the Offerings Lodge was held here last week," she said as they walked out toward the road. "Your brother made the prayer sacrifice."

There was as much censure as pride in the statements. Tribes from everywhere attended the weeklong event, the sacred occasion a source of strength and fulfillment for the people. It was a time, too, when everyone tried to focus on unity and avoid conflict of any kind. She might as well have said that Rio had failed her yet again by not having been there himself.

"He is to be congratulated," Rio replied, refusing to rise to her bait. "Dusty's a good man. Mother, I came to ask you something," he continued, needing badly to get this over with.

Curious, she forgot to castigate. "Yes?"

"About six years ago, a woman…a girl," he corrected himself, because that's what she'd been at the time, "called here looking for me. I know I'd mentioned her to you, because she and I had gone to school together. Her name was Eve."

"Six years is a long time."

"Not for your memory."

She gave him a smile, but there was enough hesitation behind it for Rio to know that her memory was, indeed, as unfailing as the sunrise.

For a moment, she said nothing more. Her five feet five inches drawn perfectly erect, she simply stared straight ahead as they walked, oblivious to the ever-present wind blowing dust across the road and rattling the scrub oak lining it. "She was the girl Shana teased you about after she found you looking at her picture. You were unhappy over her. I remember.''

"You didn't give me the message."

The flatness in his tone spoke volumes. Rio was obviously aware now that the call had been made. Knowing that, he would also be aware of what was said. Maria was quick to figure that out, and just as quick to defend herself.

"I was a mother protecting her son. When you are a parent yourself, you will understand."

Rio felt his gut knot. What he wanted to do was tell her that he had long grown past needing protection by that point. He wanted to tell her, too, that making it sound as if she'd saved him because the girl had hurt him was a rather unique spin on telling someone to back off because she was the wrong race. But anger would serve no useful purpose. Especially now, when he needed calm to prevail.

"I am a parent. I have a daughter," he said, stopping her in her tracks. "That was what Eve had called here to tell me."

He could see the questions forming as she stared up at him. The accusation. The disappointment. He could see denial, too, and maybe a hint of guilt, though he knew he'd go a long way before she'd ever admit to that one. Finally, they all formed a single question. "Where is the child?"

"Eve has her."

Rio watched his mother turn away from him, her censure deliberate.

"I knew no good would come of you leaving here to go to that college. You should have stayed, worked with Willy Little Dog. Your uncle would have counseled you, taught you to farm."

It never failed. No matter what he did, everything boiled down to this one lousy argument. He was trying to talk to her about his daughter and she wanted to point out where he'd gone astray. "I wasn't interested in farming. I've told you that. Dusty's the one who understood agriculture."

"Because he was in touch with the earth and the sky,"

she pointed out, addressing the spirituality she obviously felt her younger son lacked. "He knows himself. He knows the importance of continuing what we have. Your mind is too curious, too unfocused. You should have stayed and found yourself. But no." Shaking her head, she held her arms wide, the beads on the small amulet bag around her neck catching the glint of the sun. "You go, and you abandon everything. Now you have a child who belongs neither here nor there."

"There" was the white man's world, the place Maria Redtree had never trusted. It had taken her husband and, like some men are drawn to the sea, it had lured a son. To this day, Rio knew she believed that Joe Redtree would still be with her if he hadn't had to leave the res to find work.

Rio stepped back, hating the feelings churning inside him. Everything didn't have to be black-and-white, but his mother couldn't seem to see anything any other way. His aunts and uncles weren't like that. Neither was his sister. But that didn't matter to Rio just now. It hadn't been forgiveness or understanding for himself he'd sought from his mother. He hadn't deserved or expected either. All he'd wanted was acceptance for his child.

She didn't need to say another word for him to know she couldn't offer that. And a child, any child, deserved nothing less than to be unconditionally accepted for itself. God knew he never had been. Not by her.

"She belongs where she is," he said, finality in his voice. "This isn't a place I would want her, anyway."

"You are just like your father."

"So you keep telling me."

Rio turned on his heel, fists clenched and dust puffing around his boots with each step he took.

You are just like your father. She'd pushed him away with those words for more than fifteen years, using them like a weapon and making even whatever good traits he'd inherited from the man sound like something to be ashamed of. Every time he heard them, he cursed the man whose features he bore and whose insatiable curiosity he claimed, and he cursed himself for letting his mother get to him. But, even through his own anger, he realized that this time, there had been more pain than resentment in her accusation.

The knowledge slowed his steps, his thoughts racing as he slowly turned around.

She stood where he'd left her, still and immovable as a mountain.

She had always blamed the white man's world for stealing her husband, and wanted nothing to do with it because of that. But Rio had heard the talk when he was a child that the reason Joe Redtree had abandoned his family was because he'd been a dreamer who'd never been able to handle the responsibility of a wife and children.

His father had been irresponsible, all right. But Rio suddenly had the feeling that there was more to his father's defection than what he'd heard—and far more to his mother's intolerance.

"Did he leave you for another woman?"

He saw her suck in a breath, her hand clutching her stomach as if she'd been struck.

She shook her head, turning away.

"I will not speak of this."

"He did, didn't he? A white woman."

She said nothing, but her shoulders went rigid.

"Does anyone else know this?"

Silence.

"Was she pregnant?"

She denied nothing. But her pride allowed no admissions, either.

"These are not questions for a son to ask his mother."

"They are when I'm being held accountable for my father's sins. Is it because I look like him? Is that why you've always pushed me away?"

She wouldn't answer. Maybe it was because she couldn't. Maybe it was because she didn't know how. But after thirty seconds of suffering her silence, Rio gave up and turned away himself. Not until he reached his Bronco did he look back to where she remained by the road, her hand clutching the bag around her neck and her face tipped to the sky.

He hated leaving this way. Not speaking. Yet he always did.

Revving the engine, he headed across the hardpack for the bridge, his knuckles white on the wheel.

His mother's house was a mile behind him before he felt the sting in his fingers and started to relax his grip. Yet it wasn't the distance he was putting between them that helped relaxed his hold. It was the realization that, for the first time in his life, he understood why it was so impossible for his mother to trust anything that had to do with "there"—and how hurt she must have been when she'd realized why her husband had abandoned her.

Rio knew that hurt. He'd been ten years old when his father had walked away, and he'd been devastated. He'd worshiped the man. But he understood now that being abandoned by a spouse or lover damaged a heart in a different way. He'd learned that himself from Eve. She was why he'd sworn to never again let himself care enough about anyone for it to make any difference whether they stuck around or walked away.

Maybe his mother had done the very same thing. And maybe he was more like her than either one of them had ever realized.

Eve thought he would have called by now.

Pulling her glance from the silent phone, she turned her attention once more to the typed sheets in her hand. She should be practicing her speech. It was her mother's speech, actually. The one Eve was to give in four days at a luncheon for five hundred people where she was absolutely certain she'd spill something red on the white suit she was planning to wear just before she stood up to screw up her mother's carefully chosen words. But that seemed so irrelevant at the moment. Rio had gone to talk to his family two days ago, and she hadn't heard a word from him since.

She knew he was alive because she'd seen his byline on an article about a boat wreck that had happened yesterday. She even knew he was in town because she'd called the newspaper midafternoon, only to learn that he'd just left on an assignment. Had she left a message, he might have returned the call by now. But one hadn't seemed necessary. He had to know she was waiting to hear from him. The last thing she'd said when he'd left the other night was "call me when you get back." She'd even added "Please."

Retracing the path she'd paced in the living room, she tossed the typewritten pages onto the coffee table, covering the calling card the real estate agent had left after showing the house a few hours earlier. She could either try Rio at home, try his pager number or stop worrying about it and clean something.

She didn't expect him to answer. But he did.

"Eve," he said, immediately recognizing her voice. "I was going to call you." The sound of banging metal filtered over the line. "Things have been a little crazy."

"Are you okay?"

She'd meant to ask if "everything" was okay. Or so she'd thought before the words had come out.

Gripping the receiver a little harder than she should, she sank to the sofa. The silence on the other end of the line seemed to indicate that Rio had caught the difference, too.

"Yeah," he muttered, apparently having to think about it. A rushing sound, like running water, could be heard in the background. "Like I said, just busy."

"What are you doing?"

"Laundry."

She didn't know why that made her smile.

"Listen," he began, the flatness in his tone tugging the corners of her mouth right back down, "I'm going to Denver in the morning, but I'll be back Sunday or Monday."

"You're not going to make me wait that long, are you? To find out what happened?"

He knew what she was talking about. She also had the feeling from the length of his pause that he didn't want to talk about it now—which was why he hadn't called before.

"It didn't go well. I can tell."

"No," he agreed. "She didn't take it well at all."

She. "Your mother? Is she the problem?"

"In a word."

"Can't you tell me what she said?"

"Things are just more complicated with her than I'd realized."

"Rio, come on." She hated that the rift between him and his mother may have just widened. She hated, too, that he wouldn't talk to her. "What does that mean?"

He must have sensed her frustration.

"She's always had a thing about the white community," he told her, his tone grudging. "I thought it was for the same reasons and prejudices we've always dealt with. But she has a more personal prejudice. It seems my father left her for a white woman. It's been eating at her for years."

What he said wasn't nearly as disturbing to her as the way he said it. "What else happened?" she asked, because something in his voice told her there was more that he wasn't telling her. Something that sounded like hurt.

His pause seemed to indicate that he hadn't expected her to pick up on that. "Nothing that matters."

She didn't believe that for an instant. "But something…"

"Look, I've got to go, Eve."

"Is there anything I can do?"

She thought she heard him sigh. But all he said was "No."

"Are you sure? I'll help if I can."

"I can't imagine what you could do. Anyway, it's my problem. Not yours."

"But it is my problem," she protested, needing him to see that. "Because of Molly."

"Eve," he said, sounding very patient, very certain. "My mother is my problem. You don't need to concern yourself with it."

There was no harshness in his tone, nothing to make her believe he meant to snub her. But his dismissal of her concern stung with a fierceness that took her breath away.

It didn't make her feel any better to know that she'd left herself wide-open to his rejection. After all, just because he'd opened up a little didn't mean they were growing closer. She'd reminded herself a dozen times in the past weeks that his interests were only in the investigation and in their daughter. Their relationship existed only because she was the mother of his child. He'd as much as told her that himself.

If she had the brains God gave a grasshopper, she'd take a lesson from him and be more protective of herself.

"Okay," she returned, willing strength into her voice. "Have a good trip."

"I'll call you when I get back. Maybe I can take Molly to the park or something."

The way he spoke made it sound as if he wanted to take Molly by himself. For a variety of reasons, Eve didn't let herself consider the thought any further than that. She said only that they'd talk about it when he returned. She didn't even mention that Detective Richardson had picked up the bowl that had held the gardenias. But, then, Rio probably already knew that. Determined as he was to find a lead in the investigation, she was certain he kept himself up-to-date on the details.

It was because Rio was so determined to find a lead, and because Eve needed so badly for a lead to be found, that she left a message for him on her way out the door on Monday morning. He'd called as he said he would when he returned from Denver, and they had made plans for him to spend next Sunday with Molly. In the meantime, Hal had sent over a box of things from their mother's office. Since it contained some personal files, she thought Rio might not want to wait until the weekend to go through them. That was the message she left on his voice mail at the newspaper office just before she left for the Children's Charity luncheon.

The luncheon was being held at the elegant Randolphs. From what Eve had been told by Betty Dodd, the fluttery, birdlike lady in charge of the event, it had been touch and go as to whether the wind and water damage to the spacious restaurant would be repaired in time. The work wasn't finished, but it was close enough. If anyone minded the huge sheets of plastic hanging along one side of the banquet room to keep the construction dust off the fifty beautifully set tables, they kept the thought to themselves. In Grand Springs, nearly everyone was pulling together to "make do."

"Miss Stuart, it's so good to see you again."

"Thank you," she replied, trying to remember where she'd seen the woman approaching her.

"Eve," came another voice from behind her. "You don't know me, but your mother and I were in Toastmasters together for years. It's so nice of you to do this."

A woman on her left snagged her arm. "Eve? It's Candy Hampton. Well, Billings now. We went to grade school together."

She hadn't seen Candy since the girl's family had moved to the other side of town. But there was no time for reminiscing now. Only a quick hug and a promise to call. Betty was tugging on her sleeve.

She got about three steps before she was stopped again.

And so it went as Betty led her through the room filled with volunteers, business leaders and concerned citizens. Aware of eyes on her, responding to greetings and comments as they moved toward the head table, Eve couldn't help but wonder how her mother had done this. Eve liked people, but she was more accustomed to smaller groups. Olivia Stuart had thrived on the energy a crowd generated.

All it did to Eve was make her feel nauseous.

I can do this, she told herself, smiling when a woman in a western-cut dress told her it was good to see her looking so well. Since she didn't know the woman from Adam, she could hardly tell her she was looking well thanks to nouveau peach blush and cameo beige foundation. Instead, she politely thanked her, smiled again and moved on at the prod of Betty's bony elbow.

It was one thing to represent her mother at a small tea or fund-raiser, or to donate an item to a charity in her name. But if her mother hadn't already written this speech, and had the subject not been so important to her, Eve wasn't sure she could have spoken to such a crowd.

The fact that the Children's Charity had meant a great deal to her mother allowed Eve to make it through the next hour on little more than sheer determination. She didn't even spill anything on her white suit, but that was probably due to the fact that she didn't touch her meal. When it came time to read her mother's speech, though, the case of nerves lasted only through the first few lines. After that, having nearly memorized the text, she let the steady cadence of her mother's words take over.

The words were her mother's, but as Eve spoke, it became clear to everyone listening that the passion was hers.

Rio certainly heard it.

He'd slipped in to the back of the room and stood off to the side near the door. Petite as Eve was, she wouldn't have been seen over the high podium had someone not brought in a step for her to stand on. Even then, only the shoulders of her tailored suit and her sleek blond head were visible. But once the flutter of nerves faded, her voice grew steadily stronger, its natural softness lending a power of its own as she spoke of the right of every child to grow up in a safe, secure environment. Of the growing presence of drugs on their playgrounds and in their schools. Of the need for the community to stand behind teachers and principals and law enforcement in cleaning up the problem before it reached any more of their children. Mostly she spoke of the need for children to be the first priority in every home; that a stable, secure home life, whether that child lived with one parent or both, was essential to teaching the values and accountability so many children were missing today.

That was where her mother had stopped writing. Rio heard her tell everyone that as she looked up from the pages she'd referred to. With a poise he was coming to recognize as a shield, she went on to tell the absolutely silent crowd that she would be grateful to each and every one of them if they would remember what her mother had worked so hard for, and continue that work on her behalf. But just as she was about to thank them, her voice faltered.

It didn't seem to Rio that it was emotion that got her. Apparently, it was his presence. She'd just noticed him standing there.

Seeming to recover as quickly as she stopped, she continued, finishing her remarks just as the door beside him opened. A tall man with close-cropped blond hair, a swimmer's build and an air of absolute authority walked in. Rio immediately recognized Jack Stryker, one of the detectives on the Olivia Stuart case. After a nod to Rio, the no-nonsense cop zeroed in on Eve.

The applause was still ringing when a woman with a voice like sandpaper and the presence of a pigeon took over the mike to thank Olivia's daughter for sharing her mother's convictions with them. Rio wasn't sure what was said after that. In the moments before the applause started again and the crowd went into motion, his attention was divided between the detective and Eve, and scanning the room for the man he'd come to see.

The din of conversation rose around him as he headed into the departing crowd. By avoiding the crush in the middle, he made it to Eve before Stryker did, meeting her just as the woman who'd come up to her moved off to flag down a lady in a pink lace hat.

Eve's smile for him was wary. "What are you doing here? You're not covering this for the paper, are you?"

"Somebody from Social is supposed to be doing that," he returned, referring to the section of the paper that handled the human interest stuff. "I'm looking for your brother. His secretary said he'd be here."

Eve's smile, strained as it was, faded with her disappointment. "I had understood he would be. I'd hoped he would, anyway." Seeing the man heading straight for her, concern slipped over her expression. "Why? Has something happened?"

Curious himself about the detective's presence, Rio's voice dropped. The room was clearing rapidly, but there were still several pockets of people lingering between the tables. "Not that I'm aware of. I'm just looking for Hal. I don't know why Stryker's here."

"Miss Stuart. Redtree." Straight Arrow Stryker, as he was known by those who knew him best, gave them an acknowledging nod, then swung his attention back to Eve. "When you have a moment, I'd like to speak with you. No cause for alarm," he added, obviously aware that his presence could mean just about anything to her. "I just have some routine questions. Finish with the reporter. I'll wait for you over there."

Clearly thinking that Rio wanted an interview with her, he indicated a side door to let her know where he'd be.

"We can talk now," she told the man, over the clatter of tables being cleared. "What kind of questions?"

"I need to see you alone, ma'am."

His polite but unbending tone made the reason for his insistence clear. He was a cop on official business. Rio was a reporter. He didn't want to see whatever it was they said in the newspaper tomorrow.

Rio took no offense at the man's tacit position. They were each just doing their jobs. But Rio was truly torn at the moment. He knew that Jack Stryker was working hard on the investigation, and he wanted badly to know what the detective wanted with Eve. More important than that, he wanted to make sure Eve would be all right with whatever it was. After giving that speech, she was probably running on nothing but reserves.

He didn't have to ask. Eve's hand had closed around his forearm. Though he met her eyes for only a moment, he caught her quiet plea. Not knowing what was coming next, she didn't want to hear it alone.

Don't go, she seemed to say, though it was to Stryker that she spoke.

"Rio is a friend," she said, staking more of a claim to him than he would have expected, given the shaky ground of their relationship. "He knows as much as I do about this investigation, so I'd prefer that he stay. I'll probably wind up telling him whatever we talk about now, anyway."

Stryker conceded, but only because he knew of Rio's agreement with Stone to keep certain information confidential. It was imperative that what he asked Eve remain confidential, too, for now. So, with that understanding between the three of them, they left the surreptitious stares coming their way and moved through the side door.

The sound of dishes being cleared could still be heard through the wall. But the narrow hallway, its pearl gray paint waterstained and peeling in sections, was deserted.

"I'd like to know what you know about Josephine Reynolds."

The soft wings of Eve's eyebrows arched. "Josie?"

"She goes by that name," the stone-faced detective allowed. "She worked with your mother."

"I know. Mom talked about her all the time. But why are you asking about her?"

"For starters, she's the one who found your mother."

In other words, she'd been first on the scene. Making a mental note to start cruising back files for anything he could find on the town's beautiful treasurer, Rio watched confusion wash over Eve's delicate features.

"I'd like to know what you can tell me about your mother's relationship with her," Stryker continued. "Were you aware of any rivalry or competition between them? Any disagreements?"

"Heavens, no. Mom's attitude toward Josie was almost maternal. From what Mom said, they sounded very close."

"Close enough for her to be named in your mother's will?"

Eve's expression went blank. Then, apparently realizing Josie was under suspicion and that the detective was searching for a motive, she scrambled to the woman's defense.

"She is not named in my mother's will," she told him, looking at the man in utter disbelief. "And I can't imagine what she could have possibly gained by my mother's death. You don't actually suspect her, do you?"

"Is she a friend of yours?"

The fact that he hadn't answered her question was answer enough.

Seeming to sense a trap with his last question, Eve glanced to Rio as if looking for help, then back to the man who seemed as uncompromising as a preacher on Judgment Day. "I've only spoken with her a few times. But she was a good friend to my mother, and someone I hope to know better. She seems like a genuinely nice person."

Rio couldn't help but think that if Josie were ever arrested and the defense needed a character witness, they could do worse than Eve. But the look Stryker gave her made it apparent he thought her either extraordinarily unobservant or awfully naive, and he called it quits after a few more questions that yielded nothing but more of the same. Since the detective wasn't getting anything from Eve that would help him build a case, he impatiently thanked her for her time, reminded Rio of their agreement and left the hall the same way they had entered.

Had Rio thought he could get a thing out of Stryker,

he'd have followed the guy out himself. But there were certain members of the police department who were more cooperative than others, and Stryker wasn't usually one of them. Instead, he turned to the woman whose color appeared marginally better, thanks to the agitation she'd felt on behalf of her mother's friend.

"I can't believe he actually suspects her."

"I told you before, Eve. They're checking out everyone."

"He didn't sound as if he was just checking her out."

Unable to disagree, Rio shrugged. Jo Reynolds was as good a suspect as any.

When Rio mentioned that to Eve, she simply stared at him.

"You know," she finally said, her voice as weary as the shake of her head. "I think I'm at the point where I no longer know what to believe. Or who to believe in. I wouldn't be surprised if they didn't check me next."

He could have told her that she could believe in him. But then, he thought she had. Once. "They did."

What little color she'd gained, drained again.

"You were the last person to see her alive," Rio explained, wondering how much more she'd be able to take before that surprising iron will of hers finally snapped. "You said yourself you'd given a half-dozen statements. Didn't you wonder why so many different detectives and officers talked to you?"

She shook her head, the motion as much an answer as a statement of how bewildered she was by all that was going on around her.

"I can't think about this now," she said, backing away as if she were closing herself off. Or shutting down. "I have to go. Molly went home with one of her friends after day camp and I have to pick her up." She started past him, only to turn when she reached the door. "I left a message for you...about some papers of my mother's you might want to go through. I didn't know if you'd want to wait until the weekend, or look at them sooner. Or let me know if you're not interested in them at all and I'll pitch the works," she added, her voice too passive for his liking.

He'd picked up the message a couple of hours ago. Ever since, he'd been vacillating about whether or not to go over tonight. When he'd come back from the res, he'd found it easy to stay away from her. Seeing her now, sensing how far she had just pulled into herself, his resolve to keep contact with her to a minimum didn't seem quite so important.

"Will you be home tonight?"

She said she would. So he told her he'd be over later, then felt his concern kick up a notch when she gave him a too-weak version of her brave little smile and walked out the door.

A moment later, she was gone—and he was on his way to track down the Honorable Hal Stuart, Mayor Pro Tem.

Nine

The odd deposits to Hal Stuart's checking accounts had nagged at Rio like an aching tooth. It wasn't that he didn't believe Hal should have a business interest in the community. Many of the city council members did. That was how they'd become involved in city government to begin with. But Hal didn't have an ownership interest in any of the six businesses routinely fortifying his checking accounts. Even after searching records at the Corporation Commission in Denver, Rio hadn't found a thing with Hal Stuart's name on it.

He hadn't come up empty-handed, though. After checking out the two laundromats, the restaurant, both bars and the auto repair shop in question, Rio had reduced them to one common denominator. Every one of them was owned by the same person. A local businessman by the name of Maxwell Brown.

It was late afternoon before Rio caught up with Hal in the employee's parking lot behind City Hall. He'd been waiting for him, using the time to wade through an inch-thick complaint a citizen had filed against WGGS, a local radio station. He was halfway through it when he saw the sporty silver Mercedes glide over the faded Mayor Stuart that was stenciled across the parking space by the building's rear door.

Climbing out of his Bronco, Rio tucked the back of his white shirt into his slacks, slipped his tape recorder into his pocket and intercepted Eve's brother just as the man started to get out.

The expectant look on Hal's face faltered only slightly when he realized whose shadow had darkened his door. Giving Rio a wholly unexpected smile, he got out, then reached back inside for his suit jacket and briefcase. The briefcase had his initials tooled into the chamois-soft leather. The jacket, Rio noted when Hal slipped it on, had a decided custom fit.

"Redtree," he greeted, sounding like the affable politician the public tended to see. "Sorry I can't talk right now. I'm in kind of a hurry."

"I won't take long." Rio gave him an easy smile of his own. "I tried to catch you at the Children's Charity luncheon. I'd heard you'd be there."

"I had a change of plans."

"I noticed. By the way, Eve did a nice job with your mother's speech."

The practiced congeniality slipped. Giving Rio a level look, he hit the security button on his key ring. The car door locked with a chirp.

"I'm sure Mother would be proud." Pocketing his keys, he started for the door of the old building. "That's what this is all about with Eve, you know. Making Mom proud." Something that sounded suspiciously like envy tainted his tone, stealing the last of his superficial pleasantness. "After the way she let her down, I suppose carrying on in her name is her only means of atonement."

Hal reached for the door of the building to jerk it open. Rio kept it closed with the flat of his hand.

Blue eyes narrowed on black. "What are you doing?"

"Keeping this between us." Rio's features hardened dangerously. "Atonement?" he repeated, too aware of his own role in Eve's situation to let the dig go. "Care to explain what you're talking about?"

An explanation was hardly necessary. Both men knew exactly what Hal was referring to, but Rio doubted Hal knew how supportive Olivia had been of Eve during her pregnancy. Or maybe, Rio thought, he did know, and their closeness ate at him, just as it clearly burned him to think that his little sister might be more of a hero to the town just then than he was.

Considering what had prompted Hal's chameleonlike change, Rio couldn't help but wonder if he hadn't always been jealous of his little sister.

"I'm not going to get into this with you," Hal muttered, looking as if he hadn't expected Rio to call him on his comment. "My sister lives her life and I live mine. We don't interfere with each other."

They didn't interfere? Or Eve simply didn't listen to him? Suspecting more of the latter, Rio's hand slid from the door. "I didn't come to discuss your sister," he informed him, forcing calm when what he really wanted to do was get the guy by the throat and make him understand that he didn't deserve the concern Eve wasted on him. Rio's boss wouldn't like that, though. Eve probably wouldn't, either. "I want to talk to you about a business developer. One of our locals."

Rio opened the door himself, standing back to let Hal pass. Skepticism slashed the acting mayor's patrician features, but with the reporter's focus off of him, his antagonistic attitude vanished. It could also have been the prospect of running into a city employee now that they were inside that kept him in line. In politics, image was everything.

Following him in, Rio breathed in the institutional smells of pine cleaner and floor wax and matched Hal step for step down the wide, green-and-white-tiled hall.

"If you want to know anything about a developer, check with city planning."

"I need a more personal touch on this."

"Who are you talking about?"

"Maxwell Brown."

If Rio hadn't been watching Hal, he would have missed his hesitation before the man pasted on his politician's smile. "Max? What about him?"

"What do you think of him?"

Tile gave way to gray marble when they passed from the back of the building into the more public areas. A quick right and they were heading up a wide stairway, cutting a path through the middle of the two people coming down.

"I think a lot of him. He's sharp. He knows how to make a buck, but he doesn't forget the little guy. Between all the businesses he owns in Grand Springs, he provides jobs for at least a hundred of our citizens."

The dark double doors of the mayor's office loomed straight ahead. Walking past frosted glass doors marked City Clerk and City Manager, Hal pushed through the door with the empty brass plate holder on it and entered the outer office. A beige leather sofa and a table sporting Chamber of Commerce literature formed the waiting area off to the right. To the left was an L-shaped secretarial desk.

Rio watched Hal scowl at his secretary's empty chair. The attractive young woman he'd hired to replace Olivia's faithful workhorse of a secretary was obviously occupied elsewhere.

"While the cat's away," Hal muttered, and picked up the pink message slips from the holder on her desk. Leafing through them, he continued talking to Rio. "As I understand it, Max sponsors a Little League team and he's a deacon or something in his church. Very involved in the community. He's a patron of our Winterfest and contributes to most of our charities." Folding one message slip, he stuffed it in his pocket. "That's about all I can tell you."

"What about contributions to your checking account?"

Hal's perpetual tan faded to gray when he blanched, but his recovery was impressive. The fact that he didn't demand to know how Rio had come by the information made it even more so.

"Those are consulting fees," he asserted, the flatness in his voice making it sound as if Rio had gone to a lot of trouble for nothing. "Perfectly legitimate. Now, if you'll excuse me, I have calls to return."

Hal turned toward his private office, but not before Rio

caught the red of blood pressure on the rise creeping up his neck.

"Consulting for what?"

"I give him financial advice."

"I didn't know you were licensed to do that." As quick and painless as Rio tried to be when he interviewed victims of chance or circumstance, he had no qualms whatsoever about needling a liar. And Hal Stuart was literally lying through his teeth. Rio would stake his hard-earned reputation on that fact. "Is this a sideline you're developing?"

When Rio had encountered Hal at Eve's, he'd had the impression then that Hal was precariously close to snapping. That impression was compounded tenfold when Hal spun on his heel.

"I don't know what you think you're onto," he muttered, jaw rigid. "But you can just drop it right here. Drop everything that has anything to do with me or my family. You hear? I don't imagine your editor would be too happy about a lawsuit for harassment, but you're getting damn close."

He was certainly getting close to something, Rio thought, aware of the bulging blue vein throbbing in Hal's left temple. But he wasn't the least bit concerned about the threat. He was nowhere near to harassing this guy. The fact that Hal was feeling that way made it as clear as the window glass that he was onto something, though. But what?

He didn't get a chance to ask. Hal had wadded the rest of his messages in his fist and slammed his office door behind him. As Rio turned to the outer door, he also noticed that Hal hadn't wasted any time getting to his calls. One of the lights on the secretary's telephone had just blinked on.

He was saved from having to do battle with his conscience, over whether or not to pick up the extension, by a long-legged brunette in a short red dress and lipstick to match. Hal's new secretary, a statuesque trophy in the barely twenty-year-old range, hurried through the doorway, her arms loaded with photocopies.

"Mr. Redtree," she greeted, flashing him a brilliant smile. "Mayor Stuart hasn't returned from lunch yet. Can I help you with something?"

"Actually," he said, hitching his thumb toward the door, "he's in there. He just got back."

She was about to lose the top of her stack. Taking it before it slid off, not sure how she'd pick up anything in the elastic band of a skirt she wore, he set the copies next to the calendar on her desk.

"Do you want me to let him know you're here?"

"Thanks...Stacy," he added, picking up her name from the nameplate on her desk, "but I already got what I was after."

He could feel her puzzled glance following him all the way out the door. But he had, indeed, obtained what he was after—confirmation that there was a story behind the acting mayor's finances. When he'd stumbled onto the oddities in Hal's checking account, Rio had thought he might be dealing with a case of campaign fraud or payment for political favors. He was leaning more in the direction of the latter, though the large deposits of cash also hinted at money laundering. The one thing he did not believe was that the money was fees for financial consulting. He had no way to prove that, though. Not yet.

What he did have was another investigation on his hands. Unfortunately, he didn't have time to dig into it any deeper at the moment. He had the story on the WGGS lawsuit to do, then he had to clean up his copy on the state's grant of more funds for a wider road up to the ski lodge. And tonight, he wanted to stop by Eve's to go through the things she'd told him about. He'd give anything for a break in Olivia Stuart's case. One that would actually lead somewhere. Stone had told him just yesterday that the only fingerprints on the flower bowl were Eve's. Those, they'd expected to find.

* * *

The police would come up with something. They just had to.

Eve sat on the edge of Molly's bed, the thought echoing in her mind as she quietly stroked her daughter's soft forehead. She usually found such comfort in her little girl. And she did now, she supposed, thinking how peaceful the sleeping child looked with Ted tucked securely in her arms. But the agitation that had been with her all day had yet to fade, and thoughts of what had happened to her mother were constant. Even reading three stories to Molly and staying with her until she'd fallen asleep hadn't lessened Eve's anxiety.

She pressed a kiss to Molly's temple, breathing in the clean scents of baby shampoo and bubble bath, and forced herself back from scooping her baby up in her arms. It wouldn't be fair to disturb Molly's sleep just to make herself feel better. So Eve slipped quietly from the room, leaving the dream catcher to guard her child's dreams, and headed down the stairs to finish a task she'd started earlier.

She was okay as long as she stayed busy. It was the only way she knew to deal with the unsettled thoughts that had lingered since the luncheon: thoughts of how Olivia's words had made Eve miss her mother so very much more; of the unsmiling detective's awful suspicion about Josie; of how Eve had apparently been suspected herself. Someone had actually thought she might have killed her own mother. If she let herself think about any of it too much, she just might go out of her mind.

With the house on the market to be sold, keeping it constantly presentable was welcome duty. So she focused on that as she scanned the long counters in the kitchen to make sure there was nothing on them that shouldn't be. The glass panels in the beige cabinets sparkled, revealing neat rows of dishes and cups. Dried herbs, in muted shades of sage and lavender, hung in fragrant bunches above the window. Copper pots gleamed.

A dozen red gladiolus, still in their clear plastic wrapper, stood in a pitcher of water on the counter. Eve had bought them at the grocery store that afternoon, thinking to replace the bouquet of mums on the dining room table with something more dramatic. Taking a tall crystal vase from the cabinet, she thought of the real estate agent's comment about how beautifully the house was showing. Eve was doing her best to see that it continued to do so. She just wished she didn't feel so ambivalent about everything she was doing lately. Every effort she made toward helping the house sell brought her one step closer to losing the only place that had ever truly been home.

That disquieting thought had just joined all the others when she heard the faint knock on the front door. She knew it was Rio. She also knew that ignoring his knock wouldn't do any good. Even if he went away this time, he'd be back. After all, she'd invited him.

Setting the vase on the counter, she wouldn't even let herself acknowledge where he fit into the mental mess she was trying to cope with. Her rule of taking one thing at a time had just been reduced to taking things one minute at a time. One second, if need be.

"I figured Molly would be in bed," Rio said, walking in as soon as she opened the door. He was still wearing the dress slacks and collarless white shirt she'd seen him in earlier, and looking every bit as comfortable in them as he did in faded jeans. The ever-present black beeper was clipped to his belt. "That's why I didn't ring the bell. Is she asleep?"

He wanted to see his daughter. Since he hadn't seen her in a week, that was understandable.

"I'm afraid she is" was all Eve said, then motioned behind her. "The boxes are in the study. Hal packed up Mom's personal things when he moved into her office, but he just got around to sending them over. Help yourself."

Leaving him by the door, she headed back to the kitchen, her sneakers silent on the thick patterned rug. She had no idea what he thought of her abruptness, but she could feel his glance moving over the back of her blue cotton shirt and faded jeans. When she'd returned after picking up Molly and running her errands, she'd pulled on her work clothes and oiled every inch of the wood on the banisters and newel posts, along with most of the downstairs baseboards. If she couldn't sleep tonight, she'd finish the rest.

Not until she'd passed through the kitchen doorway did she hear Rio move. When he did, he walked through the foyer and straight into the study.

The vase had been filled with water and she was cutting the ends from the flower stems when she heard movement behind her. Glancing over her shoulder, she watched Rio set three black, vinyl-bound volumes on the counter by the hunter green canisters. Barely meeting his eyes, aware of the curiosity in them, she turned back to slice off another stalk.

"I'd like to take her day planners with me."

Not at all sure why her hand was shaking, she stood a long stem of bright red gladiolus into the vase beside her. "No problem."

"The one for this year is missing. Can you find out where it is?"

She looked toward him again, her glance barely skimming his jaw. "I think so. Let me call Hal."

"You don't have to do it right now."

"I don't mind."

Rio watched her pick up a dark green towel, thinking to tell her there was really no rush. The call could certainly wait until morning. But seeing her wipe her hands as she headed across the room and snatched up the phone hanging above the counter, he wasn't so sure it would have made any difference. There was a stiffness to her usually graceful movements that spoke of intense preoccupation; an abruptness that made him think she was focusing only on what she was doing at that very moment and nothing more.

"Hi, Hal. It's Eve," he heard her say, her tone making him think she was surprised she'd reached him. "I'm sorry to bother you," she went on, one arm holding her stomach as she faced a dish cabinet. "But Rio wants Mom's day planner for this year. It's not in the box you sent over. Do you know where it is?"

It wasn't too hard for Rio to guess Hal's reaction. Especially once she'd mentioned his name. Eve's whole body went stiff as a plank.

"I know the police are working on it," he heard her say. "But it can't hurt to have…"

Hal must have interrupted her. Going silent, she closed her eyes, then proceeded to destroy the smooth line of her hair by shoving her fingers through it while she listened to her brother rant.

Wishing he'd stopped her from making the call, Rio started toward her. He was three feet away when she decided she'd had enough.

"Thank you very much, Hal," she said, her tone clipped, and hung up.

Her back was still to him when she crossed her arms.

"He said he needs it so he can keep her appointments. It has Mom's agenda for the rest of the year. He also said to tell you that the sheriff's already seen it." Turning, she found him standing behind her. Seeming puzzled to find him there, she scooted right back to the sink.

There wasn't a doubt in Rio's mind that Hal had said far more than what Eve had repeated. But she reminded him a little too much of an overwound spring at the moment, so he didn't ask her what she'd left out. He could pretty much guess, anyway.

Eve hands were always busy, especially when she was nervous or uncertain. But she didn't continue arranging her flowers as he'd thought she might. Or start fiddling with the towel or wiping an imaginary speck off some already pristine surface. She just stood with her arms wrapped around herself, staring at the night-blackened window.

As he watched her, the wide pane of mirrorlike glass reflected the light haloing her short and slightly disheveled hair, the partially filled vase of spiky crimson flowers, and his own guarded features. He would have felt a whole lot better about whatever was going on with her if she'd started fidgeting with something. The way she held herself so tightly made it look as if she feared she might fall apart if she let go.

"What do you want with the day planners?" she asked, meeting his glance in the window. "Is there something specific you're looking for?"

He heard the hope in her voice, along with the brittle tension he'd seen in her the moment he walked through the door. When they parted after the luncheon, he'd thought then that she looked a little rocky. At the time, he'd figured that was to be expected, considering the emotional energy giving that speech would have required. She hadn't bounced back as she usually did, though. That wasn't like her at all.

Ignoring the self-protective voice that told him to stay where he was, he moved toward her. A lesser person would have broken down long before now. But he knew there was a backbone of solid steel beneath all that softness. The problem with that was that steel didn't bend or bow with its burdens. When the load became too much, it simply snapped.

"I just want to reconstruct her schedule." She was looking to him to ease some of the anxiety she carried over her mother's murder. He hated that there was nothing of substance to tell her. "It's a long shot, but maybe there's something the sheriff missed. Some name that's been overlooked."

She pulled a steadying breath, seeming too numb to be disappointed. "There are some files in the boxes. Was there anything in them that might help?"

"According to the labels on them, they were for newspaper articles, but the files themselves were empty. I'd say either Hal or the police kept them."

"Was there anything else in there? In the boxes, I mean?"

"You haven't looked?"

She shook her head, the tips of her fingers turning nearly white as she tightened the grip on her arms.

She hadn't been able to bring herself to do it. She didn't have to say a word for Rio to know that encountering another aspect of her mother's life would do nothing but bring fresh pain.

"Nothing that helps," he had to tell her. "Pictures, vases, that kind of thing."

His shadow fell on her as he curved his hand over her shoulder. In the window he saw her head jerk up. Beneath the soft fabric of her shirt, he felt her tension increase. Ignoring it, he turned her around to face him.

The sudden wariness in her eyes made him even more aware of the shadows beneath them. They made her look terribly, frighteningly, fragile.

"Are you all right?"

Eve closed her eyes, drew a breath. The man didn't play fair. As tenuous a hold as she had on herself, his concern threatened what little composure she could claim.

"I will be." Come morning, the awful feelings would have passed. It was just a matter of getting through the next nine or ten hours. Then, getting through them again the next time. "I just wish I could be like you," she told him, slipping sideways to break his hold. "I wish I had your ability to keep things from getting to me."

She made it about three feet before he snagged her arm. Blocking her retreat with his body, he scanned her face, concern for her etching his lean features. "I don't know where you got the idea that nothing gets to me," he informed her, sounding as if he already had an example to the contrary in mind. "But that couldn't be further from the truth."

"Oh, come on, Rio. You're always in such...control. You always have been."

"And you're not?"

"Not here. Not since any of this started. And not like you. Never like you. I can't...I feel..."

She shook her head, frustration piling onto everything else when the words seemed to fail her.

"You feel...what?" he encouraged, tugging her closer.

She tugged back. "Don't, Rio. Please."

"Just talk to me." Though he eased his hold, he didn't let go. "We could always talk. Remember?"

Relaxing her grip on her arms enough to restore the flow of blood to her fingers, Eve gave him a nod.

"Are you upset about what I told you today? That the police checked you out?"

"No. Maybe," she amended, because denying it didn't change the fact. "I understand that's how these things work, but... Yes," she finally admitted, because rationalizing didn't help, either. "That's probably part of it."

"What about the rest? Is it your brother?"

"Not entirely, but he's in there."

"The investigation?"

"That, too."

"What about having to sell this house?"

She gave him another nod, but he had the feeling there was still more.

He paused, his conscience kicking him squarely in the ribs. "Me?"

"Yes."

She was looking down. Since the top of her head barely reached the base of his throat, he couldn't see her face. It was probably just as well. Everything he'd mentioned was ganging up on her, but all he considered was the certainty in her last reply. It was one thing to suspect that he added to her burdens. Hearing it when she seemed so defenseless made him feel like a snake.

"And what does all of that make you feel?" he asked, smoothing her hair. "Impotent? Alone? Scared?"

His hand slipped to her nape. With his fingers resting against her slender neck, he felt her swallow.

"For starters," she whispered.

In other words, what she felt was...overwhelmed.

The pressure of his hand increased, urging her forward. But she held her ground, refusing to move.

"I just want to hold you," he told her, not sure it wasn't his own need he sought to fill.

"I want that, too." So badly she ached for it. "But I can't let you."

Sliding his thumb along her jaw, he stepped an inch closer and tipped up her chin. Her eyes looked haunted when they met his.

"Why not?"

"Because I'm not that strong. I don't think I can handle whatever it is that's going on between us right now. Or what isn't. I don't know if that makes any sense to you, but I don't know how else to explain it."

"You did about as good a job as I could. I don't know if I can explain what's going on with us, either. But I do know," he continued, running his hands down her arms to pry her hands apart, "that when something can't be explained, it's a waste of energy to try. Stop being so stubborn and come here."

It wasn't stubbornness. It was survival. But she went, anyway, more because she couldn't not go than because he drew her closer. Rio knew her so well, knew what she felt, what she needed. He always had.

His arms were already around her. And when he pressed her head to his chest, she felt the fight drain out as surely as if he'd pulled a plug. Not that she had much left. It was just that she couldn't fight herself and him, too. Not when there was so much else demanding her energy.

That was the only thought she allowed herself as she sagged against his strong, solid body. Enveloped in his arms, she simply let herself rest against him while he stroked her hair, his palm cupping the back of her head as he skimmed from crown to nape. The motion was more soothing than she could have ever dreamed, the feel of him more welcome than she could have imagined. And, in the past few weeks, she'd imagined him holding her more times than she could count.

"That's not so bad? Is it?"

She shook her head, the motion rubbing her cheek against his shirt. He smelled of soap and fresh air, and warm, musky male. Beneath the soft fabric, she could feel the strong, steady cadence of his heart. He was a rock, and she badly needed the support he offered. The way they'd been lately, he was the last person on earth she would ever have expected to offer it.

His arms tightened around her back, securing his hold. With a familiarity that shouldn't have been there, his hand curved easily around her side, the heat of his palm seeping inside her.

"I'd forgotten how small you are," he murmured, his voice as soothing as his touch. "At least now I know you won't break. The first time I held you, I was afraid you might."

Her whispered "You were?" was barely audible, muffled as it was by his shirt.

"Yeah. I was."

The admission surprised her. She couldn't picture Rio fearing anything. "But I didn't."

"No," he agreed, his breath feathering her hair. "You didn't. You're a lot stronger than you look. And a lot stronger than you think you are."

She looked up to find a faint smile curving his sculpted mouth. He was telling her that she was doing better than she thought she was, and she appreciated the encouragement more than he could possibly know. But she wasn't strong when it came to him. She'd meant that when she said it.

She might have told him that, too. But his glance drifted to her mouth, pooling heat low in her stomach when the smile in his dark eyes faded. When he met her eyes again, a faint tension seemed to have entered his body. She could feel it in his arms, see it in the strong angles of his features. For long seconds, he searched her face, looking as if he didn't know whether to pull her closer or let her go. Then he carefully tucked back the hair she'd mussed earlier.

"You're going to be okay," he told her, seeming to ignore the way his body hardened against hers. "A lot of it will just take time."

He was right, of course. But she couldn't think why. She couldn't even remember what they were talking about. All she could think of was how safe she felt at that moment, how protected. Nothing could intrude when he held her. None of the uncertainties, or questions, or hurts. Even if the feelings were an illusion, for now she needed them desperately.

"Rio?" Her voice sounded thready, hushed. "Please don't go home tonight."

The motion of his hand stopped, his fingers still threaded through her hair. "If that's what you want," he finally said, sounding as if he found it understandable that she didn't want to be alone, even if he hadn't expected the request. "I'll sleep on the sofa."

She shook her head. "I mean stay with me. Holding me."

"Eve. I can't do that."

She didn't know which hit harder. The absolute certainty in his voice, or the look in his eyes that clearly said he thought she'd finally slipped over the edge. She ducked her head, embarrassed for having asked, feeling like a fool for confusing his concern with caring.

"Honey, don't." He refused to let her go, his expression as tormented as his words when he saw the hurt clouding her eyes. "I didn't mean it like that."

"It's okay."

He swore, the whispered epithet harsh and unforgiving. "No. It's not okay." Knowing her as he did, he knew she'd never have asked such a thing of him unless she'd been desperate. And all he'd done was make her feel worse than she already did. "I said I just wanted to hold you, but that's not true." It had been when he'd said it. When he'd reached for her, he'd meant only to offer comfort. But the moment he felt her sag against him, altruism had gone to battle with want, sensibility with need. "I've never stopped wanting you, Eve. Even after all these years, all I can think about when I'm with you is how you taste and feel and move. Don't you know that?"

Her heart hammering in her throat, she slowly shook her head. "When we're together, you never come anywhere near me."

"There's a reason for that."

He didn't trust himself around her. Eve got the message clearly enough when his eyes, dark and glittering, settled on her mouth. The knowledge did something very freeing to her spirit. As controlled as he so often appeared, inside he was a man doing battle. And she was a woman who very much needed that man.

"I'll stay." He would do that because he knew how long and lonely some nights could be, and heaven help him, he couldn't stand the thought of her here by herself. "But you know what will happen if we're in the same bed together."

"I think so." She touched his chest with her fingertips, her fingers trembling. "But it's been so long, you'll probably have to show me all over again."

Her words were too honest to be deliberately provocative, but the images they evoked of the first time they'd made love played pure havoc with Rio's brain. She'd told him then that he'd have to teach her what to do. And he had. Too impatiently, he was sure.

Clasping her hand in his, he drew it to his mouth and brushed a kiss to her wrist. Beneath his lips, her pulse leapt. "It's like riding a bike," he whispered, threading his fingers through hers and drawing her arm behind her back. "It'll come back to you."

His last words were murmured against her mouth, his breath hot against her cheek. When his tongue touched hers, Eve thought her legs would buckle, but he caught her to him, letting her use his body for support. Long moments later, her breathing altered, his just as erratic, he bent and picked her up in his arms.

"Get the lights," he told her, swinging her toward the switch on the way out of the kitchen.

He turned off the front lights himself, using his forearm as they passed through the foyer. With the filtered lights from the porch and hall upstairs illuminating the way, he carried her up the stairs, pausing just outside Molly's open door.

"Is she okay?"

Seeing the soundly sleeping child, Eve whispered that she was. Quiet as air, he turned to the room Eve had claimed for herself and used his foot to swing the door partway closed once they were inside.

The filmy curtains were open, moonlight streaming into the tiny, atticlike room. The daybed was against one wall. A chair and dresser against another. Eve watched the shadows move over his face as he slid her down his body to the floor, then reached past her to close the door the rest of the way. In those muted shades of gray, his noble features were taut with purpose and possession.

"I can still sleep on the sofa," he told her, skimming his hand down her arm. He laced his fingers through hers, smoothing her hair back with his other hand.

She shook her head. At least, she thought she did. She was really only aware of his eyes, intent on her face, and the feel of his fingers drifting down her neck.

"I want you here," she finally said, just so there'd be no doubt.

There was none. The possessiveness in his eyes moved to his touch as the mesmerizing movement of his hand reached the collar of her blouse. With the tip of his finger, he nudged the fabric aside and drew his finger along her collarbone, trailing a line of heat to the hollow of her throat. His touch lingered long enough for him to feel the quickened beat of her heart before he carried it between her breasts, then back up to trace her jaw.

"You haunt me, Eve." His features seemed to tighten even more. "You must."

His fingers drifted back to her throat, robbing the strength from her voice. "Is that bad?"

He shook his head, but she didn't know if he meant it wasn't, or that he didn't know. It didn't matter. The way he touched her, sensitizing her nerves as he reacquainted himself with the texture of her skin, the shape of her body, made it impossible to think of anything other than what he was doing.

His mouth brushed hers, causing her to tip her head back with a little moan when he stepped closer and began to slowly unbutton her blouse. His tongue slipped intimately over hers, teasing, coaxing, while his hands worked their way down to the waistband of her jeans. When he reached denim, he tugged out her shirt, shaping her bare ribs with his hands and her breasts with his palms before he peeled the cloth back over her shoulders.

Eve whispered his name, trembling. He answered with a quiet "Sh" against her lips and worked open the zipper of her jeans.

He was so gentle. So patient. But that patience came with a price. When he pushed her jeans over her hips so she could step out of them, she had to hold his arm to keep from falling. It was like gripping marble. She felt that same raw tension in his shoulders when her arms circled his neck, and in the bunched muscles in his back when he eased her over to the bed and lowered her to the sheets. Mostly, she could feel it in herself when he leaned over her, slipping his leg between hers and meeting her lips once more. She seemed to absorb it from him, making what he felt part of her very being. He was already more a part of her than he would ever know. Not just because of Molly. But because she loved him. She wasn't sure she'd ever stopped.

She was probably certifiable for wanting him as badly as she did, but Eve couldn't be rational in Rio's arms. She didn't want to be. So she simply sought him as he sought her, arching against him to get as close to him as she could.

That small movement of her hips nearly did him in.

She remembered exactly what to do. Rio told her that, too, rasping the words against her ear while he stripped away her bra and filled his palm with her soft flesh. He felt her shiver as the warmth of his hand brushed her cooler skin. Then he shuddered himself when she told him he made remembering easy and she slipped her fingers under his belt.

He caught her wrist, trapped her hand by her head to nuzzle the fullness of her breast. Heat shafted through him when he drew her nipple into his mouth and he felt it bloom against his tongue. She was so beautifully, artlessly responsive, and she had responded like this only to him. The knowledge humbled him, aroused him. But when he skimmed his hand over her belly, knowing it had borne his child, he was filled with a sense of possession so fierce he could scarcely breathe.

He reared back, his hands quick as they worked the buttons from his shirt and he whipped back the sides to get rid of it. She was temptation itself lying in the moonlight, the skin of her shoulders smooth and pale, the centers of her breasts flushed and hard. She reached for him, her touch tentative as she ran her hand down his smooth, bronzed chest. Lean, corrugated muscles rippled beneath her fingers. The look in her eyes was part wonder, part desire, and he thought he might die if he didn't get inside her.

The rasp of his zipper gave way to the brush of denim as jeans joined shirt and shoes on the floor. Rio slowed down long enough to retrieve his wallet, finding the packet tucked inside. It had been a long time since he'd been with a woman. So long he wasn't sure how long his control would last.

Skin finally touched skin. Warm to cool. Hard to soft. Eve murmured his name, the sound shimmering through him like white heat. It took more control than he thought he possessed, but he took his time, molding her body to his, letting limbs tangle and seek, then pulling back to taunt again. He wanted her to ache for him the way he ached for her, to drive her mindless with need. But he was perilously close to the edge himself just watching her while he stroked her warm, damp flesh, then leaned down to drink in her soft little moans.

She tore her mouth from his, her breathing shallow, and begged him to stop. He would, he told her, in a while, and felt the sweat bead along his spine when her fingers dug into his back, coaxing him closer.

That urging was all it took. Need replaced want. Urgency canceled control. He moved over her, cradling her hips against him and gathering her in his arms. But when he eased into her and she began to meet his long, fluid strokes, conscious thought ceased. He was aware of nothing but the sensation of his body racing toward the missing piece of his spirit.

The moon had disappeared. Rio lay in the dark, holding Eve in his arms and staring at the shadows. She felt like the other half of him, the part of his being that made him whole. Yet he knew he'd felt that way about her once before. He'd let himself care about her. More deeply than he'd cared about another living soul. But when the going got tough, and she'd learned she was pregnant, she hadn't turned to him. When she'd seen no way out of her situation, she'd walked away from him without a word. He knew she'd tried to reach him later. He knew what his mother had then done. But he still couldn't shake the thought that she might very well walk away again. After all, she wasn't the only person who'd ever done that to him.

Ten

The sound of voices drifted into Eve's quiet bedroom. One was sweet and soft, the other low and deep. She snuggled into the warmth of the sheets, the whispered sounds feeding the sweet lethargy that filled her body. Lulled toward the welcome escape of sleep, she seemed to drift in and out of that blissful state—until those same sounds began to tease her consciousness, denying her the peace to which her subconscious clung.

In a matter of seconds, Eve's seldom-felt contentment vanished like smoke in a strong wind. Rio was still there. And Molly was awake.

A rush of anxiety annihilated the last vestiges of peace. Moaning to herself when she saw her clothes strewn over the floor, doing it again when she swung her protesting body from the bed, she grabbed her robe from the closet. She had no idea how Molly had reacted to finding Rio there. Or what he might have said to her.

Another groan, this one mental, and she shoved her fingers through her hair. She had all but begged Rio to make love to her last night. She couldn't begin to imagine how badly that had complicated their situation.

Conversation came to a halt the moment she swung open the door. Rio and Molly were in the middle of the wide hallway, Molly in her pink Pocahontas nightgown holding Ted, and Rio crouched in front of her. His shirttail hung over his slacks, and when he stood and turned, he was buttoning the middle button.

Her heart bumped her breastbone when his dark eyes locked on hers.

"Hi," she quietly said, tightening the belt of her white cotton robe.

"Hi yourself." His glance was steady, his tone remarkably normal. "We were just discussing who gets the bathroom first."

"He said I could go first 'cause girls take longer," Molly informed her, still looking half-asleep. "But I told him I don't take as long as you."

"You did, did you?"

The little girl nodded.

Seeming totally nonplussed to have found Rio coming from her mother's bedroom, she gave a yawn and leaned against her mother's leg for a hug. A moment later, having received what she was after, she peeled herself away and headed toward the end of the hall.

Eve had no sooner glanced back toward Rio than she felt his hand slip between her shoulder blades. "You can go share with her. I'll be downstairs."

"You're not leaving yet, are you?"

"Do you want me to?"

"No! No," she repeated, too relieved that he wasn't preparing to bolt to worry about how anxious she might sound. "I just thought…" She cut herself off, shaking her head. "I don't know what I thought."

His hand slipped over her shoulder, kneading the tight muscles there. The touch was soothing, reassuring, and did more to relieve the insecurities clamoring inside her than he could possibly know.

"I'd hoped to get out of here before Molly saw me coming from your room, but she was already awake. The damage is done, so there's no need to leave right now. I need coffee, anyway." He glanced toward the door, now ajar, at the end of the hall. With their little girl out of sight, he leaned down and brushed a too brief kiss over her lips. When he lifted his head, concern slashed parallel lines between his dark eyebrows. "You look like you could use some, too. Are you all right?"

If she hadn't been before, she was now. Smiling, she whispered that she was and touched her hand to the hard line of his jaw. She wasn't sure if he'd meant to protect her or Molly by preserving propriety. She didn't know, either, if he'd asked if she was okay because of how she'd been when he'd arrived last night, or because of what had happened afterward. It didn't matter. Whatever his intentions, she loved him for them.

Still looking concerned despite her assurances, he drew her to him, kissing her with enough heat to remind her of how they'd awakened in the wee hours of the morning to make love again. And again. The memories alone were enough to turn her blood to steam, but he didn't let her go until the sound of water running in the pipes made it apparent that Molly could reappear any moment.

Decidedly unsteady, Eve let her hands slide reluctantly from him and said she'd be down in a minute to put on the coffee. He told her to make it strong, then headed for the bathroom downstairs before he could do what he looked like he wanted to do and back her through her bedroom door. It could have all been so awkward this morning. But instead of having to deal with regrets for complicating their situation, Eve was left with the feeling that this particular complication just might work out all right.

Because it had been so long since she'd felt such hope, she clung to the thought like a talisman while she helped Molly wash and got her started on her teeth. Hearing the shower go on downstairs, she had Molly dress in the bathroom with her while she dove into the shower herself. Fifteen minutes later, a casual peach blouse tucked into matching pants and her hair drying on its own, she entered the kitchen to pour milk on Molly's cereal before her daughter, two minutes ahead of her, decided to get helpful and do it herself.

Rio had beat her to it.

He sat across from Molly at the table in the breakfast nook, listening to her explain something about Ted and tea parties between bites of multicolored puffed corn. His damp hair was combed straight back, his white shirt open at the neck. Sitting as he was, with one hand wrapped around a half-empty glass of milk, he looked very much like he belonged there.

Eve didn't let the thought get any further than that. It was far too appealing, and far too close to a dream she had abandoned long ago.

Skimming a smile past them both, she reached for the coffee canister.

"Mommy, he's going to be my daddy."

The green crockery lid skittered across the counter, then split into two pieces on the shiny hardwood floor. Eve ignored it. Clutching the canister to her stomach, her glance darted straight to Rio.

He'd told her he'd wait until *she* was ready before anything was said to Molly.

With more disbelief than accusation, she watched Rio calmly rise from his chair. Walking past her, he picked up the two halves and set them on the counter.

"It's not what you think." His voice was as tight as his expression when he took the canister from her before she dropped it, too. "She asked me if I'd be her daddy."

"Just pretend," Molly piped in. "Like when I'm the mommy and Ted comes to my house for tea."

Rio leaned against the counter, arms crossed. It was as clear to Eve as the sunlight streaming into the spacious room that he didn't appreciate her reaction. It was just as clear that he was waiting to see what she'd do next.

What she wanted to do was go back to bed and start over. What existed between her and Rio after last night was far too new for this sort of test.

"So what did he say?" she asked Molly, making herself sound as if she was into their little game.

"He said sure."

"That was nice of him, wasn't it?"

"Uh-huh. And you know what?"

"What?"

"He said I can call him daddy if I want."

"You asked him if you could do that?"

Molly gave a nod, then shoveled in another spoonful of cereal.

"Well," Eve continued, turning to the man silently watching her. "Tell you what. Since you're the daddy, you get a washcloth for her face and find out where she left her blue hair ribbons, and I'll get the coffee on. Her bus will be here in a few minutes."

She held his glance, feeling as guarded as he looked— until she saw his jaw relax. "Hair ribbons?"

"She'll help you."

Still aware of the tension lingering in his body, she pulled the empty carafe from the coffeemaker and turned on the water.

Rio moved with her, voice low. "Do you have anywhere you have to be this morning?"

"Not for a while. Why?"

He pushed the coffee canister toward her. "We need to talk."

"I want a braid today, Mommy. Not pigtails."

"Okay," she replied, speaking to the man, responding to the child and trying to not think of anything other than the physical tasks at hand. Concentrating only on what needed to be done at that moment was the only way she knew to avoid the anxious feeling building in her chest.

Less than ten minutes later, as Eve walked back into the kitchen after putting Molly on the church bus for day camp, that anxiety compounded itself.

Two mugs of coffee sat steaming on the counter. Picking up both, Rio handed her one and motioned toward the table.

"Let's sit down."

She gave him a nod, uneasily aware of his caution as he

settled into the same chair he'd vacated earlier and cupped his strong hands around his mug.

She took Molly's chair, moving the bowl and spoon off the hunter green place mat to mirror his position. There was something so civilized about discussing matters over coffee. But the atmosphere wasn't conducive to comfortable conversation. Without Molly's chatty presence, there was nothing to buffer the tension suddenly filling the room.

"I'm sorry about before," she began, unwilling to let silence add to the strain. "I was just caught so off guard...."

"Don't worry about it. There wasn't much else you could think."

Her gratitude for his understanding was reflected in her soft smile. But she didn't get to tell him that the betraying thought had lasted only a second. Or that she truly couldn't imagine him breaking his word.

"I don't want it to be 'just pretend,' Eve. I want to tell her."

Sucking in a quiet breath, her fingers tightened on the handle of her mug.

"Children need to know what to expect from their parents. You said that yourself in the speech you gave yesterday," he reminded her, searching her face for signs of resistance. "I want Molly to know she can count on me to be there for her if she needs me."

Like my father wasn't.

He didn't need to say the words. She could practically hear them, anyway.

There was a loose thread on the fringe of the place mat. Pulling it out, Eve absently balled it between her fingers.

"When did you want to tell her?"

"I leave that to you. But soon."

"We can tell her tonight, if you want."

His eyes narrowed on hers. "You'd be all right with that?"

More than all right. His desire to commit to his daughter

fed the hope that, despite all her efforts to restrain it, had taken root in her heart. ''She adores you.''

''We'll tell her together,'' he said, seeming to weigh what was best for all of them as he absently stroked the back of her hand. ''But we need to be ready for any questions. That means we need to talk about taking care of the legalities, too.''

''Legalities?''

''I want joint custody. If we work out the details before we go to an attorney, the process shouldn't take long. We just need to decide when she should come here and when I should go there. As long as we're both in Grand Springs, sharing her isn't a problem. We can just keep doing what we're doing now,'' he added, a certain hesitation slipping into his expression. ''But if you leave, we'll have to handle things differently. It'll be better if we have it all figured out ahead of time.''

If you leave, he'd said. Not *when*. But the distinction was lost on Eve at the moment. His words, so reasonably spoken, snatched back the hope she'd been so foolish to harbor and left her feeling completely exposed. She'd been so careful to avoid picturing them as a family, but the desire had been there, anyway. And joint custody meant he wasn't thinking about them that way at all.

Pulling back, she felt her stomach knot.

''You have this all figured out, don't you.'' She rose, picked up her mug and Molly's bowl, then turned from him to hide her pain. It was important that they stay calm. This was about Molly, after all. Not her. Even after last night, she still didn't matter that much to him. ''Tell me,'' she said, deflecting the hurt with the activity of rinsing away the remains of Molly's breakfast. ''How long have you been thinking about this?''

Chair legs scraped against the floor. ''A couple of weeks.''

''And you're just now bringing it up?''

"What would I have said? I had to know what we needed to do, first."

"You could have said, 'Eve, I'm thinking about filing for joint custody, but I don't know what we have to do so I'm looking into it.'"

"I wanted to talk to my mother, too."

"You did that a week ago. And I know more happened there than what you told me. You could let me in on it, you know."

She caught the incomprehension shadowing his face just before she glanced back to the bowl in her hand. Or maybe it was defensiveness.

"No, I don't suppose you could," she told him, all too familiar with the wall of protection he'd built around himself. It had always been there. Years ago, she'd just been too young and naive to recognize it. "You don't share anything unless you have to. You don't even realize what a hypocrite you are, do you?" Honest disbelief softened her voice. "It's all right for you to dig into people's lives, to tear them apart to see what they're thinking and feeling, but you never let anyone know what's going on with you. What is going on, anyway?"

It wasn't anger she felt. It was frustration. And a numbing sort of hurt. Knowing how much she loved him, especially that.

Reaching past her, Rio took the bowl she still held and set it aside, then turned her around. There was as much irritation as confusion in his expression, but the irritation died the moment he saw her eyes.

He'd been about to tell her she had no business thinking him the hypocrite. Not when she was the one who'd taken off without a word, rather than talk to him about a problem. But he couldn't attack when she already looked beaten, and he couldn't defend himself without pointing out how much metal she'd added to his armor.

"I'm getting lost here," he admitted, not willing to let the situation disintegrate. "What's going on with what?"

"With you and me." Physically, she had been as close to him as she could get. He'd seen to it. Emotionally, he was light-years away. "You pull me with one hand, Rio, and push me away with the other. You've been doing it ever since I got back."

"I'm not trying to push you away."

"You just did."

He stepped back, letting his hand fall. With her arms crossed so tightly, it didn't seem she wanted him to touch her, anyway.

"How?"

For a moment, she said nothing.

"Eve?"

"By wanting to bring an attorney into this."

Rio pulled a breath. "Look," he began, wanting to reach for her but not willing to risk having her pull back. "I don't want to make things any more difficult for you than they already are. If it'll help, we can wait a while to work out the details. I just need to know that I won't lose contact with Molly."

He was being as understanding as he could be, and as honest. She should have been grateful for that. And she would have been, had that honesty not just told her what this was all about. Rio didn't trust her not to disappear again. But then, he was hardly giving her any reason to stay, either.

"You're going to be late for work," she said, her tone too quiet.

Hesitating, he lifted his hand toward her, leaving it to hover like a benediction between them before he finally curved it over her shoulder. Drawing her to him, he folded her in his arms. "Don't worry about this right now. Okay?"

He didn't want to make things harder for her. She truly believed that. Just as she believed he'd never back down from what he wanted. Once Rio made up his mind, he didn't let up until he'd accomplished his goal.

As attracted to that quality as she was threatened by it, Eve echoed a quiet "Okay."

"I'll see you tonight."

His lips brushed her forehead. Seconds later, with nothing resolved and the set of his jaw marking his own agitation, he turned away.

Eve sagged against the counter, listening to his footsteps fade and the sound of the door as it closed behind him. Concerned as Rio had seemed to be about her last night and this morning, she doubted he'd have raised the subject at all had Molly not so innocently brought it up. Still, she couldn't feel relieved by that. Not when it was so apparent that he didn't trust her not to let him down.

Having lived for the last six years knowing how terribly she'd disappointed her mother by getting pregnant, Eve couldn't bear the thought of letting down someone else that she loved. But the only way Rio would ever trust her would be if he believed she truly wanted him to be in Molly's life, and that she wanted Molly to be fully a part of his. She could think of only one thing that might prove that to him. It was something she had to do, anyway. She needed a better understanding of Rio, of his roots. For herself and for her daughter. It was also time she faced whatever it was she and Molly were up against with his mother.

Less than an hour later, Eve had picked up Molly from day camp in her little red compact and the two of them were heading north on the two-lane mountain highway out of Grand Springs. She had canceled her attendance at the women's shelter meeting that morning, something she'd hated to do because the meeting was about creating a memorial for her mom, but once she made the decision to drive to the reservation, she hadn't been able to think of anything else. She wasn't even sure Mrs. Redtree would be there. But she was winging it a lot these days. She had a map and an address, and she could get directions when she got there. After driving from Santa Barbara last month, an eighty-mile trip was nothing. And Molly was always up for a ride. She especially liked the idea of seeing where Rio once lived.

It was almost noon when Eve saw the sign indicating that they'd passed onto tribal land and she stopped at a tiny store with tobacco ads plastered all over it. Because she asked the two Indian women behind the counter there for directions to Rio's mother's house, news of a white woman and an Indian child headed for Maria Redtree's preceded their arrival. Fifteen minutes later, when Eve crossed a narrow bridge over a dry wash and pulled into the open area between a small enclave of neat, rectangular houses and an old gray-and-white mobile home, she was met by a welcoming committee of three.

A middle-aged woman stood with her arms crossed, a few feet from the mobile home's open front door. Her black hair was drawn back from a gently rounded face and hung over her shoulder in a thick braid. The loose white blouse she wore was tucked into a full blue skirt, and a fist-size beaded amulet hung by a leather thong around her neck.

On her right was a woman in her early twenties wearing blue nurse's scrubs and a photo ID tag. Despite the worry etched in her brow, she possessed the same exotic beauty promised in Molly's fragile face. Gleaming sable hair framed features that were more angular than the woman's beside her. Her nose was thinner, her jaw and cheekbones more defined.

Eve knew Rio's sister was a nurse at the reservation clinic. Even had she not been privy to that information, the woman resembled Rio so closely, she had to be his sister. Considering that they'd obviously been warned of her arrival, Eve would be willing to bet that the thirty-something, dark-haired man in the plaid shirt and jeans protecting the older woman's left flank was Dusty. Eve knew he worked for the tribal government as an environmentalist. He was about the same height as Rio, but he bore a much closer resemblance to his mother than did either of his two siblings. His features were fuller, his build stockier. Clearly, Rio and his sister had taken after his father's side of the family.

Not allowing herself to question what she was doing, Eve handed Molly her books from the back seat. "Stay here," she told the child, and stepped out of the car.

There were more people there than she'd first thought. Skimming a nervous smile past the trio ahead of her, she became aware of movement in the windows of the houses, of inquisitive eyes and small faces being snatched out of sight. Two tricycles sat abandoned in the shadow of a blue minivan. Toys were strewn over the clumps of grass and atop a long, oilcloth-covered table beneath the branches of the yard's only tree.

From the looks of it, the children had all been chased inside.

"Mrs. Redtree?" Eve asked, suddenly feeling too vulnerable, too unprotected.

Dark eyes flicked over Eve's face before Rio's mother nodded. "I am Maria Redtree."

"I'm Eve. Stuart," she hurried to add, since they apparently went by whole names here. "I'm a friend of Rio's."

"I know who you are."

The younger woman glanced toward Maria. From her hesitation, it appeared she was waiting for her to say more. When nothing else was forthcoming, she stepped forward herself.

"I'm Rio's sister," she said, introducing herself as Shana Holt. "This is Dusty, our brother." She waited until the big man gave Eve a tight nod. "I'm afraid your arrival has caught us unprepared."

Though the woman made it sound as if some courtesy had been left unattended, Eve felt certain that the preparation she'd referred to was as much mental as anything else. Knowing that, knowing, too, that she'd put them on the spot, she directed her apology to them all.

"I'm sorry for the intrusion, but I was afraid that if I

called ahead, you wouldn't see me. All I want," she continued, certain from Maria Redtree's starched stance that
she was right, "is to talk to you. Not for me, but for Rio
and Molly."

Maria glanced toward the car and the road. "You are
alone?"

"My daughter is with me."

That didn't appear to be what the woman had meant.
"My son is not coming with you?"

"He doesn't know I'm here."

The older woman paused, something like disappointment, or grudging curiosity, causing her brow to pinch.

Shana's curiosity took a different course. "Molly is your
daughter?"

"Our daughter. Rio's and mine." Eve nodded toward the
car herself. Only the top of Molly's head was visible over
the dash. "We haven't told her he's her father yet, but
we're going to tonight. Molly asked him if he could be her
pretend daddy, so he figured there was no need to wait any
longer." She hesitated, thinking how much more sense this
had made before she'd said it out loud. "May we talk, or
is this really a bad time?"

No time would have been good. Eve was definitely left
with that impression during the long moments of silence
that passed between Shana and her mother. Finally, looking
as if the two women had just engaged in a battle of wills,
Maria looked to her son.

"What do you think?" she asked the man, as if she
expected him to know exactly what had taken place.

"That you should listen to your daughter. Blood is
blood."

"I'll put on tea," Shana announced, and pulled open the
screen.

It opened with the arthritic groan of hinges in need of
oil, and closed with a bang.

Apparently, that meant she could stay. It meant that
Shana and Dusty thought she should stay, anyway.

It also seemed to mean that Dusty could now leave. Something for which he appeared quite grateful. From the cautious once-over he'd given her, he seemed to view Eve's presence with a skepticism that was only a shade less promising than his sister's forbearance. He did not, however, appear to see her as a threat. "I've got to get back to work," he said to his mother. "You don't need me for this."

He skimmed one last glance over the slender five feet of blond, blue-eyed potential trouble he'd apparently been called to attend to, then gave her a nod. "Eve Stuart," he said, his eyes avoiding hers, "I trust we will meet again."

With that, Rio's older brother headed to the pickup truck parked at the end of the mobile home, casting a quick glance toward the child reading her book in the little red car as he passed it on the way.

Left alone with Rio's mother, Eve offered her a faltering smile.

Maria didn't return it. But then, she wasn't looking at her, either. Her focus was on the car, too.

The door had opened and Molly was getting out.

Eve's protective instincts shot to the surface. Meeting her daughter a few feet from where Maria remained rooted by her door, she whispered, "I told you to stay in the car." She didn't want Molly exposed to the woman's disapproval. It was difficult enough facing it herself. "Why didn't you listen?"

Innocent blue eyes blinked back at her. "'Cause I have to go to the bathroom."

"I will show her where it is."

At the sound of Maria's voice, Eve turned around, hugging the little girl to her side as if she were prepared to block her with her own body if need be.

"Thank you," she returned, but Molly didn't seem inclined to move at the moment.

With her arm wrapped around her mother's hip, the little girl smiled up at the stranger quietly watching her. When the woman didn't smile back, Molly focused on the intricate and colorful designs beaded into the leather circle around her neck.

Innocent of the tension skittering in the air, her little face immediately brightened. "I know what that means," she said, ungluing herself from her mother to point at the amulet. "That's a simple of the people!"

The woman's dark and uncomprehending eyes narrowed on the child. Eve didn't understand what Molly was talking about, either, but now was not the time to figure out what she meant. Or so she was thinking when she folded her hand over her daughter's to remind her that it wasn't polite to point.

"A symbol?" Maria suggested, obviously accustomed to interpreting children.

Molly nodded vigorously. "Uh-huh. The three blue circles. Men have them on their chest and women get them right here." She pointed to the middle of her forehead. A second later her angelic little face screwed up in a frown. "I forgot what the feather is. But I got one over my bed."

Maria's glance shot to Eve. "Who tells her of *Inunaina*? Our people?" she clarified.

There was as much puzzlement as curiosity in the question. Clearly, the woman couldn't imagine how Molly had come by such knowledge.

"Rio," Eve replied, then wondered why the woman looked as if she hadn't expected that, either.

The screen door screeched open again, drawing their attention to the woman carrying a small tray with two steaming mugs and a sugar bowl. The noise caught Eve's and Molly's attention, anyway. Maria's attention had returned to the child.

Shana set the tray on the toy-strewn table under the shade of the sprawling cottonwood. With the smile she had yet to manage for Eve, she walked over to Molly and crouched down in front of her. The moment Molly smiled back, Eve knew Shana's heart was lost.

"I'll bet you're Molly." Dark eyes searched familiar features. "I'm your Auntie Shana. Nearly everyone is Auntie around here," she added, giving Eve a glance that told her she remembered that the child hadn't yet been told that Rio was her father. "I know where there are six other children who would love to share their swing set with you. Would you like me to get them?"

"I need to take her inside first." Maria extended her weathered hand to Molly, her voice gentler, though her features were still guarded. "And I think we need cookies."

The change in Maria's manner was subtle, but it was enough for Molly to give the woman a heart-melting grin before climbed up the stairs after her.

Shana pulled a white scrunchee from the pocket of her scrub shirt. "I had a feeling she'd change her mind once she saw her. I've seen this happen too many times to believe she'd be any different." Turning from the door, she pulled her hair into a low ponytail and began looping it through the elasticized fabric. "A young girl is unmarried and pregnant and the grandparents swear they want nothing to do with the baby. They even threaten to disown their own child. I saw it in nursing school in the white community and I see it here in our clinic. All it takes is to put that baby in the grandparents' arms. Ninety percent of the time, they turn to mush."

Though Eve would hardly interpret Maria's attitude as "mush," since Shana seemed to think her mother had softened, that was good enough for her. For now. "Had she told Rio she didn't want anything to do with Molly?"

"I don't know what she said to my brother. All she said to us was that he'd come here and told her he had a child. You say you've come to talk about Rio and your daughter?"

"What I really want to do is listen," Eve explained, sensing more caution than unfriendliness in this woman. "If someone will talk to me, that is. I need to learn about him. For Molly. I didn't know how else to do that without coming here.''

"You speak as if you and my brother are not together.''

"We're not. Not exactly," she amended. "I mean, we see each other and we're... That's an entirely different problem," she concluded.

Understanding lit the woman's warm brown eyes. "I see. But if you're talking to him, why come here to learn about him?''

"Because getting Rio to talk about himself is like pulling teeth.''

"Ah, yes. The infamous Native American male stoicism. What I wouldn't give for the elders to teach that they can be strong without being silent." Her hair now neatly restrained at her nape, she glanced at her watch. From the way she winced, it was apparent she was late.

"I have to get back to work." She paused, seeming torn between two sets of conflicting duties. Or maybe it was loyalties. "The person you need to talk with is our mother. That is the proper way. I don't know that she'll tell you what you want to know. I don't know if she'll even talk to you at all after I leave. Still," she added, "your coming here was a good thing.''

There was enough reserve in the woman's manner to let Eve know that while Shana thought her actions were commendable, the other woman hadn't totally made up her mind about her. Eve could accept that. All she cared about was that Molly and Rio had an ally in his sister. For that, she was truly grateful.

That gratitude faded back to anxiety the moment Rio's straight-faced and dignified mother returned with Molly. Eve had no sooner removed a cookie crumb from her little girl's face than Shana, telling Molly she'd show her where the other children were, took the child by the hand and headed to the house directly across the wide yard. Without knocking, she poked her head inside. Almost immediately, four exuberant, brown-haired children raced out into the yard. Another woman, this one wearing jeans and a football jersey, appeared in the doorway. Shorter and more rounded than Shana, she had a baby on her hip and a toddler tugging on her hand. After the briefest of conversations, the baby went into a playpen by the porch, the toddler climbed onto a tricycle, and Shana got into the minivan. With a honk of the horn and a wave, she drove out across the bridge covering the dry wash, a cloud of dust slowly settling behind her.

Maria Redtree, standing still as the dry air, said nothing. She simply studied the child leaning over the playpen to see the baby. Her newest granddaughter had eyes the color of cornflowers, but other than that, there were too many similarities between her and the other children for her to ignore. From the way her features had softened, Eve suspected there were more similarities than she'd expected to find.

Maria's glance brushed over Eve's golden hair, then down to her pale, tightly clasped hands. The softness faded.

For the first time in her life, Eve knew what it felt like to be totally out of place. She was out of her element here, an outsider in the truest sense of the word. The sense of distrust radiating from the woman was the worst.

Not knowing what to do, afraid to say the wrong thing, she tried to imagine what the other woman was thinking. When that little exercise only increased her discomfort, she focused on the young woman surreptitiously glancing their way while she tended the children.

"Is that Fawn?" she asked, needing desperately to end the silence.

Maria's brow lowered. "How do you know of her?"

"Rio told me about her. And the rest of your family," she added, diplomatically avoiding specifics about the woman Maria had wanted Rio to marry. "He has spoken of all of you. And of his home."

The same puzzlement she'd shown when Molly had identified the symbols reappeared in Maria's expression. To

Eve, it looked as if the woman didn't believe Rio would have spoken of his home and family at all. Or, if he had, that his comments would not have been favorable.

Shana had said she wasn't sure her mother would even talk to her. Taking it as a good sign that she was, Eve drew a breath of courage. "Mrs. Redtree," she began, her voice quiet, "I know Rio has some problems here, but I hope Molly won't be one of them. You're all so important to him," she added, "but she's his family, too. He adores her. It would be so hard for him if he ever felt he had to choose between you."

The faint lines in Maria's brow deepened, her hand closing over the intricately beaded circle dangling near her waist. "He tells you he must choose?"

"No. He didn't say that. I just got the impression the last time he was here that he was being pushed in that direction. I hope I'm wrong."

The voices of the children drifted toward them, but Maria turned away from the yard. Facing the open expanse of ochre-colored land across the road, her fingers tightened around the amulet as if seeking comfort or guidance from the images it bore.

"Who do you see when you look at your child?"

Puzzled by the question, Eve studied the woman's strong profile.

"I see Molly," she replied, not knowing who else she was supposed to see. "A beautiful, loving little girl."

Like every other glance Rio's mother had sent in her direction, the one she shot toward her now was unreadable. Like the others, too, it also failed to meet her eyes for more than an instant.

"You see only her?"

Her initial response had been knee-jerk, and totally honest. The one she gave now was more considered. "And I see Rio," she added, because the resemblances were definitely there and that was probably what his mother wanted to hear.

"But first you see your daughter."

Not sure if she was making points or losing them, Eve gave her a nod.

The horizon drew Maria's attention once more. "I cannot look at Rio and not see my husband."

There was chastisement in her words, but it didn't seem to be for Eve. It was directed inward, like her thoughts. "I did not realize until he came to tell me of his daughter that I had never truly seen my son. I never meant to drive him away," she whispered, but she was speaking to herself and not Eve.

Seeming to realize that, Maria drew a deep breath and quickly glanced toward her again.

"I thought I'd lost Rio to the white man's...to your world," she corrected herself. "Like I lost my husband. But I see from what he teaches his daughter that is not true. He is intelligent like his father, and his mind seeks many answers. But he does not abandon us. For Rio, his heritage must be important to him, otherwise he would not pass it on to his child." She pondered the thought for a moment, her voice growing quieter. "You can tell who a man is by his actions, Eve Stuart. It is not always the words he speaks. Pretty words can deceive. It is his actions that tell who he is and what he believes."

Maria said nothing else. From the way she moved to the table and handed a mug of tea to Eve before picking up a basket of mending, it appeared that the discussion was over. It would have been over, anyway. An impish toddler with short black hair, sparkling ebony eyes and the deepest dimples Eve had ever seen, ran over and threw her arms around her grandma's legs, begging to be picked up. With the deftness of a pro, the older woman swung the little girl up onto the bench and handed her a coloring book. Moments later, Fawn was chasing another toddler by them, this one in the two-year-old range, and Maria was off to get another mug so the younger woman, who seemed more shy than reticent, could join them.

Nothing else was said about Rio. Nothing was said about anything controversial at all. And while the next hour wasn't the most relaxed Eve had ever spent, because most of the time she was holding, rocking or chasing a small child, she began to realize that Molly might well be a bridge between Rio and his mother—and to understand why Rio had been so concerned about Molly feeling accepted. It had little to do with being Indian in the white man's world. It had to do with his mother never having accepted him simply as himself. It was no wonder he'd felt he didn't belong.

As Eve and Molly started back for Grand Springs, after promising to bring Molly for little Alanna Redtree's birthday celebration next month, there was something else Eve considered. Rio had been physically abandoned by his father and emotionally abandoned by both of his parents. Every time his mother had looked at him she'd been reminded of the hurt her husband had caused her. But Maria had compounded the pain by pushing her own son away from her—before he could leave her first.

Whether Rio was conscious of it or not, Eve knew that was exactly what he was doing with her. She had hurt him, and every time they started to get close, he pushed her away. Not that she could blame him. He'd probably grown up feeling that he couldn't count on anyone; that any person he grew to trust would eventually let him down. As she had done. If it took the rest of her life, she needed him to know he could always trust her.

That resolution had scarcely been made when she heard the honk of a car behind her. The dark sedan had been following her little red Altima ever since she and Molly had come off tribal land. The only reason she recognized it was because it had been parked on the side of the road and had pulled out right behind them. Now, thirty miles later, it seemed the driver wanted to pass.

The road had started climbing upward, leaving the flats to enter forest. Because the highway was two-lane and

twisting, passing was difficult at best. Having no desire to
have an impatient driver honking at her for the next fifty
miles, she slowed down and pulled over as far as she could
to let him go by.

She slowed to thirty and he didn't pass.

She dropped to twenty and he was still on her tail.

A quick glance in the rearview mirror and she could see
two men in the car, both with dark stocking caps on their
heads.

"Mommy? What's wrong?"

Dear God, Eve prayed as, fear surging, she told Molly
to hang on and she gunned the engine to pull back out. The
moment she did, the dark sedan pulled up, edging alongside
her—and ran her off the road.

Eleven

Rio had an uneasy feeling. It had been with him all day, but by four-thirty he was ready to pace the walls. Not much had gone right. Because he'd stayed to talk to Eve this morning, he'd been late for a staff meeting. They'd waited for him to arrive before starting, so that had then made him late for an interview he'd scheduled yesterday. And this afternoon, he totally spaced a deadline. That had never happened to him before. Never. But then, he wasn't usually this preoccupied.

Molly's unexpected request had filled his heart near to bursting. He was crazy about that kid. But he could have settled for telling Eve that he wanted their child to know he was her father for real, and let it go at that. The custody stuff could have been addressed later. As overwhelmed as Eve was already, the last thing she needed was another legal matter to contend with. Dumping something like that on her less than an hour after leaving her bed hadn't been his most brilliant work, either.

He reached for the telephone, thinking of how withdrawn she'd been when he'd left. He'd tried to ease her mind, but he knew it hadn't worked.

He got her answering machine. Thinking little of it, he left a message that he'd call back later, then called again before he left the office. He got the machine that time, too.

Figuring Eve had errands to run or a meeting to attend, he left another message, this one telling her that he'd be there by seven. They had agreed to talk to Molly tonight, so he was sure she'd be back by then.

She wasn't. She was still gone when he stopped by again at eight, and her answering machine was still picking up when he finally stopped calling at midnight. It wasn't like her to not be where she'd said she'd be. Or not to let him know if something had come up and she'd be late.

When he knocked on her door at eight-thirty the next morning, she still hadn't shown up.

He knew she wasn't inside and just not answering the telephone. Her car was gone.

Growing more worried than puzzled, Rio turned back to where he'd parked his Bronco in the tree-shaded driveway. Birds scattered in a dark, chirping cloud when he slammed the door and revved the engine. There could be a perfectly logical explanation for her absence. Unfortunately, he couldn't think of a single one at the moment. Eve should be out front with Molly even now, waiting for the bus for day camp—unless something had happened to the little girl. Had Molly become ill? Been hurt?

If that was the case, why hadn't Eve called him?

The questions had him cutting a U in the middle of the quiet street and heading straight for Millicent's house. The woman, wearing a blinding yellow caftan, immediately invited him in, but all he wanted was to know if she had any idea where Eve was. She didn't. She hadn't seen her since the day before yesterday, but being her always-helpful self, she said she'd be sure to have Eve call if she saw her.

Something about those words, about having Eve call him, jerked hard at his memory. Eve's mother had once said that very same thing to him, and six years had passed before he'd heard Eve's voice.

She wouldn't do it to him again. Would she? They hadn't really argued yesterday. No more so than they had a half dozen other times, anyway. Had she been more upset than he'd realized?

A sick sensation roiled in his stomach at the thought.

"No," he said aloud, refusing to consider that possibility taunting him. "She wouldn't," he repeated, reaching for his cell phone as soon as he was back in his Bronco. "She can't."

He had Vanderbilt Memorial on the line by the time he reached the end of the street. The hospital, however, had no record of Molly Stuart being treated or admitted. Not letting himself consider all the reasons it was so imperative that he find Eve, he had them check for her, too.

He was headed for town and St. Veronica's Church when he was informed by the admitting clerk that there was no record of Eve Stuart having been there, either.

Rio pulled a deep breath, the only acknowledgment of relief he could allow himself. He was probably overreacting; he who always thought twice, weighed the possibilities and didn't draw a conclusion until all the evidence was in. But with Eve, his objectivity had long since taken a hike.

Struggling for it, anyway, he jogged across the church parking lot. The sound of children singing directed him to the activities, but the closer he got, the harder it was to escape the feeling that something was terribly wrong.

The education rooms were in the long wing projecting from the back of white, spired church. That was where the preschoolers were, or so Rio was told by the prim, blue-haired woman who assailed him the moment he entered the open double doors.

The voices grew louder the farther down the hall he went, the words to "I'm a Little Teacup" becoming clearer when he opened the first door and poked his head inside. There had to be forty kids in there. Every one of them had a hand on one hip, the other in the air, and was bending at some angle or another from the waist.

There was blond hair and brown, a few shades of red and a couple of kids wearing baseball caps. When his glance swept to a head of long black hair pulled up into pigtails, he almost sighed. But then the pretty little Asian girl turned around to see what the other children were suddenly looking at and the relief he wanted to feel vanished like a ghost.

A woman in grass green shorts and a Swing Into Summer Camp T-shirt was leading the energetic group. She turned, too. Her hand still waving in time to the song, she backed toward him.

"May I help you?" she asked, checking him out without missing a beat.

"Is Molly Stuart here?"

"Molly?" she returned, her eyes narrowing. "Who are you?"

She wasn't being rude. She was just protecting her charges. "I'm her father," he said without hesitation. "I just want to make sure she got here all right this morning."

It was the truth. Part of it, anyway. But it was enough to satisfy her.

"Molly's not in my group. She's in Mrs. Ankeny's next door. Hold on."

She turned to a skinny teenager helping one of the smaller children with his spout. Motioning her over, she asked the girl to check the next room for Molly Stuart, then, directing the music with both hands, she left Rio standing in the doorway.

The freckle-faced teenager was back in less than a minute.

Twisting the end of her curly ponytail, she spoke to the middle of his chest. "Mrs. Ankeny said she hasn't seen Molly since her mom picked her up yesterday."

"Eve picked her up?"

The girl nodded. "Right before snacks, she said."

Something cold gripped Rio's chest.

"What time would that have been?"

"We do snacks at ten-fifteen."

He thanked the girl. At least, he thought he did before he backed away, oblivious to her puzzled glance. As he blinked at the too-bright hall, the cold sensation in his chest began to slowly seep through his body.

Posters lined the cream-colored walls, colorful scenes from Bible stories drawn by the children's own hands. The cheerfulness of the images mocked him as he retraced his steps, his stride steady as he broke into the morning sunlight. Mind racing, Rio felt a red haze settle over his brain.

Eve had picked up Molly right after he'd left yesterday. Right after he'd told her he wanted joint custody. He knew how overwhelmed she'd felt with all she was dealing with, and he knew his timing had been lousy, but he couldn't have garnered any sympathy for her had his life depended on it.

She had done it again. There had been no discussion. No chance to work anything out. Instead of believing they could resolve the issue together, she'd run off and left him—just the way she'd done before.

Hurt melded with anger, clouding his thinking and stealing rationality. But the pain was so much worse than it had been before. It hurt enough to know that Eve had felt so desperate to get away from him. But she'd also taken his little girl.

This time wasn't going to be like the last, though. This time, he knew where to find her. And how.

"Hey, Rio. How's it going?"

Rio didn't answer. He merely lifted his hand in the general direction of the classified ad rep who'd voiced the greeting and kept heading for his desk.

Heads rose from computer terminals as he strode past, the other reporters in the room looking up from telephones and monitors to turn curious glances to one another. It wasn't unusual for any one of them to dive for their desk when they were hot on a story. But the only thing that looked hot at the moment was Rio himself.

Someone had left a package on his chair. He tossed it onto the day's copy of the paper that appeared on everyone's desk, intent on calling the *Herald*'s travel agent to book him on a flight to Santa Barbara. Eve was driving. With any luck, he could be on her doorstep when she got home. She wasn't going to continue doing this to him. And there was no way in hell she was going to keep him from his daughter.

"Mr. Redtree, you'd better check that out." The adolescent male voice cracked, causing the young man with the mail cart to blush as he pointed to the package. "Wendy said it was urgent."

Wendy was the receptionist. Since Wendy had received it, that meant it had been delivered, not mailed.

Rio could hear the travel agent clicking away at her computer keyboard on the other end of the line. In no mood to think about anything else, he started to ignore what the young man had said, then decided that ripping into something might not be a bad idea.

With the phone cradled to his ear, he leaned forward and grabbed the package. It was a large, padded manila envelope, thick on one end and surprisingly light. He didn't bother to read the bold writing on the front. Gathering one corner in his fist, he simply ripped—then went stock-still when he saw the battered blue teddy bear inside.

The note with Ted froze the air in Rio's lungs.

You now know how easy it was to get your girlfriend and your kid. Drop your story about Olivia Stuart or next time you'll be burying them. You have from now until ten o'clock Thursday morning to decide what you're going to do. You will be contacted at your office with their location at that time.

He'd dropped the phone. Picking it up, he told the woman on the other end of the line to forget the flight and blindly reached for the cradle with the receiver.

The note had been typed on plain white paper. There was no signature. The outside of the envelope bore only his own name and the name of his paper in black block letters.

Rio closed his eyes, willing himself to concentrate. He

knew how to be logical, sensible, calm. That was what he needed to be now. Eve hadn't run off. In a way, he almost wished she had. At least then he would have known she and Molly were safe.

Focus, he reminded himself, and somehow, just knowing that Eve hadn't betrayed him, his senses cleared. A totally different brand of anger kicked in. There was only one person he could think of who wanted him off that story. The same person who wanted him out of his and his sister's life.

Lettie Meyers stepped out of her office as he jammed the note into the pocket of his slacks. "You okay?"

"I'll let you know," he muttered, and stormed out the door.

Rio was barely through the double doors of the mayor's office when Hal's secretary looked up from the nail she was filing. Berry red lips curved in a smile.

"Is he in?"

A quiet, dangerous kind of rage simmered in Rio's cool ebony eyes. That anger honed his features, tightened his voice and made anyone within twenty feet of him want to back away. From the way Stacy's smile faltered, she looked as if that was exactly what she wanted to do herself, had there been any place for her to go.

"He's on the phone, Mr. Redtree. If you'll wait a..."

Stacy didn't get a chance to finish. Rio was already through the door, his eyes glaring a hole through the back of Hal's meticulously combed hair.

The red leather executive chair swung around. With the phone pressed to his ear, Hal furrowed his patrician features in annoyance.

Leaning across his desk, Rio pressed his finger to the button on the handset and ended the call. He had the negligible satisfaction of seeing Hal's face turn red.

"Damn it, Redtree!" Eve's brother slammed down the phone, shooting out of his chair in the same motion. "That was the governor's office! What do you think you're doing?''

Rio leaned closer. "That's exactly what I want to know," he said, biting off the words in a voice so cold, so controlled that the other man shrank back. "I don't care how important you think you are, how connected you might be or what kind of game you think you're playing, but I don't deal well with threats against people who matter to me."

"What are you talking about?"

"I'm talking about the tactics you're using to get me to back off the investigation into your mother's murder." Snatching the note from his pants pocket, Rio flipped it onto the desk in disgust. He couldn't believe how badly he wanted to wipe the imperious glower off Hal's pretty face as the man's manicured fingers snatched up the note. "I suspected you were scum, Stuart, but I didn't think you'd stoop so low as to use your own family. Where are they?"

For a moment, Hal didn't answer. The glower left his face, along with most of its color. "Where did you get this?"

"You had it delivered to me."

"No." His hand was trembling when he shook his head. "No," he repeated, distress filling his eyes. He set the note away from him on the desk, then pushed at it again to get it as far from him as possible. "I don't know anything about that."

"You're telling me you haven't seen them?"

"Not for a couple of weeks. Neither one of them."

Hal suddenly looked smaller, weaker. Watching him drop into the thronelike chair and fumble for his cigarettes, Rio felt the anger pumping through him begin to slowly leak away. In its place crept a real and harrowing fear. Hal hadn't sent the note. The man was far too stunned, the look in his eyes far too worried, for him to know what was going on. At least that was the way it seemed to Rio as the enormity of Eve's and Molly's disappearance hit. This wasn't some pathetic attempt on the part of a crooked politician to get a reporter off his tail. Rio's woman and his daughter had truly been kidnapped.

"When did you get that?" Hal asked, using the shaky motions of lighting his cigarette to avoid the other man's eyes.

"It was delivered early this morning." Rio picked up the note, his mind racing. It was because of him that Eve and Molly were in danger. "But they've been gone since yesterday."

He wasn't sure when they had disappeared...if it had been shortly after Eve picked up Molly, or later that day. He didn't even know why she would have taken the little girl out of day camp. To his knowledge, she'd never done that before.

He needed to talk to Stone.

Hal was on his feet again, looking as unsteady as he sounded. "Where are you going?"

"Where do think I'm going?" Rio shot back. "I'm going to the police."

Had Rio not already been out the door, he would have seen the fear wash over Hal's face. But Hal was saved that humiliation. He might have even felt grateful for it, had he not been so busy trying to calm the roiling sensation in his stomach.

Frightened for his sister and her child, he grabbed the bottle of antacid he kept in his bottom drawer and swilled a mouthful on his way across the room to close the door. He nearly shut it in his secretary's face, but he couldn't worry about having offended her. He'd deal with damage control later. Right now, he needed to know why an agreement had been broken.

"Hold my calls," he barked into the intercom a moment later, then punched through for an outside line.

He was pacing a trench in the carpet by his desk, the phone cord limiting his distance, when the man he needed to reach deigned to take his call.

"For God's sake," he hissed, keeping his voice low. "My sister and her kid aren't supposed to be involved in any of this!"

"Now, now" came the placating voice. "*You* couldn't get that reporter to drop his investigation, so we had to do something, didn't we?"

"I'll work on him. I'll think of something. Just let my sister and the kid go."

"Not until the reporter realizes we mean business about him dropping his story. And by the way," the man added, his tone turning ugly with chameleonlike ease, "forget about going to the authorities yourself. You're the one who said your mother was getting too close to us. So the way I see it, it's your fault she's dead. You're in this up to your eyebrows, pal. I can leak the dirt on you and your family, I can make you look like the murderer, or we can just keep things running on the old status quo. You choose."

There was nothing else to say. With a click on the other end, the line went dead.

Hal's hand was shaking when he hung up the phone, but it took only a couple of minutes for that to pass. He had a helluva headache, though. Opening the door, he gave Stacy a contrite smile and asked if she had any aspirin. If he played it right, maybe he could get her to rub his temples.

It was Stone Richardson's day off, but when Rio called him from the *Herald*'s office, told him that Eve and Molly had been kidnapped, and asked him to meet him at the station as a personal favor, the burly detective was there in minutes.

Rio waited at Stone's desk and watched his friend weave his way through the noisy, open room filled with desks, ringing telephones, cops and their captives. Ignoring the controlled chaos, he extended his hand the moment Stone stopped in front of him.

The bigger man clasped his hand in a solid grip, popped

him on the shoulder with his free hand and muttered, "What the hell's going on?"

There had never been any discussion between the two men about Rio's relationship with Eve. There was little now as Rio related what had transpired in the past hour. Any question Stone might have had about why the journalist was taking such a personal interest in the disappearance of the former mayor's daughter and granddaughter was answered just by watching his friend. Though his tension was leashed, Rio couldn't have masked the agitation etched in his features if he'd tried.

As a man whose life had recently been impacted by a member of the gentler sex, Stone could well imagine the horrors going through Rio's mind. He could also understand the quiet fury causing Rio's jaw to work. Anger, fury, rage. They were all easier for a man to deal with than fear.

"They have her daughter, too, you say?"

"Our daughter. Molly is mine."

The detective's eyebrows arched. "We'll have to celebrate that one later." More fully appreciating the worry taunting his friend's formidable control, he nodded to what Rio held. "Let me see what you've got there."

The desk looked neater than usual. Instead of the entire top being obliterated, only half of the gunmetal gray surface was cluttered with files and paper cups. Holding the bag by the corner, Rio set it on the coffee-ringed blotter. He held the note by the corner, too, and dropped it on the bag.

"You'll find my fingerprints on that," he said, indicating the note after Stone had read it. "And Hal Stuart's."

"Why his?"

"Because I went off half-cocked and threw it at him. I thought he was behind this...that he was holding them at his house or something." He could still remember the look on Hal's face, the disbelief, the apprehension. "He wasn't."

Eyes of unblinking obsidian met eyes of shrewd gray.

Stone had never known Rio to go off half-cocked over any-thing. Rio hadn't known *himself* to do it. But today, in less than an hour, he'd jumped to conclusions not once, but twice, and missed both by a mile.

"Why would you have suspected him?"

"Because I was making him uncomfortable. I'll tell you about it later, okay? Right now, Eve and Molly are out there with God only knows who. How are we going to find them?"

Rio thought for sure that Stone was going to tell him that "we" weren't going to do anything. But all his friend did was turn his attention to the child's well-loved teddy bear, the typed note and the envelope Rio wished he'd been a little more careful about opening.

"I take it that the toy is your daughter's."

Rio's jaw hardened. "She never goes anywhere without it."

His own jaw set a little firmer, Stone grabbed a couple of evidence bags from the next desk. But when he reached for the blue bear, Rio stopped him.

"Let me keep Ted."

"Ted?"

"The bear," Rio explained, and held Stone's glance until the detective caved in.

"They'd never be able to get prints off that fuzzy stuff, anyway," Stone said, and refrained from adding what they were both thinking. If the stuffed animal was needed to match fibers with those found at a scene, they'd know where to find it.

Not wanting to consider what else might be found at a scene, Rio concentrated on pacing while Stone sent the evidence bags containing the note and the messenger envelope to forensics, and had a patrol car dispatched to Olivia's house to search for any signs of forced entry or foul play. He said those same officers would check with neighbors to see if anyone had seen Eve and her daughter leave. After getting the make and license number of her car from Rio, not wasting time by asking why he happened to know the latter, he had an APB put out on it. Then he had another patrol car head for St. Veronica's so Mrs. Ankeny, Molly's camp counselor, could be questioned about whether or not Eve had been alone when she'd picked up Molly yesterday and what her emotional state had been at the time. Had someone been waiting for her in her car, having threatened some sort of retaliation if she didn't do as she was told, it was a sure bet she wouldn't have been her normal, friendly self.

"We should hear back from the patrols in the next ten minutes," Stone told Rio, motioning for Jack Stryker to join them when he finished his phone calls. "While we're waiting, I want to know why you thought our acting mayor would have kidnapped his own sister."

Hal Stuart was the last person Rio wanted to think about right now. Suspecting Stone was asking as much to keep him from climbing the walls as out of curiosity, Rio rubbed his breastbone as he paced past the man leaning against the desk. Guilt over thinking Eve had betrayed him burned in his chest like acid.

"I'd been checking out his mining investments as part of the murder investigation," he began, thinking there ought to be something else somebody could be doing to find Eve and Molly right now. "While I was at it, I came across something interesting about his finances. He hadn't wanted me to work with Eve on their mother's case to begin with, and when I started asking him about his income, he made it clear that he wanted me to stay away from anything that had to do with the Stuarts."

Stone's eyebrows merged. "Define 'something interesting.'"

Pacing like a caged panther, Rio told him, starting with why he'd been suspicious of Hal's spending habits and ending with how he'd learned that Hal claimed to be some sort of "consultant" on various businesses owned by Maxwell

Brown. Rio also told Stone that he suspected Brown was buying political favors, but he couldn't prove that. Yet.

The detective sucked in a slow whistle through his teeth. "How did you come up with this? Never mind," he immediately added, holding up his hand the moment he saw Rio frown at him. "You have to protect your source. I know. It wouldn't help us with our current problem, anyway."

Stone's phone rang, bringing Rio to an abrupt halt. From Stone's end of the conversation, he could tell that the officers in the first patrol car had found nothing unusual at the house. When Stone confirmed that himself, Rio didn't know if he was supposed to feel encouraged or not. All he knew was that he didn't care at all for the conclusions he was drawing as he reread the words Stone had copied from the kidnapper's note.

The purpose of the kidnapping was clearly a show of power. But just because the note implied that no harm would come to his "girlfriend" and his "kid" this time, that didn't mean the kidnapper couldn't panic and hurt them, anyway.

He'd obviously come too close for comfort to someone involved with Olivia's murder. Possibly the murderer himself—or herself. Unfortunately, even with Stone's frustrated prodding and the intervention of Jack Stryker, who came onto the case with them, Rio couldn't come up with a single, viable clue as to who that might have been. Except for Hal, who had so obviously known nothing about the kidnapping, Rio couldn't imagine who would want him to drop his investigation. But clueless or not, whoever had Eve and Molly wanted him to sweat for a while.

He'd sweat, all right. He couldn't stand the thought of what might be happening to them, or how terrified they must be. But no way was he going to sit back and wait for the time to pass.

"Wendy," he whispered, a possible lead hitting him midpace. Aware of Stone's and Stryker's quick and questioning glances, he grabbed the phone on Stone's desk. "That package was delivered."

A minute later, Wendy, the *Herald*'s receptionist, had given him the name of the local messenger service that had delivered the package that morning. She even gave him the phone number, since it was a service the *Herald* occasionally used. The gravel-voiced woman at Speedee Towne Delivery was not as cooperative, however. She didn't care how urgent the matter was, she wasn't giving a stranger any information about anyone who used their services without the customer's permission.

She felt a little differently a short time later when the black-haired, black-eyed, granite-jawed Rio, who was doing his best to remain civil, appeared in front of her with a rugged, broad-shouldered detective who introduced himself as Stone Richardson and flashed his badge.

"He had a beard. Trimmed close, you know? And kind of an accent, like he was from back East. Oh, and a gold ring. On his pinky."

The generously proportioned brunette with the big hair and heavy makeup fiddled with the clasp of her bolo tie. On the phone, Rio had thought she might be nervous about saying anything because she'd been threatened to keep her mouth shut. The ease with which the information flowed in person told him that wasn't the case at all.

"Was anyone with him?" Stone asked.

She shook her head, the motion making the copper loops in her ears sway. "He was by himself. In fact, he was waiting here when I opened this morning. He wanted to have his package delivered right away," she continued. "And he was real specific about when the delivery was to be made. He paid extra to make sure it was the first one."

"I don't suppose he paid with a credit card or check?"

Stone and Rio exchanged a look that said neither one of them believed there was a snowball's chance in the South Seas of that happening. But they knew he had to ask.

"Cash. For both deliveries. He gave me another one

that's supposed to be made at ten o'clock tomorrow morning.''

"May we see it?" the detective calmly asked.

The woman's lips pursed. "I can't do that. We're like the post office here. When someone pays us to deliver something, it's like a contract, you know?"

"May I speak with your boss?"

"I'm the boss."

"Then this all just got simpler," Stone informed her, politely. "I know you're protecting your business and you're being as ethical as you can, but you can either give the letter to me now, or you can give it to me in an hour when I come back with a warrant. My mood will be a whole lot better if I don't have to go back to the station, do the paperwork, then interrupt a judge to get his signature. What'll it be?"

Not caring to mess with his mood, she retrieved the letter. It was in the same sort of padded mailer the stuffed bear and note had been in. Stone opened it by pulling the staples out of the end, rather than tearing the pull tab, and pulled out the single, typewritten half sheet.

Had Stone not been holding the note so he could see it, Rio knew he would have had to force himself not to rip it out of the man's hands. As it was he had no trouble reading the terse instructions.

Twenty miles north of town. The end of Logging Road 8 off the old fire service road.

"I know that place." It was out beyond Two Falls Lake. Answering him with a tight nod, Stone glanced back to the woman quietly watching them. Then, because he didn't have a warrant and because he didn't want to jeopardize Eve and Molly in case someone came back to retrieve or change the letter for whatever reason, he asked the delivery service owner to make a photocopy of the sheet and he restapled the original into the envelope.

"Mrs. Boyle," he said, having obtained her name from the pin on her blouse, "you've been very helpful. Now, if I could ask you one more thing. If anyone comes in here asking about either of these deliveries, act as if we haven't been here. Can you do that?"

Eyes suddenly wide, she quickly nodded. She hadn't expected cloak-and-dagger. "Sure. I'm in community theater."

"Then, I'm sure you'll be fine," he told her, the glance he shot Rio saying he hoped she wouldn't carry her acting abilities too far. "And if anyone does come in here asking about either of these deliveries, call the station and ask either for me or a Detective Stryker." He wrote Stryker's name on the back of his card and handed it to her. "You won't forget now, will you?"

Eyes still wide, she shook her head.

Rio didn't have a whole lot of faith in the woman's promised silence. She'd looked so antsy when he and Stone walked out the door, he figured they'd be gone about eight seconds before she'd be on the phone to her husband or a girlfriend. Desperate that Eve's and Molly's safety not be jeopardized, he sent up a prayer that the woman would keep her word. In the past hour, he'd prayed more than he had in the past ten years.

They'd barely hit the sidewalk before Stone started pumping him.

"What can you tell me about this area?"

"There's nothing there. No campgrounds. No cabins. No potable water. It's just forest, mountains and a couple of rutted roads."

"Think he's keeping them someplace else?"

Unless someone had brought in camping equipment, Rio was inclined to think so. He found that to be the consensus, too, back at the station, where he proceeded, once again, to pace the polish off the floor. By the time a map had been tacked up on a conference room wall and a time line drawn out on a chalkboard, a few other possibilities had also been agreed on. For one thing, it seemed apparent from the delivery schedule that whoever they were dealing with figured the police would be ready to trace any call made to Rio, so that little trap had been eliminated by writing out the instructions. And since it didn't seem likely that Molly and Eve were being kept at the pickup point, that could only mean that the kidnapper intended to drop them off. Careful as the kidnapper was about not having a call traced, it seemed a fair assumption that whoever was doing the dropping planned to be long gone before Rio got there.

The contingency their abductor hadn't counted on, however, was Rio obtaining his instructions ahead of time. Because he had, he and the police were waiting in the trees the next morning when the sun began to rise.

Twelve

The logging road was much as Rio remembered it. It was less than half a mile long, and ended at a clear-cut that had already begun to regenerate itself. Foot-tall firs poked through a maze of flat stumps and pinecones, the large clearing surrounded by a thick choke of scrub and towering trees. The only access to the logging road was the narrow, graded dirt lane that was used mostly for fire protection.

Because there was nothing around for miles, other than forest and rocky, steep-sloped mountains, the only logical place to intercept the kidnapper was at the intersection of the logging and fire service roads. Any vehicle coming through would have to pass there twice. Since the safety of the victims was uppermost, Stone had told him that the kidnapper's vehicle would be allowed to pass on the way in. Then, once Eve and Molly had been released and were out of harm's way, the kidnapper would be netted on the way out.

It seemed to Rio that only someone arrogant or stupid would box himself in like that. It also seemed to him that, like all plans, their own was far from foolproof.

That thought was still taunting him as he leaned against the fender of an unmarked police car, staring into the fading darkness and sucking in the sweet scent of pine and loamy earth.

The haunting hoot of an owl drifted from somewhere high in the towering trees. Leaves rustled with the movement of some nocturnal animal on the prowl. A coyote yipped in the distance. Another, farther away, called back.

It was that ephemeral time of day between dark and dawn when night creatures lie in wait for rabbits and rodents coming from burrows and dens. Nature looking for a meal before bedtime.

Lying in wait for whoever had taken Eve and Molly were half a dozen officers dressed in dark navy pants and baseball jackets. Some of those jackets had Sheriff spelled out on the back, others Police.

Rio, in dark jeans and a denim jacket, couldn't see any of them. The patrol cars were hidden in the trees, lights off. The men themselves were hidden, too. Each man had a two-way radio and his service revolver. The three sharpshooters positioned in a triangle at the intersection had sniper's rifles.

Rio had his bare hands.

"I mean it, Rio," Stone whispered from beside him. "You stay out of this."

"If he's touched one hair on either of their heads..."

"I know you want to rip out a throat," Stone cut in, "but you won't do Eve and your daughter any good in jail or dead. The only reason you're here is because you know these woods."

The faint crackle of static had Stone lifting his radio to his mouth to respond to a fifteen-minute check-in. Edgy with waiting, Rio turned to the narrow strip of dirt a few yards away. Now that dawn was breaking, the men were on full alert, all eyes trained on the roads.

Rio tried to detach himself, to step back and look at the situation as he might have under different circumstances. He should have found it all very interesting: the logistics, the timing, the heavy anticipation. He couldn't have detached himself had his life depended on it.

The summons on the radio hadn't been a check-in, after all.

"Station 2's got 'em in sight."

Stone made the announcement in a flat whisper, pointing to his right to indicate the direction, then motioned to his partner. Brad Canfield slipped silently out of the car, his features masked beneath the brim of his dark baseball cap, and took position behind a tree at the edge of the road.

It was only seconds before Rio heard the hum of a car engine and the crunch of gravel being eaten up and spewn out by tires. Whoever was driving wasn't taking time to enjoy the sunrise.

Even if he hadn't heard the vehicle, Rio would have known the course of the car by the radio reports traveling from man to man as they closed ranks behind the unsuspecting sedan. The car was dark in color. Midnight blue or black. No one could tell yet. There were three adults inside—two appeared to be male and were pulling on ski masks. One driving and one in back. The woman in the front passenger seat was blindfolded. The child couldn't be seen.

"She's probably in back," Stone said to Rio. "They're keeping them separated as insurance."

Rio didn't have to ask what his friend meant. If something went wrong when Eve got out, they would still have Molly.

He heard the car's engine change pitch when it slowed to turn onto the logging road. Its headlights momentarily illuminating the pine boughs camouflaging the unmarked car, it picked up speed again as it shot past where Rio, Stone and Canfield waited.

Rio had been told that he and Stone would head for Molly and Eve to make sure they were all right, then he would stay with them in the trees while Stone joined Canfield, who was to block the road with their vehicle after the sedan passed again. The other two police cars were already pulling into position on the road from which the sedan had just turned.

From their station halfway between the clearing and the three-way intersection, Rio watched the sedan's taillights dim, then brighten again as the brake lights came on.

He was about to move, anyway, when Stone motioned

him forward. The pale light of morning was beginning to reveal shades of green amid the gray. That meant they would be seen on the road. Not willing to risk that, they moved just inside the protection of the trees, covering the ground like two dark, powerful cats intent on prey. Coming to a silent stop in the thicket at the edge of a clearing, they saw that the sedan had stopped twenty yards away.

The driver was already out. Of average height and slender, his red ski mask defying anyone to guess hair color or features, he jerked open the passenger door. Every muscle in Rio's body tensed when he saw him haul Eve out by the upper arm, then shove her away. The white cloth tied around her eyes made it impossible for her to see, and she stumbled on the uneven ground. Catching her by the front of the same peach-colored shirt Rio had last seen her in, her captor shoved his finger at her face and said something Rio couldn't hear. Eve couldn't see the intimidating gesture, but whatever it was her captor said made her nod and stand perfectly still.

She had to be positively terrified.

Neither Rio nor Stone took their eyes from the car as the second man emerged, but Rio felt Stone's restraining hand on his arm. The warning wasn't necessary. As hard as it was watching Eve being manhandled, he wasn't about to endanger her more by tearing out after the guy.

The second man was shorter, stockier, and his black mask and dark clothes gave him the ominous look of an executioner. Seeming more annoyed than impatient, he exchanged a few words with the red mask before pushing the passenger seat forward and pulling Molly out much as his partner had done with Eve. Instead of making her stumble her way to her mother, though, he picked her up by the shoulders, her bare feet dangling, then set her down next to her mother. Whatever he said to the child; it had her nodding the same way Eve had done.

Stone's attention was on the men as the driver climbed back into the car. All Rio cared about were the two people clinging to each other in the clearing of stumps and short, feathery pines. For all Eve knew, she and Molly were being left in the middle of nowhere without food or water. And though his relief to see them visibly unharmed was enormous, he could only imagine what was going through Eve's mind as she tried to soothe her daughter.

Stone lifted his radio to his mouth. The driver had turned the sedan around and was about to head back down the logging road. At least, that was what it appeared he was going to do until Stone realized that the other abductor wasn't getting in with him.

Canfield hadn't waited to hear that part. A second after Stone reported that the sedan had turned, the rumble of the unmarked car's engine being fired had the man in the black mask spinning around.

Rio saw Eve's head snap toward the sound, too. Then all hell broke loose.

Moving faster than Rio would have thought possible for someone his size, the man in the black mask bolted for the sedan. He caught up with it as it stopped just beyond the clearing, jerked open the passenger door and dove inside. Seconds later, the sedan shot backward, engine roaring and gravel flying from under the front wheels like shrapnel spray.

The sedan was nearly even with Stone and Rio when an arm appeared out the passenger window. The sharp pop of a gun echoed through the forest, frightened birds scattering. Seconds later, an answering shot rang through the air. At the same instant, a white spiderweb glazed the middle of the sedan's windshield, a neat black hole forming its center. The car swerved as its back wheel rolled up and over a stump, but neither man appeared to be hit.

The gunfire had Eve ripping off her mask. Swinging Molly up in her arms, she looked frantically left then right.

Seeing how unprotected she was, Rio crouched to run.

Stone swore, then yelled for him to stay down.

"Behind you!" Rio shouted to Eve, realizing she could

take cover long before he could get to them. "Get into the trees behind you!"

She couldn't see him. "Rio?"

"Go!"

Eve was far closer to the shelter of those trees than she was to him and Stone. Shoving Molly's head to her shoulder, she ran for a copse of aspen as the driver of the sedan gunned the engine, trying to move the car from where he'd high-centered it on the stump. That wasn't where Rio wanted her to go. He'd meant for her to head into the pines. They were thicker, their trunks more dense. But, small as she was, she darted between the slender white trees with the agility of a doe, then seemed to fade into the shadows.

Rio had no idea what Stone had barked into his radio, but the unmarked police car was suddenly at the head of the road, skidding to a stop at the edge of the clearing. Its door flew open, and Canfield, revolver drawn, fell into a crouch behind it, using it as a shield. The passenger side of the kidnapper's sedan faced Rio. Tilted as it was with its right rear tire in the air, its driver's door popped open, too, the thug in the red mask mirroring the cop's position as a quick succession of echoing blasts returned Canfield's fire.

The noise was deafening, the cacophony growing with the thunder of the other two police cars barreling up the road. But it was the flash of movement that had Rio's muscles primed. The guy in the black mask had crawled out the driver's side and was darting for the aspens. Within seconds, he was inside the copse. The shadows there shielded him, but a red stripe across the back of his shirt was as clear as a beacon to Rio.

The man wasn't trying to get away. He was following Eve and Molly.

He was after hostages.

Rio didn't think. He just moved. Leaving Stone yelling after him, he tore into the clearing at a dead run, jumping the stumps he didn't skirt and bolting behind the sedan.

Whatever Stone yelled had the barrage of police fire suddenly stopping, but Rio could hear the sharp report of the
kidnapper's gun and the shrieking hiss of a bullet whizzing
past his head as he dove into the aspens. A second bullet
ricocheted off one of the white trunks, leaving the splin-
tered wood looking like a spray of toothpicks.

Ahead of him he could hear what sounded like a bear
crashing through brush. Pure adrenaline pumping through
his veins, he stayed on that sound, instinctively following
the path of small broken branches on the trees. From above
him came the escalating drone of a helicopter. From behind,
the whine of bullets ripping the air.

He thought the helicopter was getting closer when he
caught sight of the red stripe on the dark shirt. But all he
cared about as the aspens opened onto a dry and rocky
streambed was that the moose in the black mask was ten
feet behind Eve and that there was no way in hell he was
going to let him touch her.

The early morning light glinted off the man's silver pistol
just before Rio, heart hammering, closed the five-yard gap
between them and dove for his legs.

"Son of a..."

The angry oath ended in a grunt as the man hit the
ground. He went down hard as a felled oak, which meant
Rio did, too, since his own body was first to meet the unyielding bed of football-size rocks. There was no time for
pain to register. The moose twisted around with a feral
growl, arms swinging as Rio grabbed for the gun in his fist
and a scream rent the air.

The scream was Molly's. Eve was too terrified to make
a sound. She just kept stumbling backward, trying to protect
Molly and watching in horror as the monster that had tormented her with details of what would happen to her
daughter and to Rio if he didn't drop his investigation of
Olivia's murder grappled with what she swore was an ap-
parition. She couldn't believe Rio was there. Yet she
couldn't bear to believe that he wasn't.

As if in slow motion, she saw Rio twist her abductor's arm away, heard his vicious oath as the other man's beefy body bucked trying to break free. A gold ring flashed like a flame as a thick fist swung at Rio's head.

The oath from the man in the mask was even more profane. He'd missed.

The look on Rio's face would have scared her to death had she not been scared to death already. Pure rage leaked from every pore of his body, power rippling from him like a panther in full attack. What the other man had on him in size, Rio had in the visceral fury of a man protecting his own. But the other man still had a gun. And his hand was now free.

The muffled pop melded with the shouts coming from behind them. Rio jerked back, grabbing his arm. The monster scrambled to his feet, but before he could take better aim, the double ping of two rifles fired a split second apart registered over the blood pounding in Eve's ears. The monster's arms flew out, his whole body lifting from the ground before sprawling on the rocks a few yards away.

Eve's legs threatened to buckle in the scattered seconds before the rustle of brush being trampled gave way to the sight of four men in dark blue running toward them. She was moving herself, fear still pumping through her veins and nothing but instinct driving her. She and Molly had to get to Rio. That was her only thought as, arms tight around her trembling child, she started back across the rocky streambed.

He was there before she reached the other side.

"Thank God," she heard him breathe as he caught her to him with one arm, trapping Molly between their bodies. "Tell me you're all right."

She nodded, shaking. From the moment she'd realized what was happening—just before she'd been run off the road—she hadn't believed that she'd ever be all right again. "We are now. How did you know where we were?"

"I'll tell you on the way back." He let his arm slip a

little, his hard black eyes searching her face, her windblown hair. Apparently believing her enough to let the questions go for now, he turned his inspection to the little girl clinging like a vine to her mother's neck. "How about you, honey?" He started to brush her uncombed hair from her eyes. Seeing the blood on his hand, he pulled it back before Eve could reach for it. "Are you hurt anywhere?"

Blue eyes huge in her face and impossibly solemn, Molly slowly shook her head. "I'm scared."

"It's okay now." He delivered the promise with a wince and reached for his right arm again. "Honest," he added, far more concerned with her than he appeared to be with the blood leaking between his fingers. "Nobody's going to hurt you."

Coming from Rio, the assurance seemed to relieve some of the tension Eve could feel in her daughter's body. But Eve wasn't feeling all that reassured herself. Not with Rio bleeding. She told him that, too, but he wouldn't admit to her how badly he was hurt. Nor would he let her help him by tying his handerchief around the wound. It was fine, he told her.

He was lying through his teeth. His arm felt as if it were on fire, and the pain was making his head ache, but he didn't care about anything right now other than getting Eve and Molly out of there. Taking his little girl from Eve with his uninjured arm, keeping his other hunched, he turned to the officer approaching them.

Someone had pulled off the mask of the motionless body on the ground. Blocking Eve's view of the man, he turned Molly so she wouldn't have to look at him, either, and asked what the situation was with the other kidnapper. As the syncopated whap-whap of helicopter blades grew louder, he was told that the driver of the sedan was as dead as his partner.

"Who ordered aerial assist?" one of the other officers called out.

"It's not ours," another replied.

Someone else swore. A heartbeat later, Eve saw a gray chopper appear over the tops of the trees and the order to head for cover had everyone darting for the woods. Like a giant mosquito, the aircraft started to descend into the clear-cut, only to change direction seconds later. As if the craft had just played out the give in a bungee cord, it suddenly shot upward, arced east and disappeared over the tops of the trees.

"Get them out of here before that chopper decides to come back," a senior officer ordered, pointing to the wounded man and the two females holding on to him. "And radio for a meat wagon."

The emergency room at Vanderbilt Memorial was not Eve's favorite place. The last time she'd been there, her mother had been carried in on a stretcher and had died soon after. At least she, Rio and Molly, hugging the blue bear Rio had brought with him, had walked in under their own steam. That had been an hour ago.

Now, running on nothing but nerves but feeling a little more human since she and Molly had washed up in the rest room, Eve followed a nurse in green scrubs past rows of empty gurneys and curtained-off cubicles.

"He's right here." The nurse pulled back part of a curtain so she and Molly could enter. "Stay as long as you want."

Thanking the woman, concern battling caution, Eve ushered Molly inside and pulled the curtain behind them. Rio sat on a narrow, sheet-covered gurney, naked to the waist and looking terribly impatient.

Pulling her eyes from the well-defined muscles of his chest and the blood leaking through the thick gauze pad on his arm, she saw his impatience turn to hesitation. They had ridden together in the back seat of the patrol car with Molly cuddled between them. But the ordeal had left them all too drained to do anything more than relish the fact that they were safe. Very little had been said that wasn't necessary.

"The nurse said you wanted to see us."

"I wanted to make sure you were still here."

Molly, her feet encased in blue paper hospital slippers, moved to the edge of the silver gurney. Looking past Rio's long, denim-clad legs, she frowned in distress at his wounded arm. "Does it hurt?"

"Not really," he replied, soothing away the furrows in her brow with the tips of his fingers. "Did you eat?"

Molly told him she had, but that her mommy hadn't wanted anything. Assuring her that her mommy would probably eat something later, he shifted his concern for her to her mother. "Did you finish giving the officer your statement?"

"Just a few minutes ago." Not as convinced as Molly by his claim that he wasn't in pain, she motioned to his shoulder. Around the temporary bandage, a wash of orange-brown antiseptic darkened his shoulder and upper arm. "The nurse said you need stitches."

"That's what I'm waiting for. Listen, if you and Molly don't need to be here, the officer can take you home. I'll be over as soon as they're finished with me." He touched the little girl's hair again, the gesture seeming to seek assurance that she was really all right. "There was something we were going to do."

They were going to tell Molly who he was. Eve hadn't forgotten. Through all the uncertainty she'd experienced at the hands of her captors, she'd recalled a dozen times what she and Rio had planned to do two nights ago.

Knowing he'd been dealing with his own fears where Molly was concerned, she didn't blame him for wanting to get their relationship straight as soon as possible.

"Why don't we do it now?"

"Do what?" Molly wanted to know, her glance darting between the adults.

Neither one of them answered. For a moment, it didn't

appear to Eve that Rio even breathed. Still holding her glance, he finally gave her a tight nod. "Go ahead."

He was looking to her to take the lead, something that made little sense to Eve. Not after the way he'd taken control and risked himself to save her and his daughter. That was the impression he gave her, though, and she was more than willing to supply whatever reinforcement he needed just then.

Picking up their little girl, she sat her next to him on the gurney.

"Molly," she began, wondering at how much easier this was than she'd thought it would be. "Do you remember the other morning when you asked Rio if he would be your pretend daddy?"

Hugging Ted, Molly nodded.

"Well, it isn't just pretend, honey. He really is your daddy."

Molly's little brow furrowed again. Lifting her chin from where it had rested on Ted's head, she looked up at the big, half-naked man beside her. Seconds later, she looked to her mom. "He is?"

"He is."

"Like you're my real mommy?"

"Just like that."

It seemed as if it had been forever since Eve had seen her little girl smile. Now Molly's whole face brightened as she turned back to Rio. "Are you going to live with us?"

Eve felt her heart jerk as she caught Rio's totally unreadable glance. But she'd scarcely opened her mouth to explain how the joint custody Rio wanted would work, when the curtain was whipped back.

Rio was promising a grinning Molly they'd talk later as Dr. Amanda Jennings walked in. With her short blond hair brushed back from her attractive features and her white lab coat starched and pressed, she gave the immediate impression of professionalism and efficiency. Since she had worked on Eve's mother, Eve knew she was far more than that. Amanda Jennings was also one of the most sensitive people she'd ever met.

Right behind her was Stone Richardson, still wearing a dark blue baseball jacket and slacks.

"It's only a flesh wound," Dr. Jennings assured Eve, since she looked more worried than either the stoic, dark-haired man sitting on the gurney or the blond bear of a detective who'd stopped next to it. "The X ray shows it didn't even nick bone."

Rio scowled up at his friend. "Did I ever mention that I hate guns?"

"Several times," Stone returned, using the excuse of handing Molly to her mother to avoid seeing what was under the gauze Dr. Jennings removed.

Stone looked rushed. He also looked extraordinarily sympathetic. But as Eve settled in the plastic chair at the head of the gurney with Molly on her lap, she figured that was probably because Rio's wound wasn't far from the same spot where he'd caught a bullet three weeks ago.

"You know, buddy, at the rate you're going, you'll never get the roof on your cabin before the winter. You won't be able to use a hammer for another month."

"You're building a cabin?"

At Eve's quiet question, Rio turned to her. He really wished Dr. Jennings would hurry up and get started with the stitches. Not because of any discomfort. With his arm already pumped full of anesthetic, the only place he hurt was where his ribs had hit the rocks after he'd made his flying tackle. But he wanted to be alone with Eve. There were a few things he needed to tell her. But now that Stone had arrived he had the feeling that getting her alone wasn't going to happen any time soon.

"It's just a foundation at this point. But, yeah, I am.

"Have you learned anything?" he asked the detective, turning to him.

"Actually, we have." Snagging the empty chair with his foot, Stone pulled it over and propped a size eleven on the marred gray plastic. "An officer at the scene recognized the driver as a low-level gun for the syndicate. He remembered him from a new batch of FBI posters. I have a feeling that the bearded guy was the same." Since Rio was too numbed-up to wince, Stone did it for him as Dr. Jennings took the first stitch. "I have someone running a picture of him over to the messenger service now to see if he's the one the owner talked to."

"You know," he added, his voice low, though there was no way to keep any of the morning's events quiet. Anyone with a police scanner would know what had happened on Logging Road 8. "These guys weren't amateurs. Their car was a rental. We found the papers in the glove box. And we believe that chopper was coming in to pick them up. That was the only way to avoid encountering another car in daylight who could identify them as having been in the area.

"They weren't going to risk Eve getting anywhere for help before they were long gone, either," he continued. "Taking Molly's shoes meant she had to carry her. That would have slowed her down in case she'd figured out where she was and tried to make it to the highway before her rescue arrived."

He paused, glancing from the doctor to Eve and back to Rio. For different reasons, he knew he could trust them all. Still, dropping his foot, he moved closer to Rio and lowered his voice to a demanding whisper.

"What in the hell did you stumble onto, anyway, Redtree? Olivia Stuart's murder just went big-time. We're talking mob connections here."

Rio held up his left hand, every bit as perplexed as his friend. "You know what I know. If you can figure it out, you tell me."

Though he'd been over every note he'd taken in the investigation, Rio honestly didn't know where he'd triggered the events of the past thirty-six hours. Once it had become apparent to him that Hal had nothing to do with the kidnapping, he'd drawn blanks. Unless Hal knew who...

With the force of a strong wind slamming a door, Rio shut his mind to that enticing bit of speculation. He wasn't about to tease himself with possibilities he had no intention of pursuing. He'd mention the thought to Stone later and the detective could take it from there. He had other questions he wanted answered, anyway. Starting with what Stone was talking to Eve about at that very moment.

"I know you've already been through this with Detective Chang," Stone was saying to her, "and I won't ask you to go through all of it again. We're just trying to figure out where it was that they held you."

He flipped open a spiral-bound notebook much like the one the other officer had used, and his foot went back on the chair. "Give me times, if you can. Starting with when you first noticed their car behind you."

Had it not been imperative that the police work quickly, Rio would have told his friend he could ask his questions later. Eve was holding up better than anyone would have expected, something Rio now realized was equal parts facade and backbone, but she looked exhausted. If they hoped to find anything that would lead them to the pilot of that helicopter, however, they had to move now.

Aware of Rio watching her, aware too of the faintly protective glint in his eyes, Eve smoothed her hand up and down Molly's little back as she spoke.

"It had to be right around five o'clock," she said, grateful that she didn't have to repeat what she'd told the other officer about the awful hours she and Molly had spent blindfolded and huddled together on a bed in what she thought was a cabin. "We'd left the reservation at fourthirty, so it couldn't have been too much later than that. They blindfolded us right away, so it was impossible to tell when it got dark or even what direction we went."

She went on to recall what she could of how long they had driven in their captor's car, the turns they had taken, the types of roads they'd been on. She knew that Rio's attention had sharpened the moment she'd mentioned the reservation, but he said nothing. Nor did he move. Not that he could with Dr. Jennings sewing up his arm. She could tell he was itching to get up, though. She was beginning to sense impatience in him again.

Hoping that wasn't because he was upset with her because of what she'd done, but knowing it could well be, since he'd made it clear that his mother was not her problem, Eve kept her focus on Stone. Mercifully, it took him only a couple of minutes to ask the rest of his questions. Wasting no time once he finished, he told Eve to call him if she remembered anything else, chucked Molly under the chin, then caught himself just before he could jog the doctor's last stitch by giving Rio a friendly slap on the arm. Instead, he told him he'd be in touch and disappeared through the curtain.

That curtain was still swaying when Dr. Jennings snipped catgut from the suture and the scissors hit the metal tray with a quiet clatter. "These can come out in about a week," she told Rio, ripping open a paper packet. A thick pad of sterile gauze went over the wound. Securing the six-inch squares with white paper tape, she gave him the rest of his instructions and told him the nurse would be in shortly to give him an injection for tetanus. She seemed very aware that, the entire time she was talking, her patient had been watching the woman uneasily watching him.

It was apparent to Amanda that Rio and Eve needed to be alone. What they didn't know was that there were two reporters hovering in the waiting room. While it was entirely possible that they were friends of Rio's wanting to see for themselves that he was all right, their presence meant he and Eve would have little peace for a while yet.

Stripping off her gloves, she dropped them on the tray and walked over to where Molly still sat on her mom's lap. "Do you know what you look like you need?" she asked the little girl.

"Not a shot."

"No," she returned with a laugh. "Ice cream. Since I could use a break, and I happen to know where they serve chocolate sundaes around here, why don't you and I go get one?" She looked at Eve. "Is that all right with you?"

"It's all right with me," Molly announced, already climbing off her mother's lap.

It was okay with Eve, too, though the moment she agreed, she wondered if being alone with Rio just then was all that wise. The way she was feeling, agitated, fatigued and desperately in need of his arms, she couldn't handle it if he got upset with her. Thanking the doctor despite her second thoughts, Eve rose from the chair as soon as Molly and Ted shuffled off, led by the kind doctor's hand.

"So," Eve began, unwilling to let silence feed the attack of nerves. "Tell me about your cabin."

Of all the subjects she could have raised just then, that one caught Rio totally unprepared.

"My cabin?"

"What's it like?"

He watched her move to the head of the gurney, her attention seemingly on the blood pressure gauge and oxygen port on the wall. Wondering if she simply couldn't handle talking about anything taxing just now, he decided to give her whatever space she needed.

"It's not much. Just a place to come back to after I leave here. A couple of rooms. A porch." He started to lift his shoulder in a shrug, then caught himself when the movement sent a jolt of pain from shoulder to rib. "If I don't finish it this year, there's always next summer."

"You're leaving?"

Something like disappointment shadowed her face. He didn't question why he found that so encouraging. "I'd thought I would. Eventually." He'd thought that for a long time. Getting as far from the reservation as he could had always been a goal. But he'd never made it any farther than Grand Springs. In the past hours, he'd come to realize that maybe there'd been a reason for that. "I can't go anywhere yet. I've just taken a promotion."

"You've been promoted?"

"To assistant editor. I got the offer a while ago, but I've just decided to accept it."

He made it sound as if the decision had been made in the last minute. Too agitated to wonder why that was, Eve told him she was happy for him, that she knew he'd do well because he could do anything he put his mind to, then made herself say what she could no longer avoid.

"There's something I need to tell you."

"About what you were doing on the res?"

There was more curiosity than irritation in his expression. Encouraged by that, she unconsciously began twisting the edge of the sheet two feet away from where he sat, and gave him a nod.

"I had to go. For several reasons," she admitted, hoping he would understand. "I'll sign your custody agreement, Rio. And that will make everything legal, so you'll know you always have access to your daughter. But I need you to believe that I want Molly to be part of your life without a court saying she is.

"I know you don't trust me," she told him, pulling back so she wouldn't be so close to him. "And I know you can never feel about me the way I do about you. I accept that. But you need to accept that I really thought you meant it when you said you didn't want children. Now I think I know you better."

"I don't think you do."

Her glance flew to his.

"First," he said flatly, "I do trust you. And second," he added, looking as cautious as she felt, "I don't blame you for not telling me. My pride was hurt, Eve. But I know the impressions I gave you, and you were right. I didn't want children. I didn't want to do to them what my father had done to me."

"But you wouldn't have," she protested. "You're a wonderful father."

That meant more to him than she could possibly know. "All I knew was that my mother kept telling me I was just like him. I believed her."

"She knows that. She knows how that hurt you, too."

"She does," Eve insisted, because Rio's scowl made it obvious that he doubted her. "And I think she feels awful about it, but that's for the two of you to work through. You will, though. I'm sure of it. And I think she's going to be all right with Molly, too." Her arms tightened over the knot. "She and I don't stand much of a chance, though. She wouldn't even look me in the eye."

"Eve." His tone was utterly flat, the look on his face one of extreme patience as he snagged her arm to pull her closer. "The reason my mother wouldn't hold your glance is strictly a cultural difference. We believe that the spirit is visible in a person's eyes, and the spirit is private. It's a sign of disrespect to invade another's privacy. Those of us who've lived off the res had to learn that we weren't being insulted when someone looked us in the eye when they spoke. Just like we had to learn not to insult them by looking away." He smiled, some of the tension fading from him. "Those who've lived their entire lives on the res, like my mother, don't understand the difference in customs."

"There's so much I don't know."

"Don't worry. I'll teach you."

He'd pulled her a foot closer, but it was his words as much as his proximity that caused her heart to hitch. Eve didn't get a chance to consider why that was, though. He was edging her closer still.

"You said you knew I couldn't feel about you the way you feel about me," he reminded her. "How do you feel about me, Eve?"

He posed the question simply, but she sensed a faint uneasiness in him, a guarded anxiety that wasn't like him at all. Far more familiar with the feeling than he seemed to be, she ducked her head, intent on the tear at the knee of his jeans.

She'd no sooner noticed the raw scrape and dirt beneath that tear when he nudged her chin back up.

"How do you feel about me?" he repeated, quietly insistent.

"The same way I always have."

"Try again."

"Rio…"

"Eve…" he mimicked. "Come on. You made the statement."

She took a deep breath, blew it out, then felt the subtle warmth of his hand skimming up her arm. This man had given her her daughter. Once she'd allowed him to be, he'd been there for her whenever she needed him. Especially at the most crucial time of all. He had saved their lives. "I love you."

"Then you're wrong again," he informed her, drawing her between his legs. "Because I love you, too. I was just too unfamiliar with the feeling the first time to know what it was."

The admission was spoken simply, his eyes moving over her as he cupped the side of her face in his hand. The way he touched her made her feel as fragile as glass, as precious as gold. "You'd once asked me if I'd found what I was looking for," he said, brushing his thumb along her jaw. "And I told you that I had no idea what it was I wanted to find. Except I had found it. Six years ago."

A muscle in his jaw jerked, the fatigue etched in his face seeming more pronounced. "You were the only person who didn't demand that I conform to their idea of what I should be. You accepted me just as I was. But I lost you," he said, his hand slipping to curve around the back of her neck. "Then I found you again, and you gave me the child I'd never thought I'd have."

He paused, searching for the words he needed as he studied her face. "I've done a lot of thinking in the past hours," he finally said. "It made me realize what was really important to me, and that I don't ever want to lose you again. We're better now, Eve. And we need to do it right this time. We need to be a family."

For a moment, Eve couldn't speak. She couldn't seem to do anything but stare into his eyes while her own filled with tears. She didn't want to cry. Not now. But the sting behind her eyelids refused to go away.

"Hey," he whispered, catching a tear with his thumb.

"I'm sorry."

"Don't be." Slipping his arm around her, he pulled her to his chest. As many times as he'd seen her pushed to near breaking, he'd never actually seen her cry. That this should do it made him feel like a louse. "My timing is rotten. The last thing you need right now is to deal with getting married."

"You're proposing?"

"I was getting to it. But we can talk about it later."

She shook her head, pulling back to frame his face with her hands. The tears were still there, brightening her eyes, but she didn't care. All she cared about was him. "There's nothing to talk about. Can we have the ceremony on the reservation?"

His entire body seemed to go still. "I take it that's a yes."

She didn't actually answer him. She merely gave him a nod that had him sucking in a low breath before his hand slipped over the back of her head.

"I hope you're into feathers," he murmured, his breath warming her lips moments before his mouth claimed hers.

There was as much promise as passion in his kiss, as much hope as desire. Eve kissed him back just as fiercely. She loved this man. She always had. And, by some miracle, she had been given back the dreams she'd been too young to handle the first time. But as she felt her body relax against his when he carried his kiss to her temple and he pressed her head to his shoulder, she had to admit it was more than having his love that mattered to her. She had his trust.

From the other side of the curtain came the drone of voices and the squeak of a gurney wheel as it rolled past their cubicle. The happiness filling her heart dimmed as reality hit.

Lifting her head, she searched the strong lines of Rio's face. "You're giving up the story, aren't you."

The worry was back in her delicate features, stealing the light from her eyes. Seeing that concern, hating what had put it there, Rio brushed her hair back from her drawn and pale face.

From the moment he had realized what had happened to Eve and Molly, there had been no question in his mind about what he'd do. He'd give up his own life before he'd jeopardize the lives of the two people he loved most. As long as there was a breath in his body, he'd do whatever he had to do to keep them safe.

Drawing her back to him, he brushed his lips over her forehead. "Yes, I'm giving it up," he whispered, then drew her closer again and kissed her with all the newly discovered love in his heart.

The truth about Olivia Stuart's murder would have to be discovered by someone else. He had far too much to lose.

*   *   *   *   *

continues with

THE RANCHER AND THE RUNAWAY BRIDE

by Susan Mallery
available in January 1998

Here's an exciting preview....

One

Brides were supposed to be beautiful and happy, Randi Howell told herself. Panic was not on the list of acceptable emotions. "It's not so bad," she said aloud. "I'm just marrying Hal. He won't be a horrible husband."

She had to smile at that one. Hal would be annoyed if he knew she thought of him as "not so horrible." Hardly praise every groom dreamed about.

"Stop it!" she told herself firmly. "Love is a difficult concept at best. How do you know you don't love Hal?"

She stopped in midpace and slowly faced the mirror. Despite perfect makeup, she was pale, her skin nearly the color of ash. The realization began slowly, a small kernel of knowledge that sprouted, then grew quickly. It wasn't that she didn't *love* Hal, she wasn't sure she even liked him.

She'd fallen into the engagement because it was easy. Easier than making her own way. "I don't want this," she whispered, suddenly certain she had only about three minutes of freedom left. "Dear Lord, this would be a really great time for a miracle."

Randi waited about two heartbeats, then figured God was busy. She was going to have to make her own miracle. She grabbed her purse, slipped off her shoes so she could walk quietly down the linoleum floors, then left the bride's room and headed for the rear entrance of the ski lodge. At least it was June and she wouldn't have to worry about freezing.

The back door of the lodge was in sight when she heard voices heading her way, and she glanced around, looking for a place to hide. The second door she tried gave way and she stepped inside. Barely breathing, she pressed her ear to the door and waited for the two people to walk by and continue on their way. Finally, Randi breathed a sigh of relief. Now to escape.

Before she could open the door, she heard voices again, from directly behind her. She wasn't alone. A quick glance over her shoulder showed a couple of jackets tossed on a long conference table. The clink of glass and the smell of coffee came from an alcove to the left.

Great. There was a meeting going on. Bad enough to be running away from her own wedding. Worse to be caught in the act.

"Jo will take care of the old broad," a male voice said. "That's her specialty."

The statement didn't make sense until Randi realized the men must be talking about a nurse. She paused for a second, then swung the door open and took a step toward the now-empty hallway and freedom. As she shifted her weight forward, her stocking-clad foot came down on a carpet tack.

Life was not fair, she thought as she yelped involuntarily.

"What the hell?" one of the men said.

Randi froze. The man approaching her was not a doctor. She'd never seen him before. But what really got her attention was the deadly looking gun he held in his right hand. The barrel pointed directly at her. This guy was going to kill her.

She waited for her life to pass before her eyes. She couldn't do anything but stand there, braced for the explosion that would end it all.

Instead, the lights went out.

Early August

Brady Jones leaned back in his chair and glanced at the woman perched in front of his scarred desk. Another hard-luck case, he thought. He'd always been good at spotting them. Too many lines of her application left blank, no home address, no relatives. He should kick her out on her shapely butt, because he didn't need her kind of trouble, or temptation.

"How about a week's trial?" he heard himself say. "You can start in the morning."

"I'd like that," she replied, brushing back the black curl that dangled by her cheek.

There was, however, one thing he had to know. "Rita," he said, his voice stern. "Are you on the run from the law?"

Her blue eyes widened, and shock parted her mouth. "Of course not," she said. "I swear."

Conversations like this were not part of her life plan, Randi thought glumly, and wondered if she would ever get used to her new name. When she'd first run away from the wedding and those men with guns, her only thought had been to stay alive. Changing her name had made her feel safer. Now she wished there was some way to convince the man in front of her that she wasn't a paroled felon. She needed this job. She was down to her last five dollars and was getting pretty desperate.

"Okay," Brady said. "I had to ask. I hope you understand. Come on. I'll show you around." At the entrance to the barn, Brady paused. "The bunkhouse is over there," he said, pointing to a long, low one-story building on his right.

Randi settled her duffel bag strap over her right shoulder. "It looks very nice."

"Yeah." Brady was lost in thought. "Tex prepares three meals a day, and he rings a bell when the food's ready. Don't be late."

She tried to ignore her growling stomach and the fact that she hadn't eaten yet that day. "No problem."

"Actually, there is." Brady shook his head and turned to his left, away from the bunkhouse and toward a white two-story house. "There are nearly twenty men on the ranch. And except for my dog, Princess, a few of the cats and some breeding stock, you're the only female around. So I'm going to give you a room up at the main house. I'm the only one who sleeps there, and I'm about as safe as they come."

That wasn't true, Randi thought, eyeing his broad shoulders and muscular thighs. She would bet he could be pretty dangerous when he chose to be. What he really meant was he wasn't interested in her, so she wouldn't have to worry. It was no more than she expected. *But for just a moment, Randi Howell wished it wasn't so!*

Welcome to the Towers!

In January
New York Times bestselling author

NORA ROBERTS

takes us to the fabulous Maine coast mansion
haunted by a generations-old secret and introduces
us to the fascinating family that lives there.

Mechanic Catherine "C.C." Calhoun and hotel magnate
Trenton St. James mix like axle grease and mineral
water—until they kiss. Efficient Amanda Calhoun finds
easygoing Sloan O'Riley insufferable—and irresistible.
And they all must race to solve the mystery
surrounding a priceless hidden emerald necklace.

Catherine and Amanda

THE Calhoun Women

**A special 2-in-1 edition containing
COURTING CATHERINE and A MAN FOR AMANDA.**

Look for the next installment of
THE CALHOUN WOMEN with Lilah and Suzanna's
stories, coming in March 1998.

Available at your favorite retail outlet.

Take 4 bestselling love stories FREE

Plus get a FREE surprise gift!

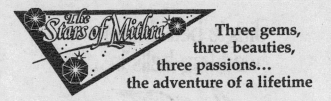

The Stars of Mithra

**Three gems,
three beauties,
three passions...
the adventure of a lifetime**

SILHOUETTE·INTIMATE·MOMENTS®
brings you a thrilling new series by
New York Times bestselling author

Nora Roberts

**Three mystical blue diamonds place three close
friends in jeopardy...and lead them to romance.**

In October
HIDDEN STAR (IM#811)
Bailey James can't remember a thing, but she knows
she's in big trouble. And she desperately needs private
investigator Cade Parris to help her live long enough to
find out just what kind.

In December
CAPTIVE STAR (IM#823)
Cynical bounty hunter Jack Dakota and spitfire
M. J. O'Leary are handcuffed together and on the run
from a pair of hired killers. And Jack wants to know
why—but M.J.'s not talking.

In February
SECRET STAR (IM#835)
Lieutenant Seth Buchanan's murder investigation takes
a strange turn when Grace Fontaine turns up alive. But
as the mystery unfolds, he soon discovers the notorious
heiress is the biggest mystery of all.

Available at your favorite retail outlet.

Jingle bells lead to
wedding bells in...

A Family CHRISTMAS

Three very captivating stories filled with the joy
of the season and the miracle of love
from three of your favorite authors:

CHRISTMAS STRANGER by Joan Hohl
JAKE'S CHRISTMAS by Elizabeth Bevarly
ROOM AT THE INN by Marilyn Pappano

Spread the holiday spirit!

Available December 1997 wherever Harlequin and Silhouette
books are sold.

 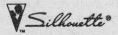

Return to the Towers!

In March
New York Times bestselling author

NORA ROBERTS

brings us to the Calhouns' fabulous
Maine coast mansion and reveals the
tragic secrets hidden there for generations.

For all his degrees, Professor Max Quartermain has a
lot to learn about love—and luscious Lilah Calhoun is
just the woman to teach him. Ex-cop Holt Bradford is
as prickly as a thornbush—until Suzanna Calhoun's
special touch makes love blossom in his heart.
And all of them are caught in the race to solve
the generations-old mystery of a priceless
lost necklace...and a timeless love.

Lilah and Suzanna
THE
Calhoun Women

**A special 2-in-1 edition containing
FOR THE LOVE OF LILAH and
SUZANNA'S SURRENDER**

Available at your favorite retail outlet.

Look us up on-line at: http://www.romance.net

Available in February 1998

ANN MAJOR

CHILDREN OF DESTINY
When Passion and Fate Intertwine...

SECRET CHILD

Although everyone told Jack West that his wife,
Chantal—the woman who'd betrayed him and sent
him to prison for a crime he didn't commit—had
died, Jack knew she'd merely transformed herself
into supermodel Mischief Jones. But when he
finally captured the woman he'd been hunting,
she denied everything. Who was she really—
an angel or a cunningly brilliant counterfeit?"

"Want it all? Read Ann Major."
—Nora Roberts, *New York Times*
bestselling author

Don't miss this compelling story
available at your favorite retail outlet.
Only from Silhouette books.